1
———

LUCKY TORE ACROSS THE YARD, CHASING A LOW-FLYING ROBIN THAT he'd caught sampling blackberries from the thorny patch at the edge of the lawn. Resounding barks announced his ferociousness to every rodent, bird, lizard, and snake in Wolf Wood. The robin flew up into a tree, which prompted Lucky to circle the house twice, as if he might scare up another bird, before recommitting to his original prey. He ran to the fir where the robin had alighted, placed his forepaws on the stout trunk, and barked up at the branches while vigorously wagging his whip of a tail.

"Does he actually expect to catch that bird?" Wendy asked.

"I don't think so," Morgen said, "but he delights in the chase."

She and Wendy were kneeling on flagstones in the lawn between the house and the barn with a witch's grimoire open between them, instructions for how to set magical wards scrawled across the pages. When active, the invisible booby traps would zap any intruders who attempted to reach the house without an invitation.

Wendy knew what to do without looking at the book, saying the chants and thrice tapping each spot with her wand, but she was also teaching Morgen so she would know how to reapply the magic in the future. The wards were supposedly strongest at repelling strangers for the first two weeks and faded after that, losing all potency after a month. Reapplying them each month would be a small price to pay to encircle the house and keep unwelcome strangers from barging in.

"He's a pointer, isn't he?" Wendy asked, raising her voice to be heard over a crescendo in the upbeat music of a video game that floated out of her nearby frog-mural camper van to compete with Lucky's barks. The mighty ferret Napoleon lay on his back on a nearby flagstone, as limp as a dishtowel as he slept through the noise. "I thought they silently sneaked into the brush, lifted a leg, and pointed their noses at their prey."

"He's a Hungarian vizsla, which is a kind of pointer, yes. As you can see, his snout *is* pointing up at the robin."

"I guess that's true."

"I'm just glad he's not sharing his hunt with me telepathically." Morgen touched her temple.

Since she'd inadvertently made Lucky her familiar, he'd shared a lot of visions of him sticking his nose into gopher holes, into bushes, and—his new favorite spot—under the recently built back deck. The mice that lived in the crawlspace under the house visited it frequently, treating it like a covered lanai.

The robin shifted on the branch and managed to drop a fir cone onto Lucky. That only incensed him. His tail wagged harder, and he barked louder.

An angry squawk came from the cedar where Amar had mounted the nesting box he'd made for Morgen's *other* familiar, Zorro. It had taken the owl a while to get used to it, but now he snoozed up there most days, unless a noisy neighbor woke him.

Zorro's head popped out of the hole, and he shrieked over at Lucky.

"He'd better be careful," Morgen said, "or he'll end up with an owl pellet regurgitated onto his back."

"Gross. I'm glad I don't have a familiar that likes to puke up bones."

"Yours is noticeably less vigorous."

"He has his moments. He likes to play." Wendy picked up a yellowed wand that had been carved from ivory—or maybe bone—and handed it to Morgen. "Here. You try."

Morgen eyed the wand dubiously. It was one of three that she'd found in the house after Grandma's death and not one she gravitated to, though she'd brought them all out. Thus far, she hadn't come across many spells that required wands and hadn't spent a lot of time studying them.

"Does it need to be this one?" she asked.

Wendy tilted her head. "I suppose not. It's hard for me to tell what the properties of them all are—such information is usually handed down from one generation to the next—but that one is the most powerful."

"I'd prefer wood to bone or ivory." Morgen tapped the other two wands, both made from wood, one lumpy and gnarled, as if it had been cut off a tree, and the other carved and sanded like a drumstick.

Not that Morgen knew what to do with any of them. Unlike her grandmother's staff, which she'd been able to use to whack enemies and take down gyrocopters, the wands did nothing when she waved them around and commanded, "Abracadabra!" Over the course of the summer, she'd learned a lot about magic and being a witch, but it would take a lifetime and then some to master everything. She wished Grandma were still around and could have taught her.

"Bone tends to be a more powerful receptacle for magic," Wendy said.

"If you don't mind wielding a piece of the skeleton of a previously majestic animal."

"I don't." Wendy shrugged. "I'm not a vegetarian. Anyway, I thought that just means you don't eat meat."

"It does, but I've always been an animal lover, so I do my best to avoid things that harm them. See the seats in my car?" Morgen pointed toward her little electric vehicle parked next to Amar's beat-up blue truck from the sixties. "Vegan leather."

Wendy raised her eyebrows. "What is *vegan* leather made from? Fake cows?"

"I think polyurethane, but it can also be made from sustainable materials like cork, pineapple leaves, and apple peels."

Wendy blinked. "Every time you get in your car, you're rubbing your butt on apple peels?"

"I might be."

"How does Amar feel about your lifestyle choice? He and the other werewolves seem to go hunting almost every night. Doesn't he come back with gristle between his teeth? What about when you kiss? Does he have meat breath?"

Morgen blushed at the realization that Wendy was aware she and Amar were kissing now. They'd almost done *more* than kissing the night of the demon summoning, but he'd suffered numerous broken ribs in that battle and was still moving around gingerly.

"His breath is fine, and I don't probe his teeth with my tongue when we kiss."

Though now that Wendy had brought up that imagery, Morgen thought about giving Amar some nice mint floss.

"I wouldn't mind having someone to kiss," Wendy said wistfully. "There's hardly anyone my age in this town. It's all old witches and retired tourists."

"Some of the Lobos are in their early twenties," Morgen said, thinking that might work for a nineteen-year-old. The werewolves were rough around the edges, but the one who fancied himself a chef—José Antonio—had some charm, and he almost never wandered around the worksite in a wife-beater tank top with pit stains.

Wendy leaned back abruptly enough to startle Napoleon. "Date a werewolf? *Me*?"

"I only brought it up as a possibility."

"My sister would kill me," Wendy said, even though she'd left the home she shared with Olivia and hadn't spoken to her in weeks. "Besides, that's super cringe. Witches don't date werewolves."

"You were in the hot tub the other day with José Antonio." Morgen waved toward the deck where the Jetmaster 3000 hummed, waiting for someone to peel back the lid and put it to use.

"That wasn't a date. I was sitting in it for therapeutic benefits."

"While a werewolf was also sitting in it for therapeutic benefits?"

"Exactly. He was way on the other side from me."

Way? Morgen had been in that hot tub. Though it purportedly seated six, that couldn't happen without a lot of knee bumping.

"Anyway," Wendy said, "Napoleon worried I was going to drown, so I shouldn't go in there again. Here. Let's focus on the wards. The ones I'm setting are the best I know. They're designed to affect all living beings, even the magical. The only thing they don't work on is machinery."

"So... I'm not protected from a robot uprising?"

"Nope, sorry. Cars can go through, too, but if there's a driver, he or she would be zapped."

The front door thumped, and Morgen's sister Sian appeared, wearing a robe and fuzzy purple unicorn slippers. She descended from the porch and padded out to them with three coffee mugs pressed between her hands. Lucky, who'd given up on his barking, trotted over to help. Or possibly to get in the way and trip Sian.

Morgen rose to block him and help with the mugs. "Thanks, Sian."

Lucky waved his nose in the air, sniffing toward the steaming coffee. He'd never shown an interest in sampling from Morgen's mug, but milk—or, knowing Sian, cream—had turned her sister's cup a lighter shade of brown.

"Dogs don't drink coffee," Morgen whispered to him.

Lucky wagged, somehow managing to whack both of them with his tail. The breed standard was to have the tail partially docked, so it was less likely to be damaged during hunting, but Morgen hadn't wanted to have that done, since it seemed cruel. Sometimes, she wondered if the docking was preferred less because of hunting and more because vizsla owners didn't want their wine glasses, coffee mugs, and cans of soda knocked on the floor every time their dog wandered through the living room.

"I did not know if your roommate would wish a mug—" Sian glanced toward the apartment above the barn, "—but there's more coffee in the pot if he does."

"Do werewolves like coffee?" Wendy wrinkled her nose as if that were a strange thought.

"He's a perfectly normal human being when he's not in his furry form," Morgen said, though that wasn't entirely true. Amar had admitted that he had sharper-than-average hearing and a keen sense of smell, even when he stood as a man. Based on the fights she'd seen him survive, and the ropy muscles that were always on display when he wore nothing but a leather vest over his torso, she suspected he was stronger than typical too. He was definitely *sexier* than typical.

Morgen smiled into her mug as she took a sip.

"I'm not sure I'd call him *normal*," Wendy whispered. "He's very ferocious, and he glowers at me a lot."

"Do men not typically glower at you?" Morgen asked.

"No, I'm super cute." Wendy grinned at them. With her freckles, brunette hair in pigtails, and daisies painted on her toenails, that was a fair assessment. "I don't know why he would glower. It's a mystery."

Sian sighed and looked at the sky, as if discussions of physical beauty and normality were beneath her. "Speaking of mysteries, why is there a basket full of berries, toadstools, and twigs on the counter next to the coffee pot, Morgen? If it's supposed to be potpourri, it's musty."

"If it were potpourri, it would be in the first-floor bathroom that the werewolf contractors were using while they did their work."

"Gross. They're done now, right?"

"I think so," Morgen said. "I've got refinished hardwood floors, a roof that doesn't leak, and a deck with a hot tub and outdoor kitchen. I can't imagine what else this house could need."

Morgen hadn't even *asked* for the deck or outdoor kitchen, but the Lobos had been so delighted that she could make them talismans that kept witches from controlling them with magic that they'd overachieved. Having since made the talismans for the whole pack, Morgen didn't feel quite as guilty about accepting all the free work. As Amar had assured her many times, it was more than a fair trade.

"I collected those items from Wolf Wood on my walks with Lucky," Morgen added. "I'm taking pictures of anything that seems unusual and isn't in my witch database. I'm hoping I can find someone in the coven who knows what they are and can teach me."

Ever since Pedro had warned Amar that someone dangerous from their past had been spotted in the area, Morgen had worried that more trouble would befall them. The more she could learn, the more capable a witch she could become. And the more she could help Amar if necessary.

"One of the toadstools is glowing," Sian said.

"Yes, Wolf Wood is full of magical stuff. That's why the witches want it left alone and not turned over to a developer. I got the water for that coffee from a mystical spring in the woods that Grandma believed had rejuvenating properties."

Horror blossomed on Sian's face as she gaped down at her half-consumed beverage. "The water for my coffee is laced with bird poop, algae, and coyote urine?"

"I put it through the filtration pitcher in the fridge."

"Those pitchers don't do anything to protect against bacterial contaminants. All they do is filter *some* metals and chemicals that affect taste and odor."

"You don't think that covers coyote pee?"

Sian gave her a scathing look before setting her mug on the porch railing and wiping her hands. She poked in her pockets, as if she might find hand sanitizer in one. Given her predilections, she might.

"I can pick up some bottled water at the store," Morgen offered.

She had no idea when the well water had last been tested, so it was possible that wasn't a safer bet.

"That's not necessary, at least not on my behalf. I spoke to the director of science at the university this morning, and she believes she can get me into a lab position doing chimpanzee research. I'm waiting to hear back on more details and a possible start date."

"You're leaving?" Morgen asked.

She'd known her sister would have to return to work eventually, but it had been nice having her visit these last couple of weeks. Since Sian had spent most of the last decade out of the country doing field work, they'd barely spoken to each other these past years. Even if Sian was stiffer than a board and grumpy at how many *housemates* Morgen had ruining the serenity of what should have been a secluded house, she was the family member that Morgen was closest to—whom she most understood. And vice versa.

"I am. I am not as enthusiastic as I would wish about the idea of lab research—studying structural, neurochemical, and electrophysiological abnormalities in the brains of chimpanzees is far from the work I was doing in Borneo—but—"

Morgen's phone rang, startling her. It was barely after eight, and since she was no longer employed and no longer married, she couldn't imagine who would be calling her so early.

Phoebe's name popped up. Odd. Her mentor usually sent her raven Zeke to deliver messages instead of relying on mundane methods of communication.

"Hi, Phoebe." Morgen held up a finger to Sian, hoping she wouldn't leave. She wanted to hear more about the job opening and if her sister would come up to visit on the weekends. It had taken some time—and a battle with werewolves in the vet's office —but Sian had finally accepted that magic and lycanthropy existed. Morgen kept trying to convince her to learn about her witch heritage. They'd been a good team during that demon fight. "What's up?"

"I have excellent news."

"You've received a new shipment of geodes from the desert?"

"That was yesterday. No, Judith is here, the treasurer from the coven, and she said that she got your dues and you're officially a member now."

"That's good."

"We're going to have our first meeting tomorrow, and we'd like you to join us."

"Really?"

"Yes, indeed." Phoebe paused, listening to someone talk in the background.

Morgen grinned. Given that some of the witches were horrible to the werewolves and a few had been making Morgen's life miserable since she'd arrived in Bellrock, she shouldn't have wanted to join them, but they weren't *all* like that. Phoebe had been advising her and teaching her useful incantations, the president Belinda had acknowledged that the database app she'd made for the coven was useful, and they were all quirky and weird. Morgen, having fallen into that category her whole life, couldn't help but be drawn to others like her.

"You're *joining* that cult?" Sian asked, her voice full of disdain.

She was also in the quirky-and-weird club, but she didn't seem to care if she had similar kinds of people to hang out with. Wild orangutans and neurologically damaged chimpanzees were more her cup of tea.

"It's not a cult," Morgen whispered. "It's a group of women with common interests that meets a couple of times a month. Like a book club."

"We do like books," Wendy said.

"That instruct you on mixing potions, making talismans, and summoning demons?" Sian asked.

"I like Harry Potter too."

Sian rolled her eyes, then whispered to Morgen, "Don't give in to peer pressure in order to gain acceptance."

Morgen rolled her own eyes. She was forty, not fourteen. "I'm not planning on it."

"Morgen, are you still there?" Phoebe asked.

"Yes."

"Judith reminded me that now that school has started up for the year, we can't use the gymnasium for our meetings. We were just discussing how lovely and secluded Gwen's house in the woods is. *Your* house now. No nosy neighbors prying into your rituals, no husbands wandering into the living room in their underwear. It sounds positively dreamy."

"Er?"

"All the werewolf contractors have left the premises now, haven't they?"

"Technically, yes." Morgen didn't mention that the Lobos liked to visit and make use of the posh outdoor kitchen they'd built, or that the hot tub was a lycanthrope magnet that drew them several times a week. "Except for Amar of course."

"Ah, yes. Amar. Our meetings are in the evenings. Perhaps he could go for a hunt?"

"He does do that regularly, but I'm sure he wouldn't bother anyone if he was here." Morgen rubbed the back of her neck. Did she *want* all of the witches up here?

She wasn't as much of a recluse as her sister, but most of the time, she preferred being by herself with a book, and the thought of near-strangers wandering around her home was moderately horrifying. She would have to talk to them. *All* of them. And would she be expected to provide food and drinks? She enjoyed experimenting with her vegetarian cookbooks, but not for *parties*. Something that might have been a burgeoning panic attack crept up in her chest.

"Hm, well as long as he stays in his barn," Phoebe said.

Someone else—was that Judith?—said, "I trust her trysts with him are *out there* and not in the house."

Morgen stared at the phone, affronted that Judith seemed to be implying that a werewolf shouldn't be let in the house. The woman might be aghast if she knew that Lucky not only came in the house but slept on Morgen's bed.

"We can fumigate for werewolves before the meeting starts," Phoebe said. Her tone was dry, but Morgen wasn't positive that was a joke.

"Fumigate?" she asked.

"Don't worry. We'll take care of it when we arrive. Tomorrow at seven. I'll let everyone know."

Morgen lowered her phone, not sure if she was stunned, flummoxed, or horrified. Or all three.

The others must not have overheard everything, for Sian and Wendy both raised their eyebrows.

"The coven has decided on a new meeting place," Morgen said. "Here."

"Did you agree to that?" Sian oozed disapproval.

"Not... exactly."

"I told you. Peer pressure."

2

THE CHAINSAW WHIRRED, PIECES OF WOOD FLYING AS AMAR sculpted a log into a squatting frog with the brim of a lily-pad hat drooping over the sides of its head. He was a gifted and usually serious craftsman, who'd made beautiful tables, armoires, and the swinging wood bench that now hung on the porch. It amused Morgen that he took on whimsical projects from time to time. Apparently, he had a few clients in Bellrock and Bellingham who adored his work and had money to spend on custom outdoor art for their yards. Since they were all older ladies, Morgen wondered if some of their interest came from the fact that Amar delivered his pieces in his fitted jeans and leather vest, with his arm muscles bulging.

When she'd first met him, she'd found his scruffy, shoulder-length black hair, roughly trimmed beard and mustache, and wood-dust-coated arms a touch wild, but she'd grown to find his look—and *him*—sexy. She would have ogled him and allowed herself bedroom thoughts as she approached him with a box of cookies and a thermos of clam chowder, but she was worried that he would be offended by the request she needed to make.

Zorro hooted from his nesting box, watching the sun set over the trees and Rosario Strait. Morgen didn't have much time before the coven showed up.

She wondered how *many* would arrive. When she'd attended —ahem, spied on—that meeting in the gym, there had been thirty or forty women sitting in the bleachers. A small number in such a large space, but, as Sian had pointed out, that many people here would be a veritable Mongol horde rampaging through the living room.

Since the average age of the witches was sixty, Morgen didn't know if she agreed with that metaphor, but the house would be crowded. Crowded with people who turned up their noses at werewolves. The thought saddened her, since the Lobos were decent guys, but the witches and the Loup pack had battled for the town years before Morgen arrived, and there was a lot of bad blood between them. The witches weren't inclined to believe the Lobos were any different from the Loups.

She waited for Amar to turn off his chainsaw and lower it before stepping forward and speaking. It was never good to startle a man with a giant serrated blade.

"Hey, Amar. I brought you some goodies." Morgen smiled and held up the box of cookies. Normally, she would have made baked goods from scratch if she wanted to give someone a gift, but these were his favorites. "Cookies and chowder. Everything you'll need when you head out into the woods to hunt tonight. By seven."

Most of the time, Amar no longer looked surly and grumpy when he gazed at her, but her words made him scrutinize her with wary suspicion. "What happens at seven?"

"A few witches are coming over. I thought you might want to vacate the premises."

His hand strayed to the talisman hanging around his neck next to a tooth on a leather thong. It always touched her that he valued something she'd made, but she hoped he wouldn't need it tonight.

"You thought *I* would want to vacate, or that is what *they* want?"

"They did suggest it would be preferable if werewolves weren't present for the meeting, but if you want to stay, I'll tell them to fumigate themselves and learn to enjoy your company." Morgen smiled again. She meant it, but it *would* be less tense all around if he stayed out of sight.

"And you brought me bribes to ensure I am willing to leave?" He contemplated the Girl Scout cookie box.

"I brought you *gifts* to keep your belly warm and your blood sugar in optimal range as you cavort vigorously through the woods after your prey. I'm sure hunting is calorically intensive."

"Uh huh." Amar still wore a dubious if not distasteful expression—probably more for the thought of witches coming near his barn than her offerings—but he accepted the cookies. "What's in the thermos?"

"Clam chowder. Fall is coming, and the nights are starting to get chillier. I thought you'd appreciate something warm."

His expression grew suspicious again. "Are there *clams* in it?"

"Ah, not technically. I'm not full-on vegan, and I do occasionally eat seafood, but I find clams to be gritty and, er, nasty, so I didn't have any on hand. I used button mushrooms."

"So, it's just... chowder."

"Or mushroom chowder, I suppose, but it's delicious. Just like real clam chowder. I have a great recipe. It uses nori to get that briny seafood flavor."

"What's nori?"

"Seaweed."

His lip curled. "You won't eat clams, but you'll eat seaweed?"

"It's delish."

"You know the fact that you're a witch isn't the strangest thing about you, right?"

"You've mentioned that before."

"Good." His eyes closed to slits, but he smiled slightly as he stepped forward and wrapped her in a hug.

Relieved, Morgen leaned into him. She'd been worried he would be offended or stomp around in disgruntlement at the thought of so many people coming onto the property. She remembered how they'd first met, by him leaping onto the hood of her car and snarling that trespassers weren't allowed.

"How late will the witches stay?" he murmured in her ear, his breath warm in contrast to the cooling evening air.

"I didn't ask. Is there a time by which you'd like me to ask them to leave?" And if she did, would he come to the house for a late-night visit? When he'd been wielding that chainsaw, she hadn't seen evidence that his ribs still bothered him. Surely, if he was fit enough for his work, he was fit enough for bedroom activities.

"By midnight, I should have stalked, captured, and devoured suitable prey."

He nuzzled her ear as he said that, which sent amazing tingles through her body, so she decided not to mention that she preferred not to hear about such things. She might, however, have that box of mint floss on hand if he came to the house.

"Midnight is a little late for me. Perhaps you could be done devouring things by ten-thirty."

"If you're tired, I could find ways to stimulate you."

"That might be all right," she whispered, wishing the thermos and box of cookies weren't crammed between them. She slid one hand up to grip his bare muscular shoulder.

"*Might*?" he asked, his voice a rumble. He drew back enough to look her in the eyes, his own eyes smoldering with intensity, and started to kiss her, but he halted and turned his head toward the driveway.

Had he heard the first car arriving? Morgen groaned, wishing she'd said no to the witch meeting so she could spend the night with Amar.

"The ferret wrangler comes," Amar stated.

"Her name is Wendy, unless you mean someone else." As far as Morgen had seen, Wendy was the only witch with a ferret familiar. The rest favored cats, ravens, crows, owls, and one lady had a snake.

"I do not care what their names are. *You* are the only witch who acts like one of the pack and cares about werewolves."

"I will admit that if you're furry, the witches aren't the easiest to get along with, but maybe if you learned their names and were civil, they'd be more likely to accept you."

"I do not *wish* to be accepted by witches."

Just when she'd been thinking that he didn't get grumpy with her as often anymore...

The sound of tires on the gravel finally reached Morgen's dull human ears, and Wendy's camper van came into view.

"I *have* completed something for that witch." Amar lowered his arms and stepped back. "Per your request."

Morgen noticed the chill once his arms were gone and again wished they could spend the night embracing. "Oh?"

Without explaining, Amar strode into the barn.

Wendy parked her van in its usual spot by the house and plugged the extension cord back in. Her ferret ran across the lawn and around Morgen's legs. Lucky—whom she'd left in the house so that he wouldn't jump on, lick, or knock over any witches—barked uproariously from the living room.

"Hello, mighty Napoleon," Morgen said.

He rose up on his hind legs and chittered at her—or maybe at the thermos.

"I don't think you'd like this." Morgen set the thermos and cookies on one of the stumps in Amar's workspace. "You're a carnivore, I'm told, so vegan clams wouldn't be up your alley."

Wendy walked over carrying a tray of cheese and crackers with a discount sticker on the plastic lid. "What are vegan clams?"

"Button mushrooms."

"You can't just call them that?"

"No, it's like the vegan leather."

"In that businesses can charge more if the name is changed?"

"Exactly."

"The meetings are usually a bit of a potluck, so I brought this." Wendy scraped the discount sticker off the tray lid. "I don't have much in the way of kitchen facilities in my van."

"You're welcome to use anything in the house. You're my graphics designer, after all. I have to treat you well."

"So far, I've designed a menu and three buttons for your app."

"I would have had to pay big money for that if I hired someone more experienced."

Napoleon climbed up the stump to investigate the thermos. The lid was secure, so Morgen trusted he couldn't get into it.

"Are you making any money from the app yet?" Wendy doubtless still had dreams of buying a house in town and having fast internet.

"No. It didn't feel right to charge people. I don't think witches generally have a lot of money."

"Most apps are under three dollars."

"Well, we wouldn't make much charging that anyway," Morgen said. "We've only got a few hundred beta testers using it right now. Also, Phoebe and the others forbade me from putting it online in the big app stores for anyone to download. Apparently, the recipe for an elixir of grout cleaning is top-secret information."

"More likely, it's only available to witches who pay their dues."

"I don't know if that's true, but thanks to Belinda's connections, we've got beta testers from all over the world. It'll be good to get feedback from more than Bellrock witches."

The barn door slid open, and Amar stepped out.

Napoleon let out a startled squeak, flung himself off the stump, and collapsed on the sawdust on the ground. Once again, he had the rigidity of a dishtowel.

Amar glanced balefully at him as he approached Morgen and Wendy, carrying a large wooden contraption full of posts supporting carpeted shelves and built-in cubes. When he set it down, the structure was almost as tall as Morgen.

"Is that a cat tree?" she asked.

"It's a *ferret* tree." Amar also gave Wendy a baleful look.

She stepped behind Morgen, perhaps not realizing that Amar had brought her a gift. Admittedly, his gift-giving demeanor could use some tweaking.

"It's unfortunate that the only ferret we know is recently deceased," Morgen said.

Amar picked up Napoleon, who drooped his head and tail dramatically over his hand, and deposited him on one of the carpeted shelves on the ferret tree. The ferret *house*. Or maybe condominium complex. It was too large and intricate to be called a tree.

"Oh." Wendy stepped out from behind Morgen. "You made it for Napoleon? I didn't think you would. You don't even like me, do you?" She eyed Amar with uncertainty.

"He adores you," Morgen said. "He's just not good at showing it."

Amar shifted his baleful expression back to her. Morgen beamed a smile at him.

"I made it," he said, "because Morgen asked for it. And I knew it would please her."

"He's a good man," Morgen told Wendy, wanting to hug Amar again, but she felt shy about doing so in front of someone else.

"Oh." Wendy stepped forward and poked Napoleon. "It's okay. He won't hurt you. He made this for you."

A single ferret eye opened, but it closed again. Napoleon wasn't convinced.

"I wonder if there's such thing as a talisman of bravery in Grandma's book," Morgen mused. If magic could keep a werewolf from being controlled, maybe it could give a ferret some cojones.

"Oh, you can make all kinds of charms." Wendy held up a bracelet that jangled with everything from metal moons and stars to a shoe that looked like it had come off a Monopoly board. "I'm only good at crafting the base trinkets, the way I can the receptacles for the talismans. But *you've* got good power for making things, Morgen. You could learn to do all kinds of charms. The ones that keep rabbits out of gardens are super popular in Bellrock. Betty, a witch in our coven, used to make them and sell them at the farmers market until she retired to Palm Springs."

"Well, I guess I can keep that in mind as a possible new career if I'm not able to make money as an app developer." Morgen smiled, though she always felt bleak when she thought about her financial future. She'd found some gold and silver coins stashed in Grandma's vault, and Wendy had returned enough of the valuable bioluminescent moss that she could pay the bills for a few months, but since there wasn't any more of it growing in Wolf Wood, she had to figure out something else if she wanted to stay up here. And as long as she had a grumpy but handsome werewolf who enjoyed spending time with her, Morgen couldn't imagine going back to a lonely apartment in the suburbs of Seattle.

Amar looked toward the driveway again and sighed. "Another car is coming."

"A lot more are coming," Morgen said. "Sorry. I should have asked you first before inviting them all. Technically, they invited themselves, but I could have said no and didn't."

"*All?*" Amar stared at her. "You said a *few.*"

"Did I? I think most of the coven shows up at the meetings." Morgen looked to Wendy for confirmation.

Wendy nodded. "There's usually food and alcohol, so that makes the meetings popular."

Amar growled.

Sian stepped out of the house in a gray sweater and jeans, the clothing drab, save for pink socks just visible when she walked. She carried a book and her purse and looked like she meant to find a coffee shop to hide out in during the meeting.

"I require your car for the evening," Sian said. "I assume you will not, as the hostess, need to leave the premises."

"Probably not." Morgen dug out her key fob and handed it to Sian. "But the bakery-slash-coffee-shop-slash-internet-cafe closed at five, I think."

"I am joining Dr. Valderas for a discussion on our passions. He is interested in my work, and he is composing a paper on acupuncture and homeopathic treatment for equines that I wish to hear about. He promised that it cites peer-reviewed studies that applied rigorous scientific methodology, and that nothing about his paper will be *woo woo*. I am skeptical but prepared to be open-minded."

Morgen blinked. "You're going on a date?"

"I do not date."

"If you're meeting a man in the evening to discuss your passions, it's a date."

"It is not."

"Does *he* know it's not a date?" Wendy asked.

"If he doesn't know now, he will before the night is over." Sian took the key fob and headed for the car as two sedans arrived and parked.

"Should we feel sorry for Dr. Valderas?" Wendy asked.

"I'm not sure." Morgen had gathered that some of the more vile witches in town—none of whom were still in the coven—had used their power to coerce the handsome vet into having sex with them. He might appreciate a simple intellectual discourse on equine acupuncture.

A car door opened, and a cranky meow floated out.

"I didn't realize they would bring their familiars." Morgen glanced toward the house a second before Lucky started barking again. "Maybe the ladies would be all right with an outdoor meeting." It wasn't that cold, and the deck did have built-in benches all around it.

A black cat leaped out of the car ahead of its owner and sauntered toward the barn. Zorro hooted several times from his nesting box, then took off, wings flapping as he flew into the forest.

"Your familiar believes tonight's company will be poor," Amar said, his eyes glinting with humor for the first time.

Napoleon rose on his hind legs as the cat approached. Unlike the ferret, the feline was fearless and prowled straight up to the group. Actually, he went to the ferret tree and sprang onto one of the lower shelves. Napoleon chittered at him and climbed higher. The cat flopped over on its back and rolled on the shelf.

"You didn't sprinkle catnip on that thing, did you?" Morgen raised a hand toward the two witches who'd stepped out of the car. A crow perched on the passenger's shoulder, making Morgen wonder how the ride had gone. A cat and a crow carpooling sounded like a recipe for chaos, if not fur and feathers everywhere.

Both women were familiar from the night of the demon summoning, but Morgen didn't yet know their names. Since her introvert tendencies included an awkwardness when introducing herself to strangers, she'd hoped Phoebe would arrive first. That feeling of panic rose up in her again at the thought that she'd have to greet everyone, ask them what they wanted to drink, and tell them where the bathroom was. Sian had been right to flee.

"I did not." Amar tilted his head and watched with bemusement as the cat kept rolling on his back, his tail swishing vigorously. "I did get the wood and carpet out of my pile of discards. Zorro visited that pile often before I made him the nesting box and convinced him to stop raiding the barn on a nightly basis."

"Raiding the barn and leaving feathers and *droppings*?" Morgen well recalled Amar ranting on that topic.

"Yes."

Wendy lifted a hand to her mouth. "Are you saying..." She trailed off since one of the newcomers had walked within earshot, a black-haired woman in her fifties. Maybe Wendy didn't want to announce her suspicion that the ferret tree was doused in owl nastiness when someone's cat familiar was rolling on it. "Hi, Sakura. This is Morgen. Morgen, Sakura. She runs the stationery store in town."

"The Lilac Blossom," Sakura said. "I also sell office supplies, wedding invitations, gift cards, and Yoku Moku cookies."

Morgen blinked at this last item.

"I have to compete with the fudge shop next door," Sakura said. "I found that the smell of baking cookies gets tourists in the door. Why is there a cat tree in your driveway?"

"It's a *ferret* tree," Morgen said.

Napoleon chittered from the top ledge.

"It's magnificent," Sakura said. "Where did you get it?"

Amar had been exchanging glowers with the other witch, a stout white-haired woman who'd stopped *well* back from the group, perhaps fearing werewolf cooties would float over and contaminate her, but at the question, he turned a surprised squint toward Sakura.

She was walking around the ferret tree, gripping her chin and examining it from all angles as her cat explored. Napoleon jumped down to the lower shelf and nosed the cat, which turned into a chase game that took place on and around the piece of furniture.

"Amar made it. He's a gifted craftsman. You should check out the bench on my porch." Morgen smiled at him, pleased to have an opportunity to praise his work to others.

"A *werewolf* made such a fine piece?" Sakura tore her gaze from the frolicking familiars.

"Werewolves are people, you know," Morgen said.

"But they're so..." Sakura peered dubiously at Amar. "Brutish."

Amar growled at her.

Morgen stepped over and swatted him on the chest. "Don't *growl*. That's why you have the reputation you do."

"Should I *purr* when I'm insulted?" he rumbled.

"No, but she likes your work. Isn't that at least flattering?"

"Yes," Sakura said, undaunted by his rumble. "How much would you charge to make a cat condo like this for me?"

"A thousand dollars," Amar said in the challenging tone of one who has no interest in the project and therefore offers an exorbitant quote.

Morgen drew him aside and whispered, "What are you doing? I thought you were in a bit of a financial pinch since you lost so much of your work and tools in the barn fire."

"The barn fire that *witches* started."

"Not *these* witches." Morgen waved at Sakura and the other woman, not including Wendy, since Wendy *had* been one of the three sisters responsible.

"I'm not sure you want to spend that much, Sakura." Wendy was eyeing the carpet on one of the shelves, perhaps searching for evidence that it hadn't been thoroughly cleaned after the owl visits.

"Nonsense. Rikido loves it. I *must* have one. That shag carpet is delightfully eccentric. I'll pay seven-fifty if you can build it and deliver it to my home in the hills. I'd never be able to fit this in my car."

"Seven-fifty for the cat tree, fifty dollars for delivery, and I will absolutely use that carpet."

Morgen opened her mouth to tell him to charge something

more reasonable—nobody spent that much on *pet* furniture—but Sakura said, "Done. I'll give you a deposit after the meeting."

Amar seemed surprised—and dismayed to have gotten another job making pet furnishings—but he nodded curtly. "Fine."

"Fine."

Another car arrived, and Morgen braced herself to greet the newcomers and perform her duties as a hostess. But before she stepped away, four wolves loped out of the woods. Three were gray and one black. Was the latter the beautiful Maria? Morgen had come to an understanding of sorts with her and believed that Amar wouldn't go back to her, but she still would have preferred not to see the voluptuous female Lobo again.

Amar stepped away from the group to greet the wolves. Napoleon, who'd been in the middle of wrestling with the cat, noticed their approach and promptly fainted again. The cat sniffed him, his tail swishing in confusion.

"Oh dear," Sakura murmured. "Come, Rikido." She picked up her cat and strode toward the other witches, casting several glances back at the wolves as she went.

"I'll show the ladies around," Wendy said, grabbing the limp Napoleon and hustling away.

Morgen, worried that the wolves' arrival meant something was wrong, lingered behind Amar.

The black and the largest gray shifted into their human forms, resolving into Maria and Pedro, as the other two sat on their haunches. Maria and Pedro stood side by side, so maybe they'd gotten back together. Since they were naked, standing hip to hip suggested some comfort with each other. Morgen made sure she only looked at their faces.

"We need to talk, brother." Pedro gripped Amar's shoulder.

He gave Morgen a pointed look, as if he expected her to leave.

The witches were waiting for her, so maybe she *should* leave, but if this was about the possible threat to Amar, Morgen didn't want to be left in the dark.

Amar also looked over at her, his face hard to read. Morgen sighed, expecting him to say this was wolf stuff and ask her to give them privacy, but after a moment, he lifted a hand in invitation.

"She has made talismans for the pack." Amar nodded toward the similar silver necklaces that they all wore—or *chains*, as he preferred to call them, the word being more manly. "She is an ally and to be trusted."

Morgen stepped closer, though she expected the cocky Pedro would scoff. He wasn't her favorite Lobo.

"Yes," Pedro said, surprising her. "She is more like a wolf than a witch, but do you wish to get her involved in this? What if our old enemy finds out she is your mate and uses her against you?"

Maria looked at Morgen, and Morgen's cheeks warmed. She didn't think she was Amar's *mate*, especially since they hadn't had sex yet. They were just dating. But the moment had too much gravity to blurt that out. Who was this old enemy who might use her against Amar?

"Has it been confirmed that it's him?" Amar asked.

"No," Pedro said, "but one of the Loups was found dead out by the campground."

"You say that like it's a bad thing."

"His throat was torn out, and massive claws destroyed his ribcage and ripped out his heart," Pedro said. "The rest of the Loups looked for the heart when they found the body, but it wasn't anywhere around. They think it was eaten. Only the *Loup Garou* do that."

"*Loup Garou*?" Morgen asked, puzzled by the similarity of the name to the Loups Laflamme werewolf pack. It didn't sound like they were related.

"Americans call them the *rougarou*," Amar said. "They came

over from the Old World. Few remain, but they are very powerful. Very dangerous. Did they catch a trail, Pedro?"

"They caught a scent. They were too afraid to go into the woods to seek its owner." Pedro spat on the ground. "If we found your body with your heart ripped out, *we* would go after the one who did it."

"I appreciate that. I better go look for myself. Until I smell him, I won't know for sure if..." Amar gazed off into the woods, his eyes growing distant.

"Who is it?" Morgen asked softly. "Someone you've met before?"

"One created from magic long ago. One far stronger than a werewolf. One the pack may have met before." Pedro looked grimly at his fellow werewolves.

"He is stronger than *a* werewolf," Maria said, "but not stronger than the whole pack."

"We will see," Pedro said. "We encountered him before you joined the pack, so you do not know. His magic is more powerful than the magic of anyone here. Even the witches."

"I'm ready to hunt him." Amar removed his vest, boots, and jeans and handed them to Morgen.

"Now that I'm a friend of the pack, I'm trusted to hold your clothes for you when you shift?"

"You are. Did you finish putting the wards down around the house?"

"Yes, though they're not active at the moment, since I knew company was coming. I have to chant commands whenever I want to activate and deactivate them. Fortunately, Wendy knew how to make it so they only keep out strangers, not the people—and familiars—who live here."

"Activate them as soon as the others leave. In the meantime, hopefully it will be safe here with so many magic users around." Amar grimaced. "*Safer.*"

"When you said you were going hunting to devour prey, I didn't imagine it would be something that chows down the hearts of werewolves."

"I didn't either."

"Do you want me to come along?" Morgen asked. "You know I'm good at whacking enemies with my staff. And if it's a demon, I might be able to banish it." She would have to stop and collect Sian to have the firepower to do that, but...

"The *rougarou* is not a demon," Amar said. "He has lived many centuries, but he is mortal."

"Barely." Pedro switched to Spanish and said more.

Amar nodded gravely. "Stay here, Morgen. I'll try to return by midnight."

"Ten-thirty," she told him.

He snorted softly and kissed her.

Morgen wrapped an arm around him, not wanting to let him go, but he broke the kiss and stepped away. Maria and Pedro had already shifted back into wolves. Amar, naked except for his tooth and talisman, changed into a great gray-and-black wolf. As he padded after the others, he looked back over his shoulder at her, his eyes the same piercing blue that they were when he was human.

She couldn't tell if he was giving her that long look because he was conveying a message or because he was afraid he wouldn't see her again.

3

MORGEN'S DUTIES AS HOSTESS AND HER CONCERN FOR AMAR KEPT her from paying much attention to what was said at the meeting. Phoebe, Belinda, Judith, and a blur of other people she was introduced to sat on the benches on the deck and talked about how the tourist season was dying down, the town would start getting back to normal, and the full-moon rituals could resume. They spoke of the rituals in the same breaths as harvesting apples and blackberries and making cider and jam, so Morgen didn't know if it was a significant magical event or simply a fall activity that a practicing witch had to check off the to-do list. Jam making, pumpkin carving, corn harvesting, nude ritual under the moon.

"Morgen?" One of the women walked out of the house carrying the glowing toadstool from the basket Sian had been mocking earlier. She was a small lady with a wizened face and curly silver hair. "Did you pick this?"

"Yeah. Is that okay? I thought it would make an eco-friendly nightlight."

"It's a rindiloki fungus."

"So... not a nightlight?"

"Not typically."

"Is it useful? I checked the internet and my database and didn't see pictures of anything quite like it. And sorry, what's your name again?" Morgen frowned, knowing she'd gotten an introduction and forgotten it.

"Ute. Or Ute the Herbalist, as some call me. The rindiloki is poisonous and is used in making a hexing liquid. You can mix it with oil of oregano and Cynar and pour it around your property, and trespassers will be cursed."

Morgen cared more about deterring trespassers than cursing them but smiled. "That sounds promising. What's Cynar?" She pulled out her phone to look it up.

"An Italian alcohol. The witches in Europe love making potions and other concoctions with it. The primary ingredient is artichoke."

"An inherently magical vegetable."

"Some think so. I trust you knew what you were doing when you gathered *this*." Ute held up a twig with silver needles and a few equally silver berries.

"That Christmas is coming, and silver wreaths are all the rage."

"Ardonix berries are aphrodisiacs. I assume you're trying to lure that strapping werewolf to your bed." Ute winked.

"Uh, he is strapping."

"I'll say. As I was driving up, I saw him get naked and give you his clothes. Talk about being hung like a stallion. He could climb into bed with me any night of the week." Ute's wink turned into a wicked grin as she made thrusting motions with her hips.

Morgen was so surprised that she almost fell over. "What did you— Uhm, never mind."

"Werewolves are suspicious about taking tea from witches. You might want to hide the berries in some beer. Something he'll swill down without thinking."

"That's not necessary. I don't need to drug him."

"I suppose not. You're still young and have your natural hair color. You don't need to resort to trickery. Or stuffing your bra." Ute studied Morgen's chest frankly. "I assume those are real."

"*Yes.*" Morgen wrapped an arm across her chest.

"How is he in bed? Passionate? Does he growl? I've never been with a wolf man, but I hear there's a lot of growling. And *howling.* Does he throw his head back and howl to the moon while you're conjoined?"

"Ute," another witch said, walking out of the kitchen with a drink. "Are you embarrassing our newest member?"

"If a little sex talk embarrasses her, she's not going to fit in at all, Harriet."

"That's true. You're divorced, aren't you, Morgen? I suppose you're not some young naive pup that we have to mind our tongues around." Harriet pointed over at Wendy. "And you did enter all those herbs that are known for enhancing sexual potency into the database on your app. I've been trying the Panax ginseng with Marv." She elbowed Ute.

"I'll bet you have," Ute said.

Morgen rubbed her face, wondering what she'd gotten herself into. These weren't the conversations she'd envisioned witches having.

But if Ute was an herbalist, maybe Morgen should befriend her. If she knew which herbs and fungi could help in defending one's home—and perhaps one's werewolf?—Morgen wanted to learn more. The wards were installed, but Amar's old enemy sounded exceedingly dangerous. If it would protect him, Morgen would happily collect every fungus in the woods and dance naked around the barn as she poured toadstool juice over every inch of lawn.

"Ute," Morgen said. "Have you ever gone foraging for ingredients in Wolf Wood?"

"I *used* to." Ute sniffed. "Until a grumpy werewolf moved in and started chasing away anyone who wandered onto the land. Gwen said she only asked him to defend against people with ill intent, but he thought *every* witch had ill intent." Her voice lost its disgruntlement as she gazed toward the trees. "I would love to go foraging out there. This place is special. There's magic in the earth, percolating into the nooks and crannies in so many spots."

"Have you ever seen shiny dots embedded in the bark of a tree?" Morgen hadn't forgotten that spot and the ominous electrical charge they'd emitted when she'd tried to scrape one off.

Ute focused on her. "I haven't, but I've heard of such things. I don't suppose you'd like to show me?"

"Not tonight." Even without some deadly new enemy prowling the county, Morgen wouldn't have gone roaming through Wolf Wood after dark. "But I could show you in the morning."

And maybe along the way, Ute could point out useful plants and mushrooms and tell her which ones could thwart dangerous enemies.

"I'd love that," Ute said. "I'll be here promptly at eight."

"Thank you."

A thump sounded as a woman with a staff navigated toward them. Belinda. The orb atop the staff glowed softly.

"Good evening, Morgen, Ute," Belinda said.

Harriet had drifted away.

"Hello," Morgen said.

"I wanted to thank you for volunteering to host the meeting here," Belinda said.

Volunteering? Was that what she'd done?

"You're welcome." Morgen made herself smile, though she wanted to suggest that another meeting location might be more ideal.

"Not everyone was willing to come to this... den of werewolf vileness, as they called it, but those who didn't come are some of the more difficult women to work with. I shouldn't admit, I suppose, that it's refreshing to have a meeting without them."

"Difficult?" Ute asked. "The Lenore cousins are the reasons tensions have been so high with the werewolves."

"I know."

"I'm sure they didn't come because they're afraid of reprisal now that all the Lobos have those talismans." Ute frowned disapprovingly at Morgen.

Morgen had hoped the witches had forgiven her for that after she, Sian, and Amar had been paramount in defeating that demon. Their acceptance of Morgen into the coven, and their presence here tonight, had to mean they had *somewhat* gotten over it but maybe not fully.

"What happened?" Morgen asked, ignoring the frown. "Between those cousins and the werewolves?"

"They and Calista and Olivia—and Nora when she was alive— liked to throw orgies with magically compelled bedroom mates," Ute said. "I like a firm young stud between my legs as much as the next woman, but it was disgusting. And criminal. I'm surprised the mayor never did anything about it. He's a wolf, too, you know."

"I've heard that," Morgen said. "One of the Loups' minions."

"Or maybe they're one of his," Ute said. "He's not a meek man or the type to do another's bidding."

"Don't the authorities here look out for the witches?" Morgen had gathered from Amar that the sheriff's department was more likely to side with the coven—those who lived here and had been citizens for a long time—than the Lobos or Loups.

"The sheriff's department treats us like little old ladies who need protection, yes," Belinda said.

"It doesn't hurt that many of us own property in Bellrock and pay taxes like upright citizens should." Ute sniffed. "The werewolves all deal in cash and barely even tip at the local restaurants."

"The mayor is more inclined to favor them though," Belinda

said, "or look the other way when a wolf chews up someone's livestock."

"I guess I'm fortunate there's not much in the way of livestock here." Morgen heard Lucky barking upstairs. He was her livestock. She would have to go up and check on him. Though he loved to be social and work the crowd for attention, Morgen had put him upstairs, afraid he would chase the avian and feline familiars all over the place if he wasn't restrained. "All I need to worry about is…"

Morgen trailed off as she spotted two women walking around the outside of the house with what looked like metal detectors. Instead of beeping, they hummed softer and louder, and lights on the head flashed more slowly or quickly depending on… Morgen had no idea what.

"Are the coven coffers low?" she asked. "They're more likely to find nails left over from construction than dropped quarters."

"It's not a metal detector, dear," Ute said. "It's a *werewolf* detector. It catches lingering odors."

A third woman came into view with what looked like a sprayer for pesticides. She walked behind the first two, a tank on her back, and squirted liquid all over the grass.

"What's she doing?" Morgen blurted in alarm. "The garden is right around the corner, and my dog rolls around in that grass. She's not spraying chemicals, is she?"

"No," Belinda said. "Werewolf bane."

"Werewolf what?"

"It's a blend of herbs mixed with water that repels their kind. Don't worry. It's all non-toxic. Though I wouldn't recommend licking the grass right now."

Morgen rubbed her face again. "Is that necessary?"

Maybe this was what Phoebe had meant when she'd spoken about *fumigation*. And to think, Morgen had thought it was a joke.

"Oh, it's ridiculous," Belinda said, "but it'll make the ladies more comfortable. Even though those witches who feared reprisal from werewolves didn't come, others were also uneasy about the presence of lycanthropes in the area. Morgen, do you have anything to drink? Non-alcoholic, please. I have to speak in a few minutes."

"Yes."

On the way to the kitchen, Morgen heard a clunk upstairs. Afraid Lucky was having trouble settling down with so much activity below, activity he wasn't a part of, she grabbed one of his favorite treats and headed upstairs.

Since Sian was gone, only a few lights were on. The empty guest rooms she passed on the way to her own bedroom were dark. When the house had been built, it had been intended for a large family with multiple generations and passels of children. Morgen wondered if Grandma had ever entertained. In her later years, she'd been a recluse, so it was hard to imagine, but perhaps this house had hosted parties before.

The beeping of the werewolf detector floated up through an open window. Maybe not parties like this.

When Morgen opened the door to her bedroom, Lucky jumped up and put his paws on her shoulders.

"I know, buddy." She only patted him for a few seconds before trying to lure him to the floor with a treat. They still needed to work on appropriate doggie manners. "It's only for a couple of hours. Do you still have enough water?"

As she glanced toward the bowl she'd brought in for him, he charged past her and into the hallway.

"Lucky," she called. "Back here, buddy. The familiars don't want to meet you."

She waved the treat, but he kept going. Surprisingly, he didn't run down the stairs. He stopped at one of the few closed doors in the hallway and snuffled loudly at the crack underneath.

Morgen frowned. It was the library with Grandma's secret

vault that held the special grimoire, *Incantations of Power*. Morgen had obeyed Grandma's wishes and not added any of the recipes, incantations, or ingredients mentioned in it to the database for her app.

Lucky jumped up again, planting his paws on the door, and looked expectantly at Morgen.

"Did someone come up here?"

Lucky dropped down, sniffed the crack, spun around twice, and put his paws on the door again.

"I'll take that as a *yes*." Morgen stepped back into her bedroom to grab the antler staff she'd used to banish the demon. She doubted its magic could banish snooping witches, but a whack on the head with the antlers might do the job. "Move over, buddy."

She nudged Lucky aside so she could grab the doorknob. But it was locked.

Hell, someone *was* in there. Morgen pressed her ear to the door but didn't hear anything. She knocked. A clunk came from inside, but nobody answered.

Damn. Was it possible the snooper knew about the vault and was trying to get in? The amulet that Morgen had found in Grandma's room unlocked it, but it hadn't occurred to her to wonder if *any* star-shaped item might do the job.

She tried the doorknob again, hoping whoever was inside would be rattled and stop whatever they were doing. Should she get Phoebe or Belinda? Morgen had encountered incantations for unlocking doors, but she hadn't planned to go into a life of cat burglary so she hadn't memorized them.

"It's rude to snoop in someone's house," Morgen called through the door, wishing she'd left Lucky to roam loose. But he wasn't a guard dog—even now, his tail was wagging, indicating he wanted to confront the person inside because they hadn't yet petted him. "And if you're looking for the bathroom, it's a smaller room with fewer books."

Lucky tilted his head and whined.

"I said fewer, not *none*." Morgen was well aware that her sister's bathroom reading habit had resulted in numerous additions to the stack poised on the back of the toilet. Sian couldn't dither on her phone like a normal person. "Oh, the app."

She rolled her eyes at herself for forgetting it, dug out her phone, and typed *lock* into the search function. To her delight, numerous incantations for opening gates, portals, and doors came up, as well as the recipe for a substance that greased hinges to help with removing them.

Pleased that her app had come in useful, Morgen pulled up the first door-unlocking incantation and gripped her amulet. It warmed in her hand, prepared for action.

"Get ready," she whispered to Lucky.

He promptly dropped his forelegs to the floor in a doggie play bow.

"Yes, very ferocious. Whoever's inside is sure to wet themselves."

He wagged his tail and whined.

"I should have gotten a rottweiler."

Morgen focused on the doorknob and whispered, "Under the moon's magic, coerce this door to unlock, so that forward I may walk."

A soft click sounded. Morgen shoved the door open and sprang into the library with the staff lowered, its antlers poised for pronging.

It was dark inside, and the only movement came from the window, where curtains stirred in a breeze. She hadn't left that window open.

As Lucky trotted past her, Morgen turned on the lights, half expecting someone to jump out at her. But it was a home library, not a university athenaeum, and there weren't rows and rows of bookcases that one might hide behind. Two reading chairs, a table, and a telescope were the only furnishings beyond the book-cases against the four walls.

Lucky ran to the window and propped his paws on the sill, snuffling loudly. It was hard to imagine one of the sixty-something witches climbing out onto the roof and shimmying down a drain-pipe to the ground, but Morgen reminded herself they weren't *all* grandmother-aged.

A breeze gusted, stirring the curtains again, and something moved on the table. A piece of paper with writing on it.

With nerves twisting in her stomach, Morgen walked over and picked it up while Lucky snuffled at the floor in front of the window.

"Your true allegiances are known," she read. "Return to the city. You are not the proper guardian of the secrets of our kind."

4

———

MORGEN SET DOWN THE NOTE AND GLANCED TOWARD THE BOOKCASE that hid the vault. The temptation to check it came over her—could the intruder have found the book?—but what if some familiar was watching from afar? Or even from in here?

She spun a slow circle, checking the tops of bookcases for rodents, ravens, and cats. "There's nobody else in here with us, is there, boy?"

Lucky planted his paws on the windowsill again.

"Yeah, yeah, I get it. We'll check outside in a minute." Morgen shooed him off the sill and closed the window—it had been open wide enough for someone to climb out. She also closed the curtains to make sure a raven perched in a tree couldn't see inside, then went to the vault bookcase.

She wanted to believe that a random visitor couldn't have possibly known about it, but she'd received the knowledge that it existed in a dream. Who was to say that someone else couldn't have had a similar dream? She liked to think Grandma would only send her relatives messages from the afterworld, but it wasn't as if Morgen knew the rules of how that all worked.

When she prodded the fang-filled snout of a gargoyle, the bookcase it was mounted on eased away from the wall. Behind it, the safe door was closed. She applied the amulet to the lock to open it and check inside.

Morgen exhaled in relief. The large book was still in the safe, as well as the more mundane valuables Grandma had left. Morgen closed everything up again and leaned against the bookcase.

She'd taken that grimoire to the graveyard for the demon fight, so any of the witches who'd been there could have seen it. Or *all* of them could have. Since she and Sian had used the staff and an incantation from the book to defeat the demon, it would have been memorable. Morgen was tempted to narrow down the possible snoopers to the witches who had been at the graveyard, but there had been more than twenty people, including Calista, who was in jail now. At least Morgen *hoped* she was still there.

Wendy's sister, Olivia, had been there and *wasn't* in jail. Just a few days earlier, her fox had been at the house, trying to eat Zorro. Amar and Zorro had taken care of the fox—permanently—but that didn't mean Olivia didn't still have it out for Morgen. Whoever had been snooping hadn't found the book, but they might try again.

Morgen opened the window and stuck her head out, peering toward Zorro's nesting box. Since it was nighttime, and there was a lot of activity at the house, he was probably off hunting, but she whistled, just in case.

"If he saw the person sneaking out of the house, that would be handy."

Lucky sat and wagged his tail. It swished on the rug.

Zorro, Morgen thought, doubting an owl would come to a whistle. *Are you out there? Have you seen anything suspicious tonight?*

She'd never confirmed that she could speak telepathically to her familiars, but they *did* seem to understand her when she thought things to them.

A vision of a dark forest came to her, and she gripped the sill for support as she smiled. Good old Zorro. Somehow, he'd heard her and understood.

But he was flying over the woods, not the house or anywhere near the yard. There wasn't a hint of light beyond what the stars provided. Even so, his superior owl eyesight came along with the vision, and she could make out leaves stirring on the forest floor far below. Abruptly, Zorro plummeted downward.

Nausea came over Morgen, and she groaned, already regretting reaching out to him. That regret only intensified as Zorro stretched out with his talons and snatched up a mouse from under the leaves. He flew up to a nearby branch and chomped down his meal.

Morgen shook her head, willing the vision to fade and for her stomach to settle. Fortunately, the magic obeyed, and Morgen found herself back in the library, staring out the window.

Lucky whined.

"Zorro didn't see anything," she informed him.

Lucky sniffed at the floor.

"Can *you* find the intruder? By scent?"

He galloped for the door, and she hurried after him. He wasn't as reliable a familiar as Zorro, but he *had* caught Calista after the demon encounter. And he did seem to understand her better now than when he'd only been a dog.

Lucky raced down the stairs and through the laundry room to the back door. When Morgen had come in, she'd closed it, but someone else had since left it ajar. He put his paws on it, pushing it fully open, and charged onto the deck.

Several women issued startled exclamations as he ran through the gathering, bumping people and running through Wendy's legs. Napoleon sat on her shoulder, and he rose up and chittered indignantly at Lucky.

"Sorry, sorry," Morgen said as she came out after her dog. She raised her hands and patted at the air apologetically. "He slipped out when I went to check on him." Sort of.

Lucky weaved through the crowd, bypassing Belinda and Ute and stopping in front of Phoebe. Morgen sucked in an alarmed breath.

Phoebe wasn't the snoop, was she? Not Morgen's mentor.

But at fifty or so, Phoebe might still be spry enough to climb out a window and down to the ground. Lucky stepped in close and nosed her jacket pocket.

Phoebe, who'd only reluctantly tolerated him coming into her store with Morgen when she'd been doing work there, gasped and scooted back. Lucky followed and kept nosing around the hem and pockets of her jacket. She hadn't taken something from the library, had she?

"What is he *doing*?" Phoebe spotted Morgen and scowled.

"Just smelling you." Morgen jogged up and grabbed Lucky's collar.

"So *vigorously*?" Phoebe backed up until she bumped into the deck railing. Lucky followed her, snuffling loudly.

"At least his nose isn't in your crotch," someone said with a snigger.

"Uhm, is there anything in your pocket?" Morgen asked the question casually while pulling Lucky back, but she watched Phoebe's face to see if anything alarmed her. Like being caught red-handed.

Phoebe only frowned and pulled out a bag of pepperoni sticks. "I didn't know if there would be snacks."

"Oh." Morgen slumped in disappointment. "Lucky."

He sat, tail swishing back and forth on the deck, his eyes locked on the bag.

"You've *had* dinner," Morgen told him. Silently, she added, *And you were supposed to be hunting for whoever climbed out the window.*

If the words were telepathically conveyed, Lucky didn't acknowledge them.

"I told you a dog isn't an appropriate familiar," Phoebe told her primly.

Napoleon chattered, sprang from Wendy's shoulder onto the railing, and ran to Phoebe. He jumped onto her arm and tried to steal the bag from her hand.

Several women laughed.

"Really, Phoebe," someone said. "If you bring meat to a gathering full of carnivorous familiars, you can't blame *them* for showing interest in you."

"Sorry, Phoebe," Wendy whispered sheepishly and plucked up Napoleon before he could successfully steal the bag.

"That must be good stuff," someone else said.

Morgen stepped back and looked around the gathering, hoping to find someone who was wiping roof shingle tar off their hands instead of joining in with the mirth.

"What's in it?" another witch asked.

"Maybe it's laced with dog and ferret nip. Is there such a thing?"

"The label just says the meat snacks are new and improved," Phoebe read. "Now even meatier."

"That'll do it."

On the long gravel driveway, a car started up. It was toward the back of the ten or twelve cars that people had driven and out of the illumination provided by the landscaping lights. Full darkness had fallen, and it was too far for Morgen to read the license plate or tell the color for certain. Gray? Pale blue? If Amar had been there, he would have given chase and ripped the fender off.

"Does anyone know who that is?" Morgen asked casually as the car turned around and drove away.

"Someone who's been hoping for a drink for fifteen minutes

and got tired of waiting?" Belinda suggested, though she was smiling. Everyone was in a good mood after ribbing Phoebe.

"Do *you* know who that was?" Morgen asked Wendy quietly.

She was admonishing Napoleon, and by the time she looked over, the car was almost out of sight beyond the trees.

"Oh, uhm." Wendy looked around the gathering. "I didn't notice anyone leaving. Maybe someone arrived, thought the werewolf fumigation techniques weren't adequate, and left."

The three women handling that duty walked past the deck again, beeping and spraying as they murmured and pointed out spots to each other.

"How could that possibly be deemed inadequate?" Morgen muttered.

"It's a mystery."

"Tell me about it." Morgen walked to the steps and willed Zorro to follow the car and find out who was driving it, but she had no idea if he was hunting anywhere near the house. By the time he returned, it might be too late.

Morgen hoped that whoever had been snooping hadn't found anything useful and wouldn't risk coming back. She also hoped that the herbs the women were spraying wouldn't affect Amar in any way. The last thing she wanted was for him to visit her for a midnight tryst, only to encounter some defensive magic that hurt him.

5

LUCKY BOUNDED DOWN THE HILLSIDE AHEAD OF MORGEN AND UTE, running from tree to bush to fern, occasionally pausing to dig or sniff. Chipmunks and squirrels chattered from the branches, giving him a tongue lashing. Or maybe that was for Morgen, since she'd brought him along.

"Sorry, woodland creatures," she murmured. "But he loves it out here."

Lucky planted his paws on a big pine and barked up at a squirrel. It chattered back at him from a safe branch twenty feet in the air.

"Fortunately, he's not a very good hunter," she added.

Morgen wished she had half of Lucky's energy, but she hadn't slept well, and even two cups of coffee hadn't helped. All night, she'd been worrying about the snooper and especially Amar. She'd woken at midnight and looked over to the barn, but it had been dark and silent. Empty.

After the Lobos had come for him, and they'd spoken of that grisly death, Morgen hadn't expected Amar to be back in time for the tryst he'd suggested, but she'd hoped he would reappear by breakfast so she would know he was safe. But when she'd checked the barn that morning, his clothes had still been hanging from the hook where she'd left them.

Ute frowned over at her. "Usually when I forage, it's less noisy, and I can enjoy the serenity of nature."

"Sorry." Morgen dug into her treat pocket and whistled for Lucky.

He cast a last longing look at the squirrel before running over to sit in front of Morgen.

"It's too early in the morning for barking," she told him. "We're going to be quiet and serene on this trek."

Lucky, who only managed something close to serene when he was snoring on the couch with all four legs in the air, cocked his head in confusion.

"I brought some twine." Ute rummaged in a basket that held scissors, a small saw, and a few other tools for gathering plants. She held up a spool of twine. "We could tie it around his snout."

"Do you tie twine around *your* familiar's snout? Or beak?" Morgen waved to the treetops, though she hadn't seen the raven that was accompanying them that often.

"No, but he's not noisy and rude."

Caws came from the woods behind them.

"That's not him," Ute said.

"Are you sure?"

Ute put the twine away and smiled. "No."

"Lucky will be a good boy." Morgen fed him another treat, put her finger to her lips, and gave him a long *sssssssh* before releasing him from his sit.

He galloped off to investigate a fern, thankfully without barking.

The caws continued as they walked, and Ute glanced back several times. Autumn sunlight filtered through the tree branches, so Morgen hoped they weren't in any danger from werewolves or anything else that hunted at night. But she jumped and blurted a surprised exclamation when a man came into view a couple dozen yards behind them. Ute screamed and dropped her basket. A second later, Morgen recognized Amar and waved, relieved he appeared to be uninjured.

"When I stopped at the barn to put on clothes, I thought it would keep women from screaming at my presence," Amar said as he walked up.

Ute, her hand clutched to her chest, shook her head. "I was startled by the abrupt appearance of a strange man in the woods."

"I'm not strange. I live here. Your sister also screamed when she saw me," Amar told Morgen.

"Sian screamed? That's unusual."

Sian had returned to the house the night before, impeccably timing her return with the departure of the last member of the coven. It had been *so* impeccable that Morgen suspected she'd been waiting across the street from the driveway, reading in the car until she was positive she could park without being forced to speak to anyone.

"She was drinking coffee on the porch swing. I believe I startled her when I walked out of the woods by the garden."

"Were you naked?"

"I was. After she screamed, she hurried inside. It's possible she's not interested in ogling me the way some people are." His gaze made it clear who he meant.

"I don't *ogle* you." Morgen blushed and glanced at Ute, who'd recovered enough to pick up her basket.

"I've often felt the scorching heat of your gaze on my ass as I walked away."

"My gaze doesn't *scorch*."

"Trust me, it does." Amar smiled as he lowered his eyelids to watch her through his lashes. Scorchingly.

"I don't think it's appropriate to flirt in front of other people," Morgen whispered, glancing at Ute again.

"Oh, I don't mind," Ute said. "Indeed, you've made me curious about his ass."

Morgen's cheeks heated even more as Ute's ribald comments from the night before came to mind. She half expected Amar's cheeks to turn red at the unexpected interest.

All he said was, "It's flat, firm, and fantasy-inspiring."

"I'll bet."

Morgen cleared her throat. "We're going to see the sparkly dots in the tree by the railroad tracks."

Amar nodded and walked beside her as they continued down the slope.

"Was your hunt successful last night?" she asked quietly when Ute wandered off to the side to trim leaves from what looked like creeping thistle with blue instead of purple flowers.

"It was not."

"I guess I didn't need to dig out the floss then."

Amar frowned at her with a puzzled crease to his brow.

"Never mind," she said. "You weren't able to find the guy who killed the Loup? This *rougarou*?"

"The other Loups were there by then and didn't let us close. They were suspicious that we were interested in the death of their pack mate, even though we told them we're only interested in the one who did it. I did catch a familiar scent at one point, a scent from my past, but when we went out into the woods to hunt for more traces of him, we couldn't find any. There are stories that the *rougarou* can leap into the tree branches and travel like monkeys for miles, so they don't leave tracks on the ground."

"The internet says the *rougarou* have the heads of wolves, the bodies of men, and kill Catholics who don't follow the rules of Lent." She'd done a quick search the night before while she'd been worrying about Amar.

He gave her a flat look. "He can be a wolf, a man, or a man with wolf features, and he kills those who've wronged him, those who are in his way, and those he simply wishes to because he enjoys the pain of others."

"Lent isn't involved?"

"No. It is not known why they were created, but some think it was to defend the estates of the rich in the Old World. They were the work of warlocks with powerful magic. The *rougarou* were spawned from the blood of werewolves but turned into something far stronger and with magic of their own. They are solo hunters, but they can take on minions to do their bidding. They can use their magic to *force* minions to do their bidding." Amar shook his head. "They're monsters, especially this one. Do you remember that I once told you my parents were killed by criminals?"

"Yes, when you were ten." She touched his arm.

"They were his minions. He stood in a nearby field, watching as they killed and robbed everyone in our town. My parents gave me a knife and pushed me under a bed and told me to hide, but I saw everything. I was furious with myself for being too afraid to help, to attack their murderers. When he came into the bedroom, I found my courage and sprang at him. I caught him by surprise and stabbed him in the eye. He was hurt and screamed with rage, and such fear filled me that I ran out into the night.

"The police arrived then, or he would have chased me and killed me. They'd been hunting him and had many weapons, so he ran off. Soon after, I found the Lobos, and they took me in. He'd also ravaged their pack, until they'd fought back against him and driven him out of the mountains. Temporarily. When he's been hurt, that only makes him angrier. More vengeful." Amar was looking off into the trees as he spoke, but his eyes were glazed as he dwelled on his memories. "The *rougarou* took more minions and returned, intending to kill us all. There were too many for us to fight. That is when we fled our homeland forever. Until this week, we had not seen or heard of him again. I'd hoped he'd died, but I've always feared he would find us once more. I wish I'd finished him off when I had the advantage all those years ago, but I was just a boy then and not yet a wolf."

"Why is he after you? If he killed your parents, you should hate *him*, not the other way around, right?"

"I stabbed him in the eye." Amar shrugged. "I don't think he's ever forgotten that slight."

Morgen wanted to ask more, but Ute rejoined them. Amar stuck his hands in his pockets, his shoulders hunched, and didn't look like he wanted to say more about his old enemy.

"It's wonderful being able to forage without being chased off by a cranky werewolf." Ute smiled and hefted her basket, oblivious to the dark conversation they'd had—and the new threat that had come to Bellrock.

"Take whatever you wish. Just know that wolves hunt all through these woods and mark their territory frequently." Amar gave the blue thistles a frank look.

"I'll be sure to wash these thoroughly before drying them," Ute said, not fazed.

Reminded of why she'd asked Ute to join her, Morgen started walking again. As they descended closer to the tracks and the water, they entered fog, and the sunlight grew weaker. Lucky returned from his wild running from tree to tree to walk at Morgen's side.

A train roared down the tracks, and through the trees Morgen glimpsed red and blue shipping containers whizzing past. She slowed down as she tried to find a tree she'd only visited once and then by accident. At the time, she'd been looking for a particular fungus for a ritual.

"Are we close to the spot with those mushrooms the wolves like to roll in?" Morgen asked Amar.

"Oh, are there blood-cap mushrooms here?" Ute asked. "Their spores are useful in many formulas."

"Yes, Amar is wearing some around his neck."

Ute peered at his chest. "Ah? Is that a Talisman of Imperviousness? I guess that makes sense. A smart choice. I wouldn't have expected a neophyte witch and crafter to have figured that out." Ute smacked Morgen's arm with her scissors handle. "Some people said you were a goober who'd inherited land you didn't deserve, but you might have some promise."

Morgen grimaced, though she was hardly surprised.

"Morgen is resourceful and carries the power of her line in her blood." Amar rested a hand on Morgen's shoulder and stared balefully at Ute.

His defense warmed Morgen's heart until Ute said, "Huh. You really do have his loyalty. If I didn't know how those talismans worked, I would guess you had him ensorcelled."

Amar's grip tightened on Morgen's shoulder. It wasn't painful, but she knew the suggestion irritated him. At one point, he'd worried about that same thing.

"I don't," Morgen said, "and he has *my* loyalty too. We're friends. Friends are loyal to each other. That's how it works."

"Friends?" Ute raised her eyebrows and looked at them, making Morgen aware that Amar had stepped close. "Does one ogle the asses of one's friends?"

"We're *more* than friends," Morgen said, glancing at Amar, though she wasn't sure she should say that until they slept together. She also didn't know why she was explaining this to someone she'd met the night before, other than that she wanted Ute's help identifying the magical dots. "Whatever we are, we're loyal to each other."

"Yes." Amar loosened his grip on her shoulder and brushed his knuckles along the side of her neck.

That sent a little shiver through Morgen that made her wish they were alone.

"Do you wish me to drive her away from Wolf Wood?" Amar asked her. Maybe he was thinking the same thing.

Ute's eyebrows flew up in indignation.

"Thank you, but that's not necessary," Morgen said. "It's enough that she'll have to deal with pee-doused thistles."

The fog thickened as they searched for the tree with the magical dots. When Morgen found it, it was as she remembered. Even though there was no sunlight to reflect on the confetti-like glints in the bark, they gleamed, and the bark around them was warm. A warning tingle buzzed her skin when her hand was close to them.

"Ah, fascinating," Ute said.

"Do you know what they are?" Morgen asked.

"Not at all, but I'll take a sample and do some research."

"Be careful. I had that same thought, and then they spat an electrical charge. I think I would have gotten zapped if I hadn't stopped."

"Oh? Fascinating." Ute pulled a magnifying glass out of her basket and stepped close to the tree.

Lucky padded off to check out the mushrooms the wolves liked to visit.

Amar stood back, his arms folded over his chest as he watched the woods around them. He hadn't mentioned why he'd come looking for Morgen, but she had a feeling he was worried about his old nemesis and that she might get caught up in the danger. Morgen hoped this *rougarou* wouldn't learn that she existed and trouble her—she had problems enough dealing with the coven members who didn't like her—but if he was a threat to Amar, she wanted to find a way to help.

As Ute emitted soft *ohs* and *hms*, Morgen stepped back to stand beside Amar and clasp his hand.

"I'm sorry she said that stuff about loyalty and ensorcelling," she whispered. "I know that's a sore spot for you."

"I am not concerned about it now that I cannot be controlled." Amar rested his palm over the talisman and gazed down at her. "And I have stopped letting it bother me that I am drawn to your power."

"That's good." Morgen smiled, though she was still bemused by the idea that she might *have* power. She was glad Amar appreciated her because she'd fought with him and made him the talisman, not only because of some magical connection they had, but if it made her a little more alluring—and even sexy?—to him, maybe that was all right. "I wouldn't want you to feel magically bound to me."

"You bind me with your *loyalty*." Amar looked down at their clasped hands, then met her eyes with his half-slitted again, and she thought of their kiss from the day before. "If we were alone and my nostrils weren't on fire, I would show you how much you please me."

"Why are your nostrils on fire?" she whispered, but what she wanted to say was, *Show me, how?*

Morgen glanced at Ute. Still engaged with the bark and the magnifying glass, she didn't seem to hear them.

Amar's eyes narrowed further, but his expression was more dyspeptic now than reminiscent of kisses. "Someone spattered the lawn all around your house with painfully strong-smelling herbs and *cayenne*."

"Oh, er. Sorry about that." Morgen had thought the women were mostly being superstitious, not that the concoction they'd sprayed would actually work to drive off werewolves. "I shouldn't have let them put that stuff down. They promised me it wouldn't be toxic to the garden. I didn't think to ask about werewolf noses."

"Offending *werewolf noses* was what they wanted to do."

"I think they just wanted to be sure you wouldn't intrude upon the meeting."

"As if any self-respecting werewolf would go anywhere *near* a witch meeting. Though I notice they weren't offended by our presence when we came to help with the demon that *they* raised."

"They'll come around. I'm working on them. I'm letting them know how much better the Lobos are than the Loups." Morgen wished she truly could ease the tensions between the magical communities in Bellrock. As a newcomer, maybe she couldn't understand fully, but she couldn't help but believe the witches and werewolves could have a less antagonistic relationship if they weren't so dead set on hating each other.

Maybe not *all* of them, such as Calista and Olivia and whoever had invaded the library the night before, but Phoebe, Belinda, and Judith didn't seem to loathe the werewolves. And Wendy was on the verge of not being terrified by them.

"You cannot change the bad blood between us," Amar said, but he pulled her into a hug and rested his chin against her head.

"Are you sure? I thought we might bribe them to change with gifts. That works with werewolves."

"Do you refer to your database? Or would you make talismans for them?"

"I'm not sure. Maybe we just have to win them over one witch at a time. What do you think about setting Wendy up with a hunky Lobo who's close to her age?"

Amar leaned back and looked at her. "What?"

"Well, maybe if there were more wolf-witch couples, the groups would start to come around."

"Or Bellrock would turn into *Westside Story*," he grumbled.

"It might not. Pedro seems to think I'm all right now, so it's possible for people to change their minds, isn't it?"

"You're more like a wolf than a witch. And you gave him a gift."

Morgen didn't know if she should be honored to be considered *like a wolf*.

"Wendy made the silver chain part of the talisman. Maybe she'd make other things for the pack if she was dating a werewolf. How do the Lobos feel about charm bracelets?"

Amar was squinting at her. She couldn't tell if it was because he thought she was crazy or if he was insulted by the idea of wearing a charm bracelet. Either way, it was a far cry from the sexy bedroom eyes he'd been giving her earlier.

"Ouch!" Ute yelped, stumbling back.

Morgen left Amar's embrace and ran over to make sure Ute didn't fall. "Did you touch one?"

"Barely, and with a tool, not my finger." Ute shook out her hand. "It zapped me."

"Yeah, they do that. I'm not sure what the reason could be, other than keeping people from digging them out of the bark."

Ute put away her tools. "I took a few pictures with my phone. That'll have to do. I'm not going to try to get a sample. They seem a little..." She groped in the air with one hand. "Strange and unfamiliar."

"Not unlike blue thistle?" Morgen asked.

"I don't think they grew here naturally."

Amar strode up to them. "It is time to return to the house."

"What?" Morgen blinked. "Why?"

Amar's nose was in the air, as if he were a hound testing the wind. The train had long since disappeared, but he was looking in the direction of the tracks and the water.

"I believe I caught the scent of the *rougarou*. I thought he preferred hunting at night, as a werewolf does, but this fog is thick, and it's *like* night." Amar shook his head. "I don't know. I caught only the barest hint, but... he may be coming here. He may be looking for me."

Morgen swore. She pulled out Lucky's leash and ran over,

wanting to restrain him before he also caught a whiff of a scary enemy and ran off. If barking irritated an herbalist witch, it would *really* irritate the cranky monster that Amar had described.

Lucky sniffed the air, as if he'd noticed the same scent as Amar had. He didn't bark. Instead, he clenched his tail between his legs and whimpered.

"Don't worry, buddy." Morgen clasped his leash to his collar. "We'll go back to the house where it's safe."

At least she *hoped* it would be safe. She'd placed those wards, and maybe the cayenne-doused grass would deter a monster as well as a wolf.

"Go." Amar pointed back up the slope in the direction of the house. "I will lead him away from you."

"Uh, why don't you come with us?" If the *rougarou* was as dangerous as he'd described, Morgen didn't want Amar to face him alone.

"Because he is powerful enough to kill me—and you. Especially if he's taken minions."

"Then you should run, not rush off to face him."

"He must be located. Also... he has ways to control wolves, not only humans. He could turn the pack into minions. He could turn *me* into one." Amar licked his lips. "That is another reason I don't want to be at your side if he shows up."

"But your talisman—" Morgen touched the jewelry on his chest.

"I don't know if it'll work on his type of magic. Go." Amar pointed again, more emphatically. "And hurry."

Before Morgen could object further, he ran toward the tracks.

"Going sounds good," Ute said and hurried back the way they'd come.

Morgen *hoped* it was the way they'd come. They'd meandered a lot before finding the tree, and the fog had grown so thick that she worried they would lose their way. It wasn't as if there was a trail to this tree.

She glanced back, tempted to implore Amar again to come with them, but he'd already disappeared into the fog.

"Wonderful." Morgen rushed after Ute, not wanting her to disappear as well. "Two women, a foggy wood, and a killer heart-devouring monster. What could go wrong?"

6

UTE HURRIED WELL FOR A GRAY-HAIRED WOMAN CARRYING A BASKET of thistles and tools, but she didn't have a good sense of direction. Morgen kept having to point her back upslope toward the house. At least, she *hoped* they were heading toward the house. Maybe it was her imagination, but the fog seemed thicker, and Morgen worried it wasn't natural and that someone *wanted* them to wander astray.

Lucky pulled on the leash as he led Morgen up the slope. Hopefully, he couldn't be led away from the location where his beloved meals appeared. But with his tail still clenched between his legs, he might not have food in mind.

An eerie howl wafted up from the water. Amar? The *rougarou*? It had sounded creepier than a wolf howl.

Ute tripped, flailed, and a pair of clippers in her basket flew out. Morgen paused to pick them up as Ute kept running.

A rumble came from up ahead and made her pause. That hadn't sounded like thunder. More like boulders grinding against boulders. As she eyed unfamiliar moss-draped rocks dotting the leaf-littered ground, Morgen groaned.

"We didn't pass those on the way down. Lucky, are you leading me the wrong way?" She raised her voice. "Wait up, Ute. I think we've gotten off track."

Another howl sounded. Whatever had made it, it wasn't close, but that didn't make Morgen feel any safer. It was in the direction Amar had gone.

Distance muffled Ute's reply. Her back was barely visible through the fog that grew thicker with every passing moment.

Lucky whined, pulling at the leash. Morgen let him take the lead again, hoping he would find the way home.

Once more, the rumble of rocks flowed down the slope, louder this time.

"Look out!" Ute yelled.

Boulders tumbled down the hillside toward them. A landslide.

Morgen swore and ran for a pair of stout trees growing close together. She dropped to her knees behind them and hugged Lucky in close. He strained against her, wanting to flee.

"Sit, boy," she ordered, hugging him tighter.

Boulders tumbled past, and rock dust flew into Morgen's mouth and nostrils. She squinted her eyes shut as Lucky whined and tugged, trying to escape.

A boulder slammed into the tree she leaned against, jolting her, and she almost lost her grip on him. Fir needles rained down from above as shards of rock flew, one gouging the back of her hand with a stab of pain.

Morgen hunkered closer to the tree and closed her eyes. Lucky finally seemed to grasp that he should do the same, and he buried his head in her shoulder and whimpered.

Long seconds passed before the sound of boulders rolling down the slope dwindled and only the clattering of pebbles remained. Even that soon fell silent. The entire woods did. Not a single bird chattered in the aftermath. Even the howls had stopped.

"Ute?" Morgen called softly, opening her eyes.

She was afraid to shout, afraid that whoever had caused the rockfall was nearby. It was possible it had started on its own... but she doubted it.

A weak cough came from farther up the hillside. "Up here."

Morgen peered around her tree in the direction of the voice but didn't see anything except boulders and gouged dirt that hadn't been there before. The smell of freshly churned earth wafted to her nose. Fog still blanketed everything.

"Can you find Ute, Lucky?"

When she released her dog, he didn't immediately charge off. He stuck between her and the tree, his tail still clenched. She couldn't blame him.

"I think she has treats," Morgen said, willing him to go out and look in case it helped. He *was* her familiar as well as her dog, after all.

He cocked his head, then ran up the slope. It was possible the promise of treats had encouraged him more than her witchly desires.

Lucky zigzagged around a clump of pines, jumped over a tree that had been uprooted in the rockfall, and ran to a thick oak with acorns littering the ground underneath. He rose on his hind legs, planted his paws on the trunk, and barked twice.

"I said find *Ute*, not a squirrel." Morgen started to prop her hands on her hips in disappointment but spotted Ute's foraging basket smashed under a rock, its contents scattered.

"I'm up here," came her voice from the branches.

Morgen navigated past rocks, roots, and Lucky to peer into the branches. A few leaves had started to turn color, but none had fallen yet, and it took her a moment to spot Ute. She'd climbed more than fifteen feet into the branches and was hugging the trunk.

"As soon as my heart stops trying to beat its way out of my

chest, I'll climb down," Ute said, resting her forehead against the trunk.

"I'm glad you're all right. That's quite a climb for someone who's..." Morgen trailed off when Ute glared down at her.

"What? *Old?*"

"A seasoned forager."

"Seasoned means old."

"Are you sure?" Morgen asked. "I'm certain a thesaurus would bring up comparables such as experienced, knowledgeable, and *sophisticated.*"

"And *old.*"

"Sorry. You're in really good shape though."

"Uh huh."

Morgen picked up the dented basket and put the thistles and mushrooms that hadn't been flattened back inside. As Ute climbed down, Lucky dropped his paws back to the ground and pointed his nose up the slope. He stared intently as his nostrils twitched and the hackles on his back rose.

"Do you smell whoever started this?" Morgen grabbed his leash, not wanting him to charge up and confront anyone like the person—the *creature*—Amar had described.

He growled.

"There are more of your sparkly dots on this tree." Ute brushed off her hands, then leaned around the trunk to point. "One zapped me as I climbed."

"Really?" Morgen handed the basket to her and looked.

Ute was right. They were a couple of feet higher than on the other tree, but Morgen could clearly make out a couple dozen glitter-like dots, winking despite the fog blocking the sunlight.

"Interesting." Morgen took photos of them. "The other tree wasn't an oak, was it?"

"No, but it was also a large and old tree. The magic could have been placed there long before Europeans came to the Pacific Northwest."

"Or my grandmother could have gotten a tree-bedazzling kit and stuck them to the trunks last year."

Just because the *trees* were old didn't mean the dots were. If anything, if they'd been there for decades, wouldn't the trees have grown and half-buried them?

"I suppose," Ute said. "It's nothing I've seen before though."

Morgen rested her hand on the trunk below the dots, and a weird feeling came over her. Déjà vu? Not quite. It was almost like the visions she received from her familiars, but she didn't get queasy and no images popped into her mind. She just had the feeling that if she could figure out the mystery, the power represented by the dots could help her.

Lucky growled again.

Sighing, Morgen lowered her hand. It was a mystery for later.

"Do we want to walk farther up the slope and see what he's growling at?" Morgen was tempted to wait until Amar returned to investigate, but they had to head in that direction anyway to get back to the house.

"So I can whap whoever was responsible for damaging my foraging tools?" Ute tugged her bent scissors out from under a rock and growled.

"You're welcome to do that, preferably with the pointy end." Morgen doubted foraging tools were what the instigator had hoped to damage. "All right, boy. Let's check it out."

She took Lucky's leash and let him pull her up the hill, though she glanced back frequently, surprised the sound of the rockfall hadn't brought Amar. What if he was battling his enemy, right now? Or what if his enemy had arranged a wild goose chase for him and was poised nearby to spring out at Morgen?

Up ahead, movement caught her eye, and she froze. Lucky

lunged, almost yanking the leash from her hands. A squirrel chittered at them from atop a boulder. He barked at it, no doubt informing it that it was delicious and would soon fall to his mighty hunting skills.

"I thought he was leading us to the bad guy," Ute said.

"He's easily distracted."

Morgen kept climbing, knowing Lucky wouldn't have put his hackles up and been growling at a squirrel. He'd caught the scent of something more ominous.

The slope grew steeper, most of the boulders having originated at a scree-covered area with a rocky cliff above it. No trails led to this part of Wolf Wood, and Morgen hadn't seen it before during her walks around the property. Thanks to the fog and having veered in the wrong direction, she wasn't even sure they were still *in* Wolf Wood.

She eyed the cliff for caves or nooks someone might be hiding in.

"Look." Ute pointed toward red lines visible on the rocks, the trees half hiding them.

Morgen's stomach turned. Was that blood?

Lucky forgot about the squirrel and snuffled at the ground. He kept tugging at the leash, wanting free rein to investigate, but Morgen was reluctant to let him off when someone dangerous might be about.

They picked their way across the scree and weaved through the trees. It wasn't blood; it was red paint. Someone had written a message on the cliff.

The past never forgets.

7

It took a half hour for Morgen and Ute to find their way back to familiar trails and reach the house. After reading the message left in red spray paint, they'd found the dented can that had been used to leave it. The perpetrator was not only a thief but a litterbug.

Morgen had it in her pocket, intending to give it to Amar to sniff, in case his lupine nose could identify the scent of the culprit. Lucky had nosed the can a couple of times, but he hadn't indicated that there was anything unusual about it. She had no idea if he would have growled and barked and raised his hackles if he'd caught the scent of Amar's enemy on it. She also had no idea if that message—and that rockfall—had been meant for her or for him.

When Morgen and Ute stepped out of the woods and onto the lawn in front of the house, they found an unfamiliar black SUV parked in the gravel driveway. A gray-haired man in a plaid flannel shirt and jeans stood in front of the porch, just outside the wards Morgen and Wendy had set up. His fists were on his hips, and he looked straight at them. Despite the gray hair, he had a broad, powerful chest and a square jaw that looked like it could take a hit from a sledgehammer if need be.

"Uhm." Morgen hadn't expected company. "Do you know who that is?"

Lucky whined, and fear flashed through her as she wondered if this could be Amar's enemy. He'd said the *rougarou* could appear as a man if it wished. But wouldn't it—*he*—have a scarred or missing eye?

"That's Mayor Ungar," Ute said.

"Oh."

"Friend of the Loups," Ute added quietly.

Morgen grimaced. If Ungar hadn't been looking right at her, she would have slunk back off into the woods and waited for him to leave. She had a feeling Sian was upstairs ignoring his arrival and pretending she wasn't home either.

Lucky whined again as they approached, then dropped to his belly. He'd made the same move when he'd first met Amar and that would have told her the man was a werewolf even if Dr. Valderas hadn't previously given her the scoop.

Morgen made herself lift a hand and smile in greeting. She was about to say *hello* when a second man walked around the corner of the house and into view. He had thinning gray hair, wore a blue suit, and carried a tablet that he was using to take pictures as he considered the siding and roof. As with the mayor, he was staying outside the boundary line created by the wards.

"Hello?" Morgen asked more than greeted them.

For the second time in an hour, she wished Amar had come back.

"Morgen Keller? I'm Mayor James Ungar." His voice was cool, his eyes tight, as if he expected trouble from her.

As if *she* was the one who'd shown up unannounced to his house with some guy who was now taking pictures of the covered porch.

"Ute." Ungar nodded curtly to her. "I hear you're indoctri-nating Gwen's granddaughter in the ways of your kind."

"If you refer to how to forage in the forest," Ute said, hefting her basket, "then yes."

"You know what I refer to." His lupine smile was unfriendly.

Lucky stopped at the edge of the driveway and didn't walk closer to either man.

"What can I do for you and, uh, your friend, Mayor?" Morgen asked.

"I came as a favor." Ungar waved to the man in the suit. "Tejas here worried that your purported roommate might drive him off. He's known to do that, after all."

Fists still on his hips, Ungar inhaled deeply as he looked around the grounds and over at the barn. His gaze lingered on it and the stump out front that Amar used for his wood-carving projects.

Morgen wondered how long the men had been on the prop-erty. Long enough to have been responsible for that rockfall? She couldn't imagine why the mayor might want to flatten her, other than that she was learning to become a witch and dating someone from a rival pack, but she found the timing of his visit suspicious.

"Tejas?" she asked.

"Yes, I'm Tejas Dhar." The man with the tablet walked up and stuck out his hand. "The county assessor."

"Uh." Morgen didn't want to shake either of their hands and pretended not to see the gesture. "What do you assess?"

"Properties. I do evaluations whenever adjustments need to be made for the purpose of determining fair property taxes."

Morgen's stomach sank. Her cousin Zoe had warned her that the taxes for the house and the surrounding land—all five hundred acres of it—would go up once the county reassessed things. Thanks to her age and having been married to a veteran, a lot of Grandma's taxes had been waived. But now that Morgen was the owner and didn't have any special conditions that would allow for exemptions, she would have to pay a lot more.

"You come to do that in person?" Morgen had never heard of that. She and her ex-husband had lived in the same house for almost ten years, and she'd never been visited by anyone from the county.

"I heard there had been some recent renovations," Dhar said. "Despite a lack of permits having been filed. I needed to ensure everything was accounted for."

Ungar squinted at Morgen. "We want to make sure everyone in the county pays their fair share. Thanks to a recent incident in town that accounted for a lot of property damage to public buildings, we're going to have a lot of extra expenses this year."

Ungar held her gaze as he radiated disapproval. He had to be referring to the demon-summoning incident, but he couldn't blame *her* for that, could he? Maybe Calista had done it because she'd wanted to take revenge on Morgen, but it wasn't *Morgen's* fault the witch had been crazy and unbalanced—and criminal. That was why she was in jail.

"I think I've got what I need." Dhar raised the tablet. "That's a nice new deck and outdoor kitchen you've got out back, ma'am."

A nice new deck and outdoor kitchen that he would make sure to include in his report and *tax* her on?

Dhar smiled and headed for the SUV.

Ungar started to follow him but paused in front of Morgen. "I hope you won't find the new tax bill too onerous. It would be a shame if you couldn't pay, and Wolf Wood reverted to the county."

At which point, he and a bunch of thugs would come by to kick her out of her grandmother's house? And Amar out of the barn?

"I'll be able to pay it," Morgen said firmly, hoping she was right.

"You can bet the *county* wouldn't let the place be used as a congregation hall for witches." Ungar sneered at Ute before heading to the SUV.

Both men climbed in and drove off, cornering fast enough to sling gravel.

"He wasn't *nearly* that much of an ass before the Loups came to town," Ute said. "He used to date Phoebe."

"Really?" Morgen couldn't imagine the big brute of a man discussing potions, crystals, and spell components with her mentor over dinner. "What happened?"

"The Loups made him a werewolf."

"So Phoebe broke up with him? Or he broke up with her?"

Ute shrugged. "I don't know the whole story, but the mayor is in their pocket now. You'd better not cross him."

"I didn't know installing an outdoor kitchen would put me on his shit list." Morgen rubbed the back of her neck.

Without a job, paying the taxes on the house would have been onerous by itself, but if Wolf Wood was redesignated as residential real estate or another *expensive* classification, she would be in real trouble. The taxes on that much acreage would have been daunting even when she'd been employed as a database programmer with a good salary.

And what if the mayor and the assessor colluded to make the taxes higher than normal? Could she get a lawyer to appeal something like that? And how much would *that* cost? She would have to call Zoe to ask for advice. Even if she was a real estate agent in another county, she ought to know all about this stuff.

"I never should have let the Lobos add all the extras to the house," Morgen muttered.

"I suspect it's who you're dating that put you on that list," Ute said. "Not your fancy six-burner grill."

"Wonderful."

8

AFTER UTE LEFT, MORGEN FOUND HER SISTER SITTING AT THE kitchen table, reading on her phone and sipping coffee. Lucky trotted in and leaned against her leg while wagging his tail.

"There were men here taking pictures of your house," Sian said without looking up.

"The mayor and the county assessor. Did you talk to them?"

"No." Sian gave in to Lucky's insistent leg leaning and rubbed his head.

"Did they knock on the door?" Morgen asked before remembering the wards should have prevented that.

"The large belligerent man bellowed several times for someone to come out and talk to him."

"And you didn't?" Morgen poured herself a cup of coffee.

"I did not. You know I don't care to interact with strangers."

"Unless they're covered with fur, dangle from branches, and hoot while scratching their armpits?"

"You're stereotyping primates."

"Do you think they'll be offended?"

"*I'm* offended." Sian sent her a baleful glare over the rim of her coffee mug.

"Sorry. The assessor was going over the deck and the outdoor kitchen and presumably the rest of the exterior with a fine-tooth comb. I guess I'm glad that you didn't respond to them. The assessor would have wanted to come in here and take pictures of the newly finished hardwood floors and the now-working windows." Morgen hadn't yet tried inviting someone through the wards who wasn't already integrated into the system, but Wendy had assured her that they could all bring guests in as long as they deactivated the wards or formally invited them in. "I'm sure you get taxed more if your windows open than if they don't."

"Undoubtedly."

Morgen sat at the table across from Sian and pulled out her phone to compare the photos of dots she'd taken from the two different trees. "I don't suppose you'd like to chip in some money to keep this place in the family's hands?"

She thought about emailing her brothers, but they'd been resentful that Grandma had left her the estate and hadn't left them anything. They might have felt differently if they'd realized the woods were overrun with werewolves, dozens of people were scheming to get the property, and Grandma had been a witch. But maybe not. Bitter people stuffed with feelings of entitlement were rarely rational.

"I'm prepared to pay you for the lodgings you've provided while I'm on my unasked-for sabbatical, even though you did not warn me that Grandma's house would be overflowing with strangers at all hours of the day and night."

"Thanks, but you don't have to do that. I was kidding. Mostly. I am going to have to figure out how to make some decent money if I want to keep this place. The idea of having it fall into the Loups' hands—paws—is almost as detestable as the thought of developers razing the woods and putting in two thousand houses built so close together that you have to watch your neighbor take a pee while you're brushing your teeth in the morning."

"You think the tax bill will be unmanageable?" Sian asked.

"I have a *lot* of windows that open."

Sian rolled her eyes.

Morgen sighed. "It's all the acreage, not the house. And after my brief chat with the mayor, I'm afraid they're going to try to make the bill even more onerous than it should be."

"You can get a lawyer if they do that."

"All the lawyers in town are probably Loups too. I understand they're a bitey clan."

"Bellingham is twelve miles away. I'm sure they have lawyers." Sian swiped to a new page on her reading app. "If you get the tax bill and find you need assistance, perhaps I can help, but I must warn you that the salary of a primatologist is lower than the salary of a database programmer."

"How about an unemployed database programmer?"

"Aren't you making money from that witch app you've been obsessively devoting all of your time to for weeks?"

"No. I built that to win the love and adoration of the local witches."

"Good luck paying taxes with that."

"Thanks." Morgen lifted her phone to show Sian the gleaming dots. "Have you ever seen anything like this while traipsing through forests and jungles around the world?"

Sian looked up for the first time, aside from the earlier glare she'd shared, and studied the photo. "I have not." She must have noticed how rumpled Morgen's hoodie was, or maybe the dirt and dust stuck to it. "Were you rolling in a pigsty?"

"No, someone started a rockfall and tried to squish Ute and me under boulders."

"Someone?" Sian's eyebrows rose.

"I don't know who, but I brought an empty can of spray paint back for Amar to sniff."

"Does he enjoy that?"

"I mean to see if he can identify the owner's scent," Morgen said. "He or she left a message painted on the rocks about how the past doesn't forget."

"Ah." Sian sipped from her mug. "Have you contemplated going back to the city, getting another job, and resuming your old life?"

"The one where I was a bitter divorcee without any knowledge of the magical power flowing through my veins?"

"The one where people didn't try to kill you on a daily basis."

"You have that power, too, you know," Morgen said, ignoring the comment. Why couldn't she interest Sian in studying her heritage? Wasn't she the least bit curious? "If you didn't, it wouldn't have worked when we combined forces to chant at the demon and blast it with the staff."

"I am not interested in becoming a witch, even if such a thing were possible. I prefer a logical world fully explained by science."

"Even if magic exists? After what you've experienced, you must concede that it exists."

"Yes, and yes."

"You're no fun, Sian."

"As you informed me *many* times when we were teenagers."

"I was astute in my youth."

The sound of tires on the gravel driveway filtered through the windows, and Lucky lifted his head.

Morgen groaned. "*Now* who?"

Lucky jumped to his feet and ran into the living room. He always seemed to believe he could bark most effectively in there, maybe because the window was larger and low enough for him to see out.

Morgen got up and looked out the kitchen window. This time, a silver truck had pulled up. Another vehicle she didn't recognize.

"That's Dr. Valderas," Sian said, leaning against the counter beside her to look out. "He said he would bring me a book that would lend evidence to support the argument he was making yesterday."

"I see you had a relaxing evening and discussed typical date-night things such as favorite music, movies, and book characters."

Sian looked blankly at her. "We are not dating."

"Right." Morgen glanced at her phone on the table, the picture of the dots still lit up. "Mind if I come out and ask him a question, or do you want to speak with him alone?"

"I am indifferent to your presence."

"Yeah, having you around makes me warm and snuggly inside too."

"You're an odd sister, Morgen."

"Yes, that's right. *I'm* the odd one."

Sian squinted at her, then led the way to the front door. Morgen might know she was as quirky as Sian, but she wouldn't admit it aloud.

After parking, Valderas headed toward the house. Lucky was still barking, his paws up on the windowsill, but he was also wagging. Apparently, he'd met Dr. Valderas enough times to recognize him.

"I'm surprised you've forgiven him for the thermometer treatment at his office," Morgen told her dog as Sian opened the door.

Lucky wagged his tail, then lunged past Sian to run out first.

Morgen whispered the command to lower the wards, and a zing of energy flowed into her as they obeyed. Huh, the magic actually seemed to work.

She wished she'd been there to see the mayor and the assessor get knocked on their asses as they tried to walk up to knock on the door. That might have been one of the reasons the mayor had been grumpy with her. .

"I don't think your dog holds grudges," Sian said as Lucky bounded up to Valderas.

"He doesn't," Morgen said. "Dogs are much better than people."

"Tell me about it."

Lucky lowered down to his belly in his meek-for-werewolves pose, but his tail kept wagging. Valderas leaned down and patted him on the head. As if that had released him from his obedient *down* position, Lucky jumped up and ran around him three times, then shoved his snout into Valderas's hand for further pets.

Valderas, his silver goatee and mustache tidily groomed, carried a thick tome in his free hand, the pages uneven and yellowed. It looked old enough to predate printing presses.

"*That's* the book you brought to back up your arguments?" Sian folded her arms over her chest. "If it was written before the microscope was invented, I am going to question its accuracy."

"Do you argue that academics throughout the ages haven't applied scientific vigor?" Valderas asked in his Spanish accent.

"It's less their vigor I question and more mankind's rudimentary understanding of science in previous centuries."

"The book isn't *that* old."

They shared smiles, and Valderas looked curiously at Morgen. Even if Sian assured her they weren't dating, Morgen felt like an interloper in their conversation.

"Hi, Doc. I was wondering if I could ask you a question about magical tree dots."

"I... suppose?" Valderas looked puzzled rather than like he knew what she was talking about, but she showed him the photo anyway. After a minute, he said, "This tree looks familiar."

"It's in Wolf Wood near the spot where you and the other werewolves get high on 'shrooms."

Sian's eyebrows climbed.

Valderas coughed, though he *didn't* look puzzled about that. "That's not exactly what we do there," he murmured. Were his cheeks coloring slightly?

"Sorry." Morgen hadn't meant to offend or embarrass him. She thought it was cute that the fearsome werewolves had a spot where they frolicked and rolled about like felines enjoying fresh catnip.

"I don't know what the dots signify, but I have a book on medicinal herbs of this area that you could check." Valderas frowned at Morgen's phone and zoomed the photo in closer. "Though I don't believe those are natural growths. They look more like confetti that someone threw at the trunk. Are you sure they're not merely stuck on?"

"No, because they zap you when you touch them. I'll take a look at your book, if you don't mind."

"Of course. It's back in my office, but you can come by anytime. I always like to share knowledge."

"From books written before microscopes were invented?" Sian might have been teasing him, but with her deadpan tone, it was always hard to tell.

"*Especially* from those." Valderas eyed her sidelong. "Because people these days are overly enamored with our modern era, we've lost a lot of knowledge from the past."

Sian waved her fingers in what could have been acknowledgment or dismissal.

"Doc," Morgen said, wondering if he could offer any insight into the mayor.

"You may call me Osvaldo." He nodded to Sian. "Both of you."

"What about Ozzie?" Morgen asked.

"No."

Sian glared at her. "Do you want him to call you Morgie?"

"Ew, no. That's awful. Doc," Morgen said, deciding to stick with formality, "you said Mayor Ungar was turned into a werewolf by the Loups when they were expanding their pack, right? And that not everyone was turned, uhm, voluntarily?" Morgen extended a hand toward him, though she didn't know how much he'd told Sian about that and didn't assume she knew.

"That's correct," Valderas said stiffly.

"Do you know if Ungar was turned voluntarily?"

"I believe he was, but I wasn't there for it. Why do you ask?"

"He came to the house this morning. I got the feeling he doesn't like me, possibly because I'm dating Amar."

"Are you sure it isn't because you called him *Ungie*?" Sian muttered.

"No, but if we become archenemies, I'll be sure to use that name when I taunt him."

"From what I've seen," Sian said, "you don't need any more enemies, arch or otherwise."

"That is true." Morgen resolved to keep unflattering nicknames to herself.

"I wouldn't taunt him," Valderas said. "Ungar had the strength of an ox even before they turned him. There was a reason the Loups wanted him on their side."

"If he's a werewolf and is in charge of the town, why are the witches treated favorably by the establishment?" Morgen asked. "More than once, Amar has implied that if he complained to the law about them, he wouldn't be believed because they're respected citizens."

"The witches have been here longer, most have homes, and they pay their taxes. The Lobos' immigration status is questionable, among other things. I highly doubt they file with the IRS each year."

"Do *most* werewolves file with the IRS?" Morgen couldn't believe the French-Canadian Loups had come into the country legally either. "One thinks of werewolves as being roguish and making their own laws."

"*I* am here legally and pay my taxes," Valderas said. "The mayor generally treats the witches reasonably. When he joined forces with the Loups, I think it was mostly because he liked the idea of having magical power and being able to turn into a wolf rather than any vast adoration for their pack. He used to date Phoebe from the Crystal Parlor."

"So I heard."

"I believe he still visits her now and then for—what's the American term?—booty calls."

Morgen blinked a few times. "Er."

It wasn't so much that she couldn't imagine Phoebe having a sex life; it was the image that popped into her head that startled her, one of the big flannel-wearing mayor getting randy with Phoebe among all the dainty crystal keychains, luck charms, and glittering geodes in her shop.

"*Still?*" Morgen asked. "Phoebe doesn't like werewolves."

"He wasn't always a werewolf." Valderas shrugged. "If you want more details, you'd be better off asking her." His eyes darkened. "It's also possible she controls him. The Loups don't have your talismans."

"Phoebe wouldn't do that," Morgen said quickly, hoping it was true.

"My experience suggests that many women, once they get a little power, choose to do things that they wouldn't have dreamed of before." He glanced at Sian.

Even though there was nothing accusing in his eyes, Morgen hurried to defend her sister.

"Sian isn't interested in learning about her power, so you don't have to worry about that. Power isn't scientific, so she doesn't approve of it."

Valderas snorted. "I wasn't worried."

"Oh. Good."

Sian seemed more puzzled by Morgen's defense than appreciative. Before Morgen could decide if she wanted to try to clarify, Valderas's phone rang. He stepped away to answer it.

"It sounds like if you just pay your taxes and avoid being a nettlesome citizen," Sian said, "the mayor will leave you alone."

Morgen wasn't so sure. She looked toward the woods, wondering when Amar would return. It was strange that he'd been gone so long.

Valderas hung up and returned. "I need to go to the office. There's been an incident."

An incident such as Amar being terribly injured and showing up in the hope that the vet could treat him? "What kind of incident?" Morgen asked, afraid to let him leave without getting the details. "A golden retriever that's eaten a sock?"

"No." Valderas headed for his truck.

"It's nothing to do with Amar, is it? Or any of the Lobos?"

Valderas opened the door but paused. "Amar isn't injured."

"Wait, does that mean he's there? Who *was* injured?" Morgen stepped forward, her worry extending to the rest of the pack. Not all of them were delights, but they'd done all those renovations for her, and after she'd seen Amar working with them and that they all cared for each other, she didn't want anything bad to happen to any of them. Some of them she genuinely liked.

"You care for them." It was more a statement than a question, but Valderas almost seemed puzzled.

"They're Amar's pack, and he's..."

"I see. It's the boy, Arturo."

Morgen's stomach sank. The kid was only thirteen or fourteen. If some monster had attacked him, she would grab Grandma's staff and ram an antler into him herself.

"I need to go. I'll let you know later if he's all right." Valderas climbed into the truck.

As he drove off, Morgen wished she'd asked to go along. She also wished Amar would start carrying a phone so she could call him. He'd once mentioned that he'd broken a number of them when shifting forms in a hurry, but she hated not being able to get in touch easily. Just because Valderas had said Amar wasn't injured didn't mean he wasn't in trouble.

"I'm going into town. Will you keep an eye on Lucky?" Morgen started for the house to grab her purse and keychain.

"If Dr. Valderas needs to perform a surgery, he won't appreciate extra people in his office making noise."

"I'm just going to get a latte and a scone from the vegan bakery." And she would. After she spoke to Amar and made sure everything was all right. Besides, Valderas had mentioned a book she could borrow. It made sense to go into town. "Do you want anything?"

"Yes." Sian rounded up Lucky and shooed him inside. "Whatever looks tasty and like it's full of butter."

"Ha ha." Morgen grabbed the spray-paint can off the railing on the way past, hoping Amar could identify the graffiti and rockfall culprit.

9

MORGEN SKIPPED THE BAKERY AS SHE DROVE INTO TOWN, THOUGH she made a note to stop on the way back to get Sian her scones. After she was sure Amar and Arturo were all right.

As she passed the Crystal Parlor, she thought about also stopping there later to talk to Phoebe and get the lowdown on the mayor. But her property taxes wouldn't be a problem for a while. She could wait until their next lesson to ask if Ungar was likely to make trouble for her.

Morgen parked behind the silver truck in front of the remodeled Victorian house where Valderas took clients on the first floor and lived on the second. Clouds had rolled in, and rain threatened, reminding her of the last time she'd visited. Her tires had been slashed, and she'd been poured on. Now that she'd been accepted into the coven, Morgen hoped vehicle mutilation would be rare.

When she reached the front door, she hesitated before knocking or pressing the buzzer on the speaker. If Valderas was performing a surgery, she didn't want to interrupt him.

The door opened while she was debating what to do. Amar stood inside, blood staining his vest, jeans, and bare arms.

Her first thought was that Valderas had lied and Amar *had* been injured, but he appeared unharmed. If he'd carried Arturo here, that could explain the blood. The poor kid.

Fear for them both flooded her, and Morgen hugged Amar fiercely, hating that some new villain had shown up. Or—to them —a very old villain.

"Are you all right?" Amar wrapped his arms around her. "Did something happen to you?"

"Someone tried to squash me and Ute under a rockfall, but I'm otherwise fine." Morgen could fill him in on the mayor and tax assessor later. "Are *you* all right? I was worried when you didn't rejoin us. And what happened to Arturo?" She leaned back to look in his eyes.

"A *rockfall?*" Amar scowled. "The *rougarou* couldn't have circled back. I'm sure of it. I followed his trail up the beach, and after he attacked Arturo, he kept going north. I would have kept tracking him, but I had to bring Arturo in for medical attention."

"Whoever started it left a message. I can show you the spot later, or— Oh, the spray paint. I picked up the can in case you're able to smell the culprit's scent on it. It's in the car."

Morgen stepped back, intending to retrieve it, but Amar's arms tightened around her, and he pulled her into a hug of his own.

"I shouldn't have left you," he growled. "It didn't occur to me that there might be another threat. It *should* have. As I said, he sometimes takes minions."

"It's all right. Ute, Lucky, and I all survived. There were some handy trees to hide behind."

"It's *not* all right," Amar whispered fiercely into her ear. "I wouldn't forgive myself if someone from my past hurt you. Or worse."

The words written on the cliff sprang to mind: *The past never forgets.*

A little shiver went through her.

"If you hadn't left, you might not have been able to help Arturo." Morgen forced aside her worries and smiled at him. "Will he be all right?"

Amar didn't release her from the hug, but he loosened his grip. She sensed that he didn't want to change the subject, but he glanced toward the closed door to Valderas's operating room and winced.

"I hope so. Werewolves have excellent stamina and heal quickly from most injuries, but... there was a lot of blood. And it was my fault. Arturo wasn't even alive when the Lobos last crossed paths with the *rougarou*. There was no reason for him to attack the boy." Amar growled again, his chest reverberating against hers. "Arturo was clamming at the beach. I don't know if the *rougarou* smelled the pack's scent on him or was simply attacking because he's a monster and that's what he does, but Arturo didn't have a chance against such a foe. The *rougarou* half-eviscerated him. I gathered him and the intestines that had fallen free—"

Morgen sucked in an alarmed breath. Would the poor kid survive that? She hadn't realized it was so bad.

"—and brought him here as quickly as possible. Dr. Valderas is operating on him now."

"Does he think... he'll survive?"

"We will see. As I said, werewolves have great stamina and regenerative powers. Our magic makes us hard to kill."

And yet, she'd seen werewolves be killed. They might be sturdier than the average human, but they weren't immortal.

Rain started falling, pounding down on the roof of the porch. Amar released the hug, but he stayed close as he drew her inside.

"Stay here." He took her keys from her hand. "I'll get the can."

Morgen almost objected, but maybe the rain would wash off

some of the blood on his clothes—and his soul. She eyed the waiting-room furniture but paced instead of sitting. Amar was gone longer than it would have taken to retrieve the can. Had he paused to examine it thoroughly?

The door opened, but it was Pedro, Maria, and José Antonio who walked inside. They nodded briefly at her and headed into the operating room.

Morgen expected Valderas to order them back out, but nobody said a word, and the door closed again. She supposed they were the equivalent of Arturo's parents. Like Amar, maybe Arturo had come to the pack as an orphan, and they'd taken him in. Though, given that someone had to be bitten to turn into a werewolf, she wondered how that had happened. It disturbed her to think of someone that young volunteering to be made into a werewolf and an adult agreeing to do it. What kid truly knew what he wanted to do with the rest of his life? Whether he wanted to be irrevocably changed?

Morgen rubbed the back of her neck and told herself not to judge the Lobos. It wasn't as if she knew the story or fully understood them. She just knew she'd been relieved when she found out that witches couldn't be turned into werewolves.

Amar came inside, closing the door behind him.

"Did you find the can?" Morgen asked.

He hadn't brought it back with him.

"Yes. I didn't recognize the scent of whoever used it, but it was a woman."

"Oh. A witch?"

"I can't know that, but if she started a rockfall, and you didn't hear any explosives detonate…"

"There was nothing like that. It just started."

"Magic was probably used then."

Morgen didn't want any more witches plotting against her, but she was a little relieved it hadn't been Amar's enemy. She didn't want him to have a reason to feel guilty about anything that happened to her. Maybe whoever had climbed out her library window the night before had been responsible.

"Do you think your *rougarou* could have turned a witch into a minion?" Morgen asked.

Just how much power did the guy have?

Amar shook his head. "He has wolf magic. It's similar to ours but more powerful. With a howl, he can draw wolves to him. Normal natural wolves and werewolves and some weak-minded humans. Not those with magic though. He could make *me* a minion but not you."

"Let's hope that talisman will protect you from that." Morgen smiled.

Amar hesitated. "I do not know if it will."

"The recipe I used for making it said it protected from moon magic. That should include wolf magic, don't you think?"

"Maybe." He didn't sound convinced. "As I said, he's very powerful. He once had dozens of bandits and commanded them to rob and kill all through the countryside. It was long ago, but I doubt his power has waned."

Amar joined Morgen in pacing. A clock on a fireplace mantel in what had once been the dining room ticked audibly. Not a sound came from the operating room.

After a time, Amar leaned against the wall and closed his eyes. A gust of wind blew rain against the windowpanes. Morgen hoped the jerk who'd mauled Arturo was stuck out there getting soaked. She resolved to hunt through her database and her grandmother's books later to see if *rougarou* were mentioned. If there was a way to fight Amar's nemesis, she wanted to find it.

She moved to stand next to him and clasped his hand, wondering how much longer it would be.

"Even though I'm sure Valderas is a capable vet, do you think it would make sense to get a doctor? A doctor who regularly operates on humans?" Morgen didn't know if such a person existed in Bellrock. Maybe people with serious ailments had to go to the city.

"Being werewolves makes us somewhat anomalous. A doctor without familiarity with our magic wouldn't be ideal."

"Oh." Morgen managed not to make that an *ew* as she imagined wolf tails sprouting from the Lobos during surgery. She'd seen Amar naked enough times to know he didn't have anything odd growing out of him when he was in human form.

Amar eyed her. "It's possible your newly awakened witch magic will make you anomalous as well."

"I have my doctor remove anything anomalous. Did you see my mole scar when you were peeping at me while I did my naked ritual around the fire?"

"I was not *peeping*. I was drawn by your magic."

"If you didn't see the scar, your non-peeping perusal couldn't have been that thorough."

His eyelids drooped. "Where is it?"

Morgen touched the side of her hip.

"That is not what I was perusing when I was drawn, but I will investigate the area thoroughly later." Amar smiled at her, though his concern didn't leave his eyes, and he glanced toward the operating room door.

"I look forward to being investigated." She leaned against him, then let out a contented sigh when he wrapped his arms around her. "Out of curiosity, what *were* you perusing?"

It probably wasn't the time for silly banter, but if she could distract him from his worry, maybe he wouldn't mind.

Amar rested a hand on her backside.

"You're a butt man?"

"Among other things. I thought I should refrain from cupping your breast while we're waiting for a pack mate to come out of surgery."

"Probably." Morgen imagined the rest of the Lobos walking out while she was getting groped. "I'm delighted that you want to."

Delighted? Was that the right word? Maybe titillated. She rested her head against his chest.

"Good," he rumbled.

A few minutes later, José Antonio came out of the operating room, making Morgen glad she and Amar weren't up to hanky-panky. The affable would-be chef of the pack wouldn't have chastised them, but she didn't want him to tell Valderas—who might tell her sister. Who definitely *would* chastise her.

"The kid's going to be all right," José Antonio told them. "He's in a lot of pain and won't be able to shift or even walk for a while, but he'll recover."

"That's a relief," Morgen said.

"Will he be able to shift by the full moon?" Amar looked at her. "It's painful if the moon calls, and you're not able to heed it. Very painful."

"He might not be able to hunt by then," José Antonio said, "but I'm sure he'll be able to shift. He can lounge on the porch while the rest of us hunt. I'll bring him back an elk for my specialty elk balls. You've got to pamper someone whose intestines have recently been mangled."

"Some people might want to be pampered with chocolate instead of elk balls," Morgen said, "but I otherwise agree with the sentiment."

"A werewolf in his wolf form wants meat," Amar said.

Morgen suspected Arturo would spend more of his recuperating time in human form on the couch playing video games, and resolved to send him a box of goodies. Non-elk goodies.

Valderas opened the door, letting Maria and Pedro out. Their heads were together, their faces grim, as they conversed with each other in Spanish. Since José Antonio had delivered good news—or at least acceptable news—Morgen suspected it had to do with the *rougarou* rather than Arturo's status.

"He's awake and wants to see you, Amar," Valderas said with a formal nod.

"Do you want me to wait out here or come with you?" Morgen asked Amar, not sure if he would want her support or consider it a private pack matter.

Amar clasped her hand and led her toward the door to the operating room.

Pedro halted Amar with a hard grip on his shoulder. Morgen tensed, afraid Pedro would blame Amar and challenge him to a fight or some such.

"I'm glad you found him in time, brother," Pedro said, then switched to Spanish that flew by too quickly for Morgen to attempt to translate. Amar's nods suggested he agreed with whatever he was saying. When Pedro wound down, he looked at Morgen for the first time. "All of those we care about will be in danger as long as our old enemy is here."

"I know." Amar's grip tightened on Morgen's hand.

"We'll get the whole pack together after midnight and hunt for him."

Amar glanced toward the window, rivulets of water running down the pane. "He'll be hunkered down because of the rain."

"Then we'll find where he's hunkered."

Amar nodded again before heading into the operating room, where Arturo lay on his back on the table, the smell of antiseptic in the air. Morgen couldn't believe Valderas performed surgeries without a nurse or assistant of any kind. She supposed one had to make do in the small town of Bellrock.

Arturo's dark eyes were glassy and half-closed, but he said, "Amar," and weakly lifted a hand.

Amar stepped over and took it. Arturo was shirtless under a blanket that hid what had to be dozens of stitches, but he wore the talisman Morgen had made for him. That touched her, but she wished it'd had the power to protect him from what must have been claws and fangs. As they spoke quietly, Arturo slurring his words, she hoped he truly would recover quickly and be healthy enough to return to his usual shenanigans, even if that meant hurling rocks through the windows of Loup-owned establishments.

"Will you take away the pain with your witch magic, Ms. Keller?" Arturo asked.

"My what?"

"Some witches possess limited healing magic," Amar told her.

"Oh." Morgen blushed, still chagrined when he had to inform her of things that she should have known. Technically, she did remember putting all manner of ingredients and spells for healing potions into her witch app, but she'd assumed it was mostly hokum. "Didn't the doctor pump enough painkillers into you to do the job? I'm guessing those are a lot more powerful than witch magic."

"They're starting to wear off." Arturo grimaced, disappointment flashing in his eyes. "I thought you might be able to use your powers." His free hand strayed to the talisman. "I know they work. One of the mean old witches tried to get me to do chores for her last week, and this kept her from controlling me."

Morgen frowned. "Who tried to control you? What was her name?"

She'd hoped that with Calista in jail, Nora deceased, and Olivia kicked out of the coven, none of the witches left would be the kind to cast spells to manipulate people. She wanted to be friends with and learn from them, but not if they were being cruel to werewolves or anyone else.

"Their president," Arturo said. "That old crank with the staff."

"Belinda?" Morgen asked with disappointment.

Belinda had been the one to sway the others and talk them

into voting Morgen into the coven. Morgen had thought she was a fair person.

"When you say chores," Amar said, "do you perhaps mean repairing mailboxes?"

"Uhm."

"Because I had *numerous* orders for new mailboxes these past few days," Amar said, "and heard from the clients that they needed to be extra sturdy and embedded in cement to protect against teenage hooligans with the hobby of mailbox baseball."

"Uhhhhm." Arturo avoided his gaze.

"They weren't able to identify the culprits because they biked away so quickly after destroying the mailboxes, but more than one reported seeing a boy on a red mountain bike. *You* have a red mountain bike, don't you, Arturo?"

"That doesn't mean I did it," Arturo said, though he looked like he wanted to pull the blanket over his head to hide from Amar's assessing gaze. "And even if I had, a lot of the people on that street are witches. Uncle Sancho said it's *okay* to torment witches, on account of so many of them being mean to werewolves."

"And yet you want witch magic to heal you."

"From *her*." Arturo nodded at Morgen. "She's your mate. And a good witch."

Morgen blushed again, this time at the belief that Arturo— that everyone in their pack?—believed she and Amar were mates.

"I wouldn't bother her mailbox," Arturo said.

"I'm sure she's flattered," Amar said.

Arturo nodded and tried a smile.

Amar gave Morgen an exasperated look.

"It's going to be a challenge to mend the rift between witches and werewolves, I see," Morgen said, losing some of her earlier disappointment. Now, she envisioned Belinda out on her lawn with her staff, forcing Arturo to pick up broken pieces of her mailbox that were strewn all over the sidewalk.

"Indeed," Amar said.

Morgen drew her phone, wondering if anything in her database might help Arturo. She couldn't make a potion here—even if she could, she would worry about it not mixing well with the drugs Valderas had used—but maybe there were some incantations to help people in pain.

Several came up when she searched, and she smiled, hoping the other witches were finding it handy to be able to peruse the offerings in her growing database with a simple search query.

"I'll try this." Morgen quickly memorized a chant, then stepped up to the other side of the table. "I haven't done this before, so I don't know how well it works. It might not do anything."

She put her phone away, rested one hand on Arturo's chest, and gripped her grandmother's amulet with the other.

"It won't accidentally turn me into a frog, will it?" Arturo's eyes widened at this thought.

"No," Morgen said. "At worst, an aardvark."

Arturo's eyes widened even further as he gaped at Amar.

"She's joking," he said.

"Are you sure?"

"Yes. Though you deserve *some* kind of punishment for your mailbox antics."

"I already *was* punished. By the harpy witch. She made me pick up her mail and apologize."

"A truly heinous sentence," Amar said.

"*Yes.*"

As Morgen chanted the incantation, the amulet warmed in her hand. She was never sure if the sensation of doing something with magic was her imagination, but its heat trickled through her, as if she were a conduit, and into Arturo.

Long seconds passed with the kid holding his breath and watching her—probably waiting for the first sign that he was morphing into a frog. She repeated the incantation, willing it to help him. More warmth trickled through her body and into Arturo.

The tension ebbed out of him, and he let out a long sigh. "Feels better," he mumbled drowsily. "Not froggy at all."

Amar snorted, though he was watching Morgen intently. Not, she trusted, because he believed she would hurt Arturo in any way. No, his eyes seemed to hold approval.

Another sigh escaped Arturo as he closed his eyes and drifted off to sleep. Morgen withdrew her hand and released her amulet.

"She's got some real power," Valderas said from the doorway.

Morgen hadn't realized he'd been there and was relieved he didn't seem irked that she'd presumed to treat his patient.

"Yes," Amar purred and smiled. That was definitely approval in his eyes, and it warmed her in a different way than the amulet had. In a far more enticing way, and she remembered their conversation in the waiting room—and his hand cupping her butt. Too bad he'd told Pedro he would go hunting again that night.

Amar stepped around the table and took her hands. "Thank you for helping the pack."

"You're welcome." If they hadn't had a witness, Morgen would have kissed him.

"I could use an assistant for surgeries if you need a part-time job," Valderas told Morgen.

"I do need to start making extra money to pay my taxes. Does operating on werewolves pay well?"

"No, but my mailbox is almost never molested."

She snorted, wondering how long he'd been listening.

"You have much power that could be used for many things," Amar said. "I'm certain you can use it to make sufficient money for your needs. After the *rougarou* is gone, I'll help you figure it out. I'm an experienced businessman."

"I have seen how your work lures even werewolf-hating witches into ordering pet furniture."

Valderas raised his eyebrows.

Judging by Amar's frown, that wasn't the kind of business he'd been thinking about.

"Amar makes *excellent* ferret trees, and he's getting into cat condos," Morgen told Valderas. "If you have any clients who need pet furniture, let us know."

Amar squinted at her, and she waited for him to protest and say he would not lower himself to making more pieces for animals.

"He offers to assist you with your entrepreneurship," Valderas said, speaking first, "and you promote his business."

Amar must have decided not to complain. He lifted his chin and said, "We are a team."

"The first witch-werewolf duo. Impressive." Valderas smiled, backed out, and closed the door.

Morgen was thinking about kisses again when a queasy feeling came over her. She groaned and gripped Amar for support.

Her vision wavered, and the living room came into view from dog height. It had been a while since Lucky shared a vision with her, but she recognized one when she received it. As usual, he was running around, and the view shifted from the living room, to the hall, to the kitchen, to the back door, and the living room again. Sian crouched in front of the door—or was she facing the fireplace?—with a broom gripped in both hands.

Morgen swore, wishing Lucky would stand still and focus on Sian, but he ran past her, and Morgen struggled to tell what was going on. He put his paws on the living-room window and seemed to be barking at something, but sound never carried through the visions her familiars shared with her.

"Morgen?" Amar rested his hands on her shoulders. "Are you all right?"

"I think someone's at the house." She glanced toward the nearest window to check if it had gotten dark out, but she struggled to see through the vision taking precedence in her mind. "Sian could be in trouble. I need to get back."

Amar swore. "It could be the *rougarou*."

What had been mild concern turned into a blast furnace of fear. Morgen tried to run for the door, but Lucky's vision hadn't relinquished her, and she crashed into the corner of a counter. Amar caught her, swept her into his arms, and ran for the exit.

"I'll drive. I've still got your keys."

"Good. I've still got dog vision." Her stomach lurched with queasiness, and she hoped she didn't throw up on her gallant werewolf. She also hoped Sian had locked the doors and that whoever was there couldn't get past the wards.

10

THE VISION LUCKY WAS SHARING WITH MORGEN FADED AS AMAR drove her home, his knees banging the steering wheel in her compact car. Rain poured down on the windshield, and the wipers struggled to keep up. Amar drove as quickly as possible in the poor conditions, with puddles like lakes covering the roads, but Morgen worried it wouldn't be fast enough.

Amar must have worried, too, for his knuckles were tight on the wheel. The car went hydroplaning twice, and Morgen was almost relieved when they turned off the slick asphalt and onto the dirt road leading up to the house. Her relief lasted only until they hit the first pothole at too great a speed and her head hit the ceiling.

She winced. "I didn't think that was possible when you've got your seat belt on."

Amar only glanced at her, then fumbled for the control to roll down his window. He was used to the hand crank on the door of his old truck. As soon as the window descended, wind-driven rain flew in sideways and spattered the side of Morgen's cheek.

She was on the verge of complaining, but he stuck his nose out and inhaled in quick bursts. Checking for the scent of his enemy? It was hard to imagine anyone smelling anything besides wet trees, but she didn't have a werewolf nose and couldn't know what it was like.

The car hit another pothole and sprayed muddy water. A bird bedded down in a bush beside the road screeched a complaint and flew off.

Zorro? Morgen didn't think it had sounded like an owl, but maybe she could reach out to him and get an update. It was surprising that there had been danger and he hadn't sent a vision —he was more reliable than Lucky with such things—but perhaps he'd been caught out in the rain and wasn't in his nesting box. *If you're near the house and can let me know if there's trouble, I would appreciate it.*

After they hit another pothole, and mud splattered and struck Amar's cheek, he rolled the window up. "I don't detect his scent, but he may not have come up the driveway. He was on foot earlier."

"Can *rougarou* drive?"

"He can take human form when he wishes."

"Yeah, but you said he's hundreds of years old, didn't you? I'd think he'd be more of a horse-and-buggy kind of guy and have a hard time strolling into the DMV to get a learner's permit."

"He's capable of learning," Amar said, "and he can pass as a normal person. Sort of. He has yellow eyes—a yellow *eye*—and a feral look about him, so he's nobody you'd ask on a date."

"Since this is a tense moment, and we've both had a rough day, I'll refrain from commenting on *your* feralness."

Amar glanced at her again but didn't dignify that with a response. Morgen supposed the fact that he hadn't gotten a haircut for a long time and wandered around in nothing but boots, jeans, and a leather vest didn't make him feral. Not in the eviscerating-young-werewolves-on-the-beach kind of way.

As the lights of the house came into view, a muzzy vision came over Morgen. Something from Zorro?

She gripped the door handle for support in case he sent nausea-inducing images of him careening through the forest. But he was stationary. *Very* stationary. The vision had her looking at a dark wooden wall. Zorro shifted, and a hole came into view, a few lights visible outside as rain slanted across the opening.

"Zorro is in his nesting box," Morgen said, not sure whether to be relieved or annoyed that her owl familiar had been *napping* while Sian and Lucky were in trouble. It was still dusk—though the heavy cloud cover made it seem like night—so it was technically Zorro's bedtime. It wasn't as if she could berate her owl for not being out and about during the day.

"He's not alarmed by anything?"

"I guess not."

As they came out of the trees, shifting from potholes and mud to the packed gravel of the driveway, Morgen peered around for evidence of invaders. Amar's truck was the only vehicle in view, parked in its usual spot in front of the barn. The lights were on in the house, so she could tell Lucky wasn't at the living-room window anymore. What if someone had arrived and kidnapped him and Sian?

Morgen ran from the car toward the porch, rain pounding onto the top of her head. Zorro's faint hoots drifted over the deluge. It sounded like he was still in his nesting box, unwilling to come out in the rain.

Aware of Amar running behind her, Morgen leaped up the porch steps and flung open the front door.

A shriek came from the fireplace. Sian spun toward them, holding not the broom but Grandma's antler staff, though she had it backward with the antlers pointing behind her. She crouched, ready to jab intruders, but she lowered the weapon with a scowl when she saw Morgen and Amar. Meanwhile, Lucky sniffed around the hearth, his attention alternating between the floor-boards and the fireplace, and didn't seem to notice them.

"What's going on?" Morgen looked around but didn't see kidnappers lurking or signs that there had been a ruckus. "Lucky sent me a vision."

"He what?" Sian lowered the staff.

"He shared what he was seeing with me. At the time, it was you crouching with the kitchen broom." Morgen waved to the staff. "I see you upgraded, though FYI, you're supposed to prong enemies with the antlers, not the butt end."

Sian scowled at her as Lucky kept sniffing at the floorboards. "Some of the tips are broken off."

"That's because I threw the staff at gyrocopter blades this summer. While they were spinning. It's a poor way to treat a magical weapon, and I regret it, but I'd still recommend using the antlers to attack."

"I didn't want to break them further." Sian pointed toward the floor. "There's something in the crawlspace under the house. At first, I thought there was something *in* the house with us, but now I'm pretty sure it's under the floor."

"Something... like an animal?" Morgen wiped rainwater off her face and frowned at Lucky, now understanding why Zorro hadn't bothered to stir. "Buddy, you're only supposed to send visions if someone's in trouble or a fearsome enemy has presented himself."

Lucky wagged his tail vigorously, sniffed at a heat duct in the floor, ran over to circle Morgen twice, and galloped back to the heat duct.

"Do you think your archnemesis is in the crawlspace?" Morgen asked Amar.

"An arch-possum maybe," he said.

A thunk came from under the floor in the hall. Lucky barked and ran to investigate.

"At least whatever it is isn't in the pantry," Morgen said,

reminded that the extensive remodeling project had all started because rodents were getting in the house.

"Something that large shouldn't be in the crawlspace either. It's possible I left the grate loose when I..." Amar glanced at Sian before looking at Morgen. "When I was hunting for tidbits to entice your owl to use his nesting box."

Morgen smiled at the memory. It had taken a few days to convince Zorro to use the box Amar had made instead of nesting and molting all over his projects in the barn. During that time, Amar had deigned to turn into a wolf, hunt for mice under the house, and drape the offerings over the box to lure Zorro to use it. He'd informed Morgen numerous times that wolves, being mighty apex predators, didn't hunt such measly prey as rats and mice, and he still seemed embarrassed that he'd done it.

"I'll go check," Amar said.

Morgen stopped him with a hand on his arm. "It can wait until morning. It's pouring outside."

"Won't your dog bark all night if the animal isn't shooed out of there?"

Morgen eyed Lucky, who was inhaling at the heat vent hard enough to launch a career in the duct-cleaning business. "Possibly."

"I'll check." Amar walked out into the rain.

"You're a good man," Morgen called after him.

"Should I have offered him the use of your weapon?" Sian leaned the staff against the wall by the door.

"He has his own weapons. His fangs, claws, and the powerful muscles of a fearsome predator capable of tearing foes limb from limb."

"Ugh."

"You don't agree? You've seen him as a wolf. And—" Morgen smirked, "—with his shirt off."

"I don't disagree. My *ugh* was because I realized you're besotted."

"Besotted? Nobody uses that word anymore."

"It's a perfectly legitimate word and conveys all the implications of the original definition of *to make dull or stupid; to stultify.* The insinuation that carnal attractions are involved came in later."

"Thanks for the etymology lesson. Here in the twenty-first century, a normal person would say *I'm hot for him.*" Morgen admitted there was probably slang more current than that. She didn't spend much time with teenagers and wasn't up to date on the latest and greatest. Maybe she would ask Wendy if she should be using something else.

"I hope you know what you're doing. You're recently divorced, you know."

"Yes, I do recall that fact. And it's not *that* recent. And Jun and I hadn't been... carnally attracted for some time."

"Details I do not want to hear about." Sian started to sit on the couch but halted mid-sit when a *thud thud thud craaaack* came from under the floor. "Did he go *down* there?"

"It sounds like it. He's deigning to hunt measly prey that's beneath him for the sake of our beauty sleep." Morgen clasped her hands to her chest. "I'm not besotted. I'm falling in love."

Sian rolled her eyes and finished sitting. "I didn't think vegetarians approved of prey-hunting."

"Normally, I wouldn't, but if it keeps you from wandering around the house, swatting wildly at things with a broom, I will withdraw my usual objections."

"I thought it was *in* the house with me. I was being prepared."

"For wild swatting."

"Like a Valkyrie with a spear determining the fate of warriors on the battlefield."

"It's good that Lucky alerted me to your peril," Morgen said. "If you'd been alone much longer, you might have broken the living-room lamps."

"Ha ha."

Morgen sat next to Sian and pulled out her phone to look at the dots. She realized she'd forgotten to get that book from Valderas. Oh, well. He had more important things to worry about. For that matter, so did she.

"I chanted that demon phrase," Sian admitted, then glowered at Morgen, as if it were her fault. "I hoped it would do something against a home intruder, which is what I originally thought I was dealing with. Given how many people—magical, furry, and otherwise—have it out for you and are happy to raid my room and fling my underwear about while looking for you... I thought I might be in trouble."

"I don't think the demon-banishing incantation is meant to get rid of—"

The door opened, and they jumped up. Amar stood naked, water gleaming on his bare torso. Morgen might have found it sexy, but he was also holding up a raccoon. A *living* raccoon, as evinced by its twisting and hissing as it tried to scratch him.

"I removed this and also the mice down there," Amar said, "then sealed the access grate so they can't return. Nothing else should disturb your night."

"Thank you, Amar," Morgen said.

He closed the door and headed for the barn—and hopefully to set the raccoon free in the woods. The poor thing must have been looking for a dry spot to hide in during the rain. Morgen was surprised but pleased that Amar hadn't killed it; she knew that had been because of her preferences. Once more, she clasped her hands to her chest, touched.

"I'm aware that a demon-banishing incantation wouldn't be designed to evict raccoons," Sian said, sitting again, "but it's the only one I know."

"I could have shown you more incantations, but you've repeatedly said you're not interested in learning any magic. Has that changed?" Morgen tried to keep the hopeful note out of her voice, but she couldn't help but want her sister to be involved in this new world with her. Since Morgen was on better terms with the coven now, she didn't feel as isolated in her witchy endeavors, but it would be fun if she and Sian could bond over them. They'd never truly done that. After forty years, Morgen still didn't know if her sister really liked her. She was so aloof and difficult to know.

"I need to leave soon and find out if that lab position will be acceptable," Sian said, "since I've been forbidden from returning to tropical countries plagued by mosquitoes spreading disease."

"But wouldn't it be better if you were armed to protect yourself from such things? With *magic*?"

"Magic can ward off the Dengue Fever?"

"It can get rid of slugs in the garden and mildew-tainted grout in the shower. It's *amazing*."

Sian snorted. "I confess that I was a little... concerned when I didn't know what was making the noise under the house."

She must have been if she'd tried chanting the demon incantation.

"It wouldn't be the worst thing if I knew how to defend myself with more than Tae Kwon Do kicks learned thirty years ago. Especially since I haven't kept up with the practice and can't get my leg up very high anymore."

"Technically, you don't need a lot of height to kick a raccoon."

Sian shot her a dirty look.

Morgen lifted her hands. "Sorry. I'm delighted that you're considering this. I'd hug you, but I know how you feel about unnecessary touching."

"Save it for your lupine lover."

A car door slammed outside, and Lucky sprinted to the window and started barking again. Morgen peered into the rain, wondering if Amar was driving off to meet the rest of his pack, but several familiar trucks were arriving. Pedro and a dozen other Lobos, at least. It seemed the hunting grounds were in Wolf Wood, and they were starting here. That had to mean they believed the *rougarou* had circled back and was in the area.

"Another reason for us both to study defensive magic," Morgen murmured.

11

Morgen laid the three wands she'd been studying on the coffee table next to a couple of Grandma's basic tomes of incantations. She'd chosen the books in case her sister preferred old-fashioned methods of learning to the phone app, but everything they needed ought to be in the database now.

Outside, the rain had let up, and Amar and the pack had taken to their furry forms and disappeared into the woods. It was getting late, but Morgen preferred to do something productive instead of going to bed and lying awake worrying about Amar. And, after her harrowing experience with the raccoon, Sian was as alert as if she'd quaffed six espresso shots.

As Morgen was debating how to start her instruction, given that she felt far too new to witchdom to be an effective teacher, Wendy returned to the house.

"Oh, good," Morgen said as her houseguest parked her camper. "Wendy can instruct you."

"The teenage girl who spends most of her waking hours playing computer games?" Sian asked.

"She's almost twenty. I believe that makes her a full-fledged adult."

"Who spends most of her waking hours playing computer games."

"She also does graphic design and is helping me with the user interface for my app. Did you see the little cartoon frog hopping into the witch's cauldron as the program loads? It's super cute."

"I haven't downloaded it," Sian said.

"You haven't downloaded my *app*? What kind of witch do you plan to be?"

"A reluctant one with minimal junk cluttering her phone's display."

"My app isn't junk." Morgen smiled, but she couldn't help but feel a little hurt by this lack of familial support. What kind of sister didn't download a sibling's app? "If you'd had it earlier, you wouldn't have been stuck only knowing *one* incantation when an enemy invaded the crawlspace."

Sian sighed. "I'll download it as long as you promise to teach me something more useful than de-mildewing the shower."

The werewolf-control incantation popped into Morgen's mind —it would be infinitely useful in a county half-controlled by a hostile pack—but her werewolf allies might consider her teaching that to a new witch to be a betrayal. They all had the talismans she'd made, so they wouldn't be affected, but she decided to ask Amar how he felt about it first.

The door opened, and Wendy poked her head inside. "Everything okay in here?"

As she tilted her thumb toward the truck-filled driveway, Napoleon rose up on his hind legs on her shoulder and chittered angrily. Wendy's hair was wet, and his fur was equally wet, so they must have been caught outside somewhere.

"For the moment." Morgen pointed at Napoleon, who

appeared even slinkier and more rodent-y than usual with his fur matted to his sides. "Is everything okay there?"

The ferret squeaked with displeasure.

"He's cranky because he's wet and up late," Wendy said.

Lucky, who'd been curled up on the couch, hopped down and trotted over to wag at Wendy. Sometimes, he barked at the ferret, but he must have been tired, for he only leaned against Wendy's leg for pets. Napoleon hissed when she deigned to deliver them.

"Do you think he wants a snack?" Morgen asked. "Do *you* want a snack? Sian has agreed to learn about her witch heritage and how to cast spells. I was hoping you might help with the teaching."

"Oh, really?" Wendy raised her eyebrows. "I didn't think she was interested."

Sian, leaning back on the couch with her arms crossed over her chest, *still* didn't look interested.

"She was the victim of a home invasion," Morgen said, ignoring an eye roll from Sian, "and has realized how helpful it would be to know a few incantations for defending herself."

"A home invasion?"

"The details aren't important," Sian said firmly. "I would like to learn how to banish intruders. *Any* kind of intruder."

"I can show you a few things," Wendy said. "Sure."

Napoleon ran down her back and jumped to the floor. Morgen lunged for Lucky's collar, afraid that a ferret cavorting around would stir up his prey drive, especially a ferret that had hissed at him.

But Lucky dropped his forelegs to the floor and wagged his tail. Napoleon chittered at him. Lucky wagged harder. Napoleon ran under the coffee table, and Lucky galloped after him. That earned him more hissing before Napoleon ran out on the other side and hopped up on the raised hearth. When Lucky went over, hoping he would play, Napoleon flopped down and played dead.

Lucky cocked his head, sniffed him, and his tail drooped with disappointment.

"I may need to get another dog so Lucky has more playmates," Morgen said. "Zorro won't play with him either."

"Maybe when your sister gets a familiar," Wendy said, "it'll be something that believes dogs are fun, instead of large fang-filled predators that are best avoided."

"When I get a what?" Sian asked in her deadpan voice.

"Most witches perform the ritual to call a familiar out of the forest," Wendy said.

"Your ferret came out of the forests of Western Washington?" Sian cocked an eyebrow.

Morgen didn't know much about ferrets but didn't think they were indigenous to the area. During her hikes, she'd never had one pop up out of a log and squeak at her.

"Uhm, actually I did my ritual under an eagle's nest, hoping for a cool raptor. But there was a pet store nearby." Wendy spread her arms. "Napoleon escaped his cage *and* the store's locked door to come to me. That's initiative."

"Did you have treats in your pocket?" Morgen asked.

"A dead fish. Sometimes, one has to help the ritual along. I didn't realize that eagles prefer to catch their own prey."

"Whereas ferrets don't mind being hand-fed delicacies?"

"Not at all."

A chitter came from the fireplace. Lucky had settled down on the rug, his forelegs crossed with his head on them, so Napoleon shouldn't have been complaining about him. But he rose up on two legs, waved his forepaws in the air, then flopped down dramatically on the hearth.

"Is there a werewolf nearby?" Morgen peeked out the window, but none of the Lobos had returned.

Napoleon stood again, made some cranky noises, scooted closer to the firebox, then flopped down again. This time, he landed on his back with all four paws in the air. He was almost *inside* the firebox, and Morgen worried he would prong himself on the grate that held the logs.

"Oh," Wendy said. "He's telling me he's wet and cold and wants a fire."

"Did he send you a vision?" Morgen asked.

"No, but I know how much he likes to be comfortable."

"If I make a fire, will you start teaching my sister some basics?"

"Sure," Wendy said.

"Do you know *how* to make a fire?" Sian asked, no doubt remembering that their brothers had been the fire-starters on their family camping trips.

"I've gained all kinds of life experience since coming up here." Morgen waved toward the lawn behind the barn at the edge of the woods. "I had to make a fire for the ritual that won me Zorro." Never mind that Amar had helped her.

"I'd wondered what made that circle of dead grass out there," Sian muttered.

"Yes. I learned that putting aluminum foil under a campfire won't keep the grass from dying."

"No kidding."

Morgen brought in kindling and logs from the woodbox on the covered porch, pausing to listen for howls that would indicate the wolves had caught the scent of their prey. But the night was quiet, the silence broken only by the patter of rain. Given how dangerous the *rougarou* sounded, Morgen didn't know whether to hope the pack found him or not.

What if she lost Amar? Just as she realized she was falling in love with him?

Napoleon supervised while Morgen piled kindling atop the grate, using a log of compressed sawdust that she'd picked up in town to make the process easier. Despite her claims of vast experience, she was a novice fire maker. She also had a ferret butting her in the arm as a distraction.

"All I need to do is memorize these incantations and say them?" Sian asked skeptically. The teaching had started while Morgen worked.

"Yes," Wendy said, "while gripping a powerful magical focus and thinking about what you want to happen. Practiced witches can do some incantations without assistance, but it usually takes them a couple years of doing it that way before they're capable of focusing their own magic. The words themselves have limited power and are designed to get you thinking about what you want done."

"So they needn't rhyme?" Sian had made disparaging remarks previously about the incantations, which, as far as Morgen had seen, always rhymed. Usually without much poetic flair.

"They *needn't*, but isn't it a delight that they do?" Wendy smiled. "It makes memorizing them easier."

Sian, who was known to remember and quote entire encyclopedia entries without any rhymes in sight, looked over at Morgen. "What is your *powerful magical focus*?" She sounded like she was trying to keep the sarcasm out of her voice but didn't quite manage it.

"Grandma's amulet." As Morgen pulled it out from under her T-shirt, she realized she hadn't seen any others around the house, and she swore under her breath. It hadn't occurred to her that her sister would need one of her own.

Maybe if Morgen tried to fall asleep thinking about amulets, she would receive another helpful dream that starred Grandma. She hadn't had any more of those since the nocturnal visions had guided her to the safe behind the bookcase in the library, but after that experience, she couldn't help but believe there was some magic in the house—or maybe even something of Grandma that lingered after her passing—that wanted to help her. Shouldn't it want to help her sister too?

"My amulet is also from my grammy." Wendy pulled a chain out from under her own shirt and revealed a silver frog with emerald eyes dangling on the end. No wonder she liked frogs so much. "My aunt had the ones for my sisters made in town by a local witch who used to live here, but Grammy said I was special."

"Do you have any more?" Sian asked Morgen.

"Uhm. I haven't seen any." Morgen almost offered to look around again, but she'd already cleaned and sorted through everything in her quest to bring an organizational paradigm to all the witch paraphernalia in and under the house. She'd even been in Grandma's hidden safe. If there were more amulets around, she would have found them, unless they were squirreled away under the floorboards somewhere. "Maybe I could make you one."

"You're going to make a powerful magical focus? You who thought *aluminum foil* would be helpful in building a campfire?"

"I didn't think the foil would help build the fire, just keep it from torching the yard. And I made Amar's Talisman of Imperviousness. I bet the same book has something about making amulets." Morgen didn't have her sister's memory, but as the words came out, she believed she was right. The book had contained rituals and ingredients for many kinds of magical jewelry, and she'd come across the word *focus* numerous times while perusing the contents.

"I'm not sure it does," Wendy said. "Talismans and charms are relatively simple to make—they don't require the crafter to have a lot of innate power—as long as you have the ingredients. Amulets don't usually require a bunch of ingredients, but the rituals are long and arduous, and you need to have a lot of power of your own to funnel into them. I've heard of witches having to combine forces to have enough."

"Can't I just wave a wand like they do in the movies?" Sian picked up the bone wand.

"You can," Wendy said, "but they're kind of like guns. They don't do anything unless you have bullets—a witch uses her own power to fire them, and they amplify and focus it."

"Maybe I should get an actual gun," Sian said, "and forget the witch stuff."

"The living-room lamps would *really* be in danger if you had a firearm. Just give me a little time. I'll figure out how to make you one, even if I have to hold hands with the rest of the coven." Morgen waved toward the fire now crackling in the fireplace, as if it were evidence that she could craft an amulet.

"I can make a chain and a pendant to ensorcel, if you like." Wendy was kind enough not to scoff and say Morgen couldn't make an amulet even *with* the rest of the coven.

"That would be amazing." Morgen smiled at her.

"I'm on the payroll now. I think it's my job to be amazing."

"Employers do appreciate that," Morgen said, though she felt guilty that she'd thus far been paying Wendy in silver coins from Grandma's stash. She needed to figure out how to start a legitimate, moneymaking business soon.

Contented clucking noises came from the hearth behind Morgen. Napoleon lay on his back again, his legs in the air, the heat from the fire warming his side. In a similar pose, Lucky was sprawled out on the rug in front of the hearth. Morgen wondered if she should invite Zorro in to warm his feathers.

She grabbed her phone to check her app to see if she'd scanned in the pages from the talisman book so she wouldn't need to dig it out. After inputting so much information, it was all a blur. But she paused when the picture of the magical dots, the last thing she'd been studying, came up on the screen.

Maybe she could try to dream about *them*. Grandma had lived in the house for decades and tramped all over Wolf Wood. It would be surprising if she hadn't come across the trees with the dots before, especially if there were multiple such trees out there. If there were two, there might be many more.

The door opened, and Amar walked in. He was back in his clothing, and it was dry, but his wet hair plastered his head and water droplets glinted in his beard. Before he closed the door, the sound of trucks starting up was audible.

"We didn't find any sign of him." Amar yawned and looked at the fire, reminding Morgen that he hadn't slept the night before. "We'll hunt again tomorrow. I know he's out there, and I know he wants something." The way Amar touched his chest implied he was certain the *rougarou* wanted *him*.

Morgen set down her phone and held up a finger, then went to the laundry room and grabbed a towel for him. When she returned, he was eyeing the photo of the dots while Sian and Wendy murmured over a page in a book.

"Do you think those do something useful?" Amar accepted the towel, rubbed it over his hair, and sat on the rug next to Lucky. The fire now burned vigorously enough to put off discernible heat.

"I haven't been able to learn anything about them." Morgen thought about mentioning her plan to try to *dream* about the dots and learn from the ghost of Grandma, but saying such things aloud embarrassed her. Just because Sian now believed in magic didn't mean she wouldn't have a snarky comment for someone who thought dead people could share information via dreams. "It's possible they don't do much, but since they have power that zaps you when you touch them..."

He squinted at her. "They zap you even when you're wearing the amulet?"

Morgen hesitated, remembering that some of the magical plants and fungi that grew around Wolf Wood—especially around the special spring—zapped her if she wasn't wearing it. "The amulet protects me somewhat, but I could tell they didn't want to be bothered. They kicked out something like lightning when I tried to remove one."

"They're on other trees out there." Amar paused and looked thoughtfully toward the ceiling. "At least one that I've seen."

"Is it the oak over by the cliff?" Morgen held up the photo.

"That's not the one I was thinking of. There's one by the spring."

"Will you show me in the morning?"

"Yes. I want to take a look at the spray-painted message you mentioned and see if the witch who did it left any other signs. It's possible that *rougarou* is working with a local or even using a weak-minded member of the coven as a minion." Amar lay back on the rug with his hands behind his head. "We'll go on a hike together." He smiled at her, though another yawn somewhat ruined the effect. "It'll be romantic."

"As nature hikes to hunt for scheming enemies so often are."

His eyes glinted through his lashes as he held her gaze. "Yes."

12

MORGEN WENT TO BED WITH HER HEAD ON THE PILLOW AND HER fingers wrapped around Grandma's amulet. She had no idea how she'd managed to conjure the visions the last time they'd come to her in the middle of the night, or if she'd had anything to do with their arrival at all, but she tried to think about the tree dots and her desire to learn what they did.

It took a while to fall asleep, and her mind wandered to thoughts of Amar, whom she'd left dozing in front of the fire with Lucky. When the magic lesson had broken up, with Sian heading to bed and Wendy to her van, he'd opened his eyes partway, proving he was aware of everyone's comings and goings, but they'd drooped shut again. Morgen had draped one of Grandma's crocheted afghans over him and left him there, assuming he was exhausted after carrying Arturo to the vet, worrying about the kid during surgery, and hunting his enemy two nights in a row.

Around one a.m., Morgen woke to colorful lights glowing in the corner of the bedroom. Grandma's amulet was warm against her fingers, as it had been the other times she'd received nocturnal visions. What formed inside the lights didn't have anything to do with trees and dots. It didn't have anything to do with Amar, either, at least not at first.

Grandma stood hunched over a worktable in the root cellar, the benches, counters, and shelves cluttered and disorganized, the way they had been when Morgen first arrived. It was perhaps a testament to her need for organization that she noticed the disarray before the fact that Grandma was completely naked, except for a silver chain around her neck. Was it the amulet that Morgen now wore? From her point of view, she couldn't see the front.

Morgen propped herself on her elbow, tempted to look away from the nudity, but she didn't want to miss whatever the vision was showing her. Besides, Grandma's back was to her, her gray braid hanging between her shoulder blades. Sweat gleamed on her skin as she lifted her hands toward the low ceiling, then back down again. She stirred something in the small crucible Morgen had used when she made the werewolf talismans.

Was this a memory of Grandma performing a ritual and making something of her own? Instead of a spoon, she used what looked like a walrus tusk to stir. As Morgen knew from her previous research on teeth and tusks, some had magical properties, especially ancient fossilized specimens.

A thick tome with yellowed pages lay open on the worktable beside the crucible, and when Grandma's arms rose, Morgen could see handwritten words and drawings. She didn't recognize the book. It wasn't the one from the vault, nor did she remember seeing it when she'd organized the shelves and scanned thousands of pages for her app.

Grandma grasped the crucible in both hands and dumped the contents onto a small object on the workbench. The liquid that poured out looked like water rather than blood or anything strange and witchy. A hiss sounded as billows of white steam rose toward the ceiling.

Just as Morgen wished the angle of the vision would shift so she could see what the object was, Grandma moved, carrying the crucible to a counter. A silver chain and pentagram pendant lay on the workbench in the puddle, steam still wafting from it. It glowed green.

Grandma returned, waved away the steam, then picked up the book and walked to the back of the root cellar. The same single bare lightbulb dangling from the middle of the ceiling lit the room, leaving much of it in shadow, so Morgen barely saw what Grandma did with the book. She would have assumed it went on one of the shelves in the back, but a scraping noise sounded as Grandma tugged at something in the shadows. A bookcase. She pulled it outward, revealing a tapestry of a mountain hanging on the bare dirt wall behind it.

Morgen stared. Though she'd cleaned everything, it hadn't occurred to her to move the furniture, so she hadn't seen that tapestry before. Grandma pushed it aside and stuck her hand into a cubby dug in the dirt. A plastic bin rested inside. She opened the lid and tucked the book in with what looked like cards, papers, and a few other books, then secured the lid and pushed the bookcase back into place.

"This house has more hidden nooks than a medieval castle," Morgen muttered, half-wondering if there might be a secret passage under the root cellar that led off into the woods.

Grandma reached for the talisman she'd made—or was that an amulet?—but paused, turning her head toward the cellar doors. For the first time, Morgen could see her face, and a twinge of sadness came over her. She wished she could reach out and say something to her, to apologize that her death had been harrowing instead of peaceful. Maybe Grandma would take some solace from knowing that the woman who'd arranged her motorcycle accident was in jail now.

Whatever she heard didn't reach Morgen's ears, but Grandma

had clearly detected something. She grabbed the familiar antler-tipped staff from the wall beside the steps and strode up them with a determined expression on her weathered face. She pushed the root-cellar doors open, and the viewpoint of the vision shifted for the first time. Morgen was able to follow Grandma out into the night as if a camera were floating along behind her.

Snow dusted the lawn and driveway, and Grandma slid her feet into a pair of flip-flops by the door. Not stopping to don anything else, she strode across the white path toward the driveway in nothing but the flimsy footwear and her amulet. It hardly seemed adequate for battling a raccoon or whatever else she'd heard. The single light mounted above the barn door did little to illuminate the yard.

A howl floated out of the woods. That wasn't a raccoon, and it wasn't far away.

A shadow stirred near the driveway at the point where it descended from the hilltop and into the trees. Grandma leveled her staff in that direction. A large gray-and-black wolf limped out of the trees. Morgen's breath caught. Even in the poor lighting, she recognized Amar.

He looked back into the woods instead of at Grandma, then collapsed on the snowy driveway. Morgen gripped her amulet tighter, telling herself that whatever had happened to him had been in the past, that it couldn't have killed him, because she'd been with him scant hours earlier.

After standing poised without moving for a long minute, Grandma crept closer to Amar. A breeze blew, tugging at her braid. She had to be freezing, especially with the sweat she'd worked up during her ritual, but she didn't show it.

"Tough old lady," Morgen whispered, again wishing she'd spent more time with her when she'd been alive.

Blood stained the snow around Amar, and he didn't move as she approached, the antler tips leading. Morgen expected her to prod him with them to see if he stirred, but she squinted into the woods beside the driveway. Several gray wolves padded out from between the trees. Were they from the Loup pack? Had they attacked Amar?

Morgen couldn't tell if Grandma recognized them, but she knew a threat when she saw one. She leveled the staff at the wolves.

They growled, lips rippling back from their fangs, as they fanned out around Amar. It looked like they wanted him, not Grandma, but she stepped closer to him instead of backing away.

"Beat it, fur balls," she said without a quaver in her voice. "Nobody likes a bully."

That only prompted more growls.

Morgen couldn't believe Grandma's audacity. Six wolves were visible, and there might have been more back in the trees. Two crouched, their hackles raised, and Morgen shouted, "Look out!" as if Grandma could hear her, as if this hadn't all happened years earlier.

On the ground, the injured Amar didn't stir.

Grandma chanted something, the words barely audible over the growls. "Under the moon's magic, bad behavior correct and this witch protect!"

One of the wolves sprang, and green light flared from the antler tips. The rest of the wolves charged, but the first one seemed to strike a wall as light flashed in his eyes. The magic must have done more than flash, for her furred assailant cried out and twisted violently in the air. The wolf stumbled and fell as the other five were pushed back by energy that burned too brightly for Morgen to see through. Even in the dark bedroom, she had to lift her arm, squint, and turn her head away from the vision.

When the light faded and she could focus on the imagery again, the wolves were running into the woods with their bushy tails clenched between their legs. Only Amar remained, bleeding on his side in the driveway.

Grandma lowered her staff and eyed him. "All right, wolf. The bullies are gone. Skedaddle."

She made a shooing motion with her hand, as if he were a blue jay munching on her raspberry bushes.

Amar didn't stir. His side barely rose and fell.

"Come on, wolf. You can't stay here, and I'm not strong enough to carry you inside."

Still, he didn't move. She prodded him with the staff.

"Are you listening to me? This isn't a Four Seasons. And I'm..." Grandma spread her arm and looked down at herself. "Naked."

Amar blurred and shifted into his human form, his equally naked human form, but he still didn't move. He had to be unconscious. If Morgen hadn't known better, she would have believed him dead. Did he know that Grandma had helped him?

"Which is apparently the fashionable way to be this winter," she grumbled.

Grandma crouched, put her hand on his shoulder, and dropped her chin to chest. Her lips moved in another chant. It was either longer than the others, or she kept repeating it over and over. This time, Morgen couldn't make out the words. Grandma shivered, the first indication that she felt the cold, and snow started falling as she crouched beside Amar.

Finally, she rose, went into the house, and grabbed a blanket off the couch. It was the same afghan that Morgen had draped over Amar before going to bed.

"You better not freeze to death out here, wolf," Grandma said as she lay it over Amar. "I don't need a dead-werewolf speed bump in my driveway."

A faint moan sounded. Amar? The wind?

"The barn's unlocked if you need someplace to go," Grandma said. "Though wolves are *supposed* to sleep in the woods."

After Grandma closed the root-cellar doors, she returned to the house. One of the living-room curtains shifted aside. She must have sat on the couch to keep an eye on him.

Several moments passed, with the vision remaining focused on Amar instead of following her inside. He rolled to his hands and knees, staggered to his feet, wrapped the afghan around himself, and shambled into the barn. A lot of blood remained in the snow, but as he'd promised Morgen more than once, he healed quickly. And Grandma might have done something to help with that. Morgen hoped he hadn't spent that night in too much pain.

Once Amar disappeared, the curtain shifted back into place, and the light in the living room went out. The images faded, and Morgen slumped back against her pillow.

She'd hoped a vision would come and teach her about the tree dots. Maybe Grandma's ghost or the magic of the amulet had felt it was more important for her to learn how to make an amulet. And how often poor Amar had been hurt in his life.

13

"THOSE ARE A LOT OF PAW PRINTS," MORGEN OBSERVED, WAVING HER staff at the ground.

She and Amar were following the trail leading to the spring, the earth squishy with mud and fallen leaves. The rain hadn't stopped until after breakfast, and the gray clouds promised it could start up again at any time.

"The pack returned this way last night," Amar said.

"So, those are all your prints? You're sure? Which ones are yours?" Morgen pointed at the paw prints trampling the mud between the leaves, the gouge marks from the wolves' claws visible.

"You can't tell?" Amar raised his eyebrows, looking amused.

Since he tended toward gruffness, when his humor appeared, it always made her smile.

"They all look the same to me, other than some being bigger than others. You're not missing a toe or something obvious I've failed to notice, are you?" Morgen eyed his boots, certain she *wouldn't* have failed to notice missing digits. Admittedly, it wasn't usually his *toes* she was looking at when he wandered around naked after shifting forms.

"I am not, but you've surely observed that I am a substantial man, and I've informed you that I have the same mass when I'm a wolf."

"You're saying you're a big-footed wolf?" She raised her own eyebrows.

He was a little taller than Pedro and the other Lobos, but it wasn't as if he was the Hulk.

"Big all over."

"No kidding." Morgen gripped her chin and studied the prints, looking for an extra-large one, but they still all looked the same to her. Since he was in a playful mood, she picked out the smallest one. "That's a nice-looking print. Is that yours?"

His eyes narrowed. "That is *Lucky's* print and was left at least two days ago." Amar waved back toward the house, where Lucky had opted to stay, since Sian had been frying eggs and bacon. "A clue would be that it's going in the opposite direction from the others."

"Sorry, I'm learning to be a witch, not Davy Crockett."

Amar sniffed—or was that a huff?—and stalked ahead of her.

She should have known his natural grumpiness would reassert itself at the first slight. Since he'd fallen asleep in front of the fireplace and spent the night on the living-room floor, his back and everything else was probably stiff. He'd also had a dog using him as a pillow, which might not have been that comfortable. Morgen had been puzzled when Lucky hadn't come to bed—his usual spot was stretched out on it with her, shoving her against the wall or off the edge—and even more puzzled to find him snuggled under the afghan with his snout on Amar's chest.

The puzzlement was because Amar had allowed the dog snuggling, rather than any surprise when it came to Lucky's habits. As she well knew, he was an equal-opportunity bed sharer who would sleep with anyone who lifted the covers and gave him a come-hither look. Apparently, that included werewolves snoring on the floor.

It had been just light enough when Morgen had come downstairs that she'd been able to get a photo before either of them woke. She'd taken it because it had touched her, but she planned to show it to Amar at future dates in case he ever tried to pretend he was disinterested in pets.

The gurgle of the stream that ran through the woods grew audible, and Morgen spotted the spring up ahead, the cement bench resting undisturbed by it. Weeks earlier, Wendy and her sisters had cut away all the bioluminescent moss that had blanketed the trees growing around the pool, but a few glowing mushrooms peeked out from under the bench.

After rounding the spring, Amar headed up a rocky slope on the far side.

"Have you gotten any updates on Arturo and how he's doing?" Morgen followed him, her shoes slipping on the damp rocks. She was glad she'd brought the staff along, though Grandma might have cringed to see her using it as a walking stick.

"Not since last night, but he's at Valderas's office. I told him to call you if there's any trouble."

"To call me? Because you don't have a phone?"

"Yes."

"Maybe, after you complete that cat condo, you'll have the money for a new phone of your own."

"I can afford one. As I told you before, I choose not to have one because I break them frequently when I shift forms."

"I know, but there are times when it would be nice to be able to call you. Such as when nefarious witches are flinging rockfalls at me or mayors are glowering threateningly at me."

Amar stopped and faced her. "I smelled Ungar's scent at the house." His eyes closed to slits. "What did he want? You say he threatened you?" His voice turned into a growl for that last sentence.

Morgen lifted a hand, realizing that he was a deadly weapon, and she had better be careful lest she inadvertently fire him at someone who didn't deserve it. "Sorry, no. Not really. He brought a property assessor by to look at the house and said the county would be happy to take it if I couldn't pay the taxes."

"That is a threat."

"Possibly, but he didn't promise to turn into a wolf and tear out my throat, so it was a more reasonable one than I've been getting lately."

"How *much* will you have to pay?"

"I won't know until the bill comes. It'll be a fun autumn surprise."

"So, you don't know yet if it's *reasonable*."

"True."

Amar growled again.

Morgen patted him on the chest, regretting that she'd given him reasons to be grumpy when he'd been in a good mood earlier. "How far are we from the tree?"

"Not far."

He resumed the trek, and she followed him up the slope, mossy boulders slick after the rain. For the most part, she managed to keep from falling and banging her knees as they climbed.

When they reached the top of a knoll, Amar rested his hand against a centuries-old stout pine. Dozens of confetti-sized dots sparkled from the trunk, and Morgen pulled out her phone to take another photo. What she would do with the collection of pictures she didn't know.

While gripping her amulet, she reached up and touched her fingertip to one. Maybe it was scientific curiosity, but she wanted to know if they were all the same.

A warning tingle went through her as her amulet grew warm against her skin. Surprisingly, the staff also reacted, heating in her hand and sharing a faint buzz of its own.

"Huh." She prodded an antler tip to one of the dots. A more intense tingle carried through the staff to her hands. "Does that mean something, or does it always do that when it touches something magical?"

As Amar raised his eyebrows in inquiry, Morgen tried to remember if she'd prodded something magical with the staff before. She leaned it against the tree trunk, watching to see if the antlers glowed or flashed or anything interesting, but once it was out of her hands, the staff didn't do anything.

"Hold this, please." Morgen removed her amulet and handed it to Amar, then brushed the dot again. It zapped her. Hard. She winced and shook out her hand. "Whatever these are, they don't want to be disturbed. Or are they only offended by witches? Do they zap you?"

Amar leaned in and touched his tongue to one of the dots. He didn't react, other than a flicker from his eyelids. Maybe he was trying to show her how much pain he could handle.

"How do they taste?"

"Like a pine tree."

"I think I've heard of pine bark having health benefits." Morgen switched to the internet on her phone to run a search. "Yup, lots of them. If this is the right kind of pine tree, the extract could boost your antioxidants, balance your blood sugars, and improve blood flow and help with erectile disfunction."

Amar leaned his shoulder against the tree. "I have no need for *help* in that area."

"That's good. I would hate for you to need to gnaw on trees, though as a vegetarian, I would prefer kissing a man with pine-bark breath to one with moose breath."

"You're an eccentric woman."

"Last time, you called me strange."

"You've grown on me," Amar said. "Eccentric has fewer negative connotations, doesn't it?"

"I think so, but we'd have to ask my sister for sure. She could give us the etymology of the word."

"I'm sure that's fascinating. To answer your original question, yes, they zap me. It's not that painful, but it would be enough to dissuade me from trying to dig them out of the bark."

"Maybe that's the point. A defense mechanism. But they must *do* something, don't you think?" Morgen supposed the mystery didn't matter, at least not enough to prioritize it over their other concerns. She ought to figure out how to make her sister an amulet and do some research on the *rougarou* to see if there was a way she could help Amar against his enemy. "Are you aware of any other trees in Wolf Wood with dots?" she couldn't help but ask.

"No, but they could be out there."

Morgen turned and gazed around, noticing that their elevated position gave her a view out over the treetops all the way down to Rosario Strait. She could also see the top of the house and the barn. With so many trees, she'd have no chance of picking out the other two on the property that held dots, but she pointed one arm toward the train tracks, guessing the rough location of the first dot tree she'd discovered. With her other arm, she pointed toward the area where she believed the rockfall had occurred and where Ute had climbed the other tree with dots.

"That's interesting. You could make a triangle, with the trees at the points, and the house would be inside of it." Morgen considered her arms, extending imaginary lines with her mind's eye. "Well, not quite. The house is more in line with the hypotenuse, assuming a right triangle."

"The what?"

"The long side. But I'm sure it's not exactly a right triangle. I can't actually *see* the other trees from here. Though I wonder..."

Morgen gazed off to the south. "Maybe it's not a triangle but a *square*. Are you up for continuing our nature walk and looking for another dot tree?"

"If your witch friend doesn't mind her cat furniture being delayed."

Morgen opened her mouth, but movement down at the house drew her eye before she could reply. Sian had walked out the back door and onto the deck. She lifted the hot tub lid and peeked inside, perhaps contemplating a soak.

"It hadn't occurred to me that there might be places in Wolf Wood perfect for spying on the house." Morgen resolved to always wear a swimming suit when she used the hot tub.

The house and the barn were on a hilltop; the pine tree just happened to be on a *higher* hilltop.

"A few," Amar said.

"Remind me to make sure the curtains are always closed when I'm in the bathroom or wandering around the house naked."

"Then how will *I* spy on you?" Amar's eyes glinted. Apparently, he'd forgiven her for implying he might need pine-bark extract.

"Do you come up here often?"

"That's not necessary. If I crane my neck just so, I can see into your bedroom from my barn apartment."

She snorted. "You could sleep *in* my bedroom. That would make spying even easier, no neck craning required."

"Is that an invitation?"

"I thought you might come up last night. Instead, you slept on the floor and let my dog use you for a pillow."

"I thought about coming up," he murmured, brushing her cheek with his fingers. "But I was exhausted, and a witch's bedroom is usually warded. I didn't feel like being hurled down the hall by magic."

Morgen blinked. She remembered being flung out of Wendy's van by a ward, but it hadn't crossed her mind to put one on the threshold of her bedroom. Two days ago, she hadn't even known how to make them. But Amar hadn't known that. What if that was the only reason he hadn't already come to her at night? What if he'd thought about it but hadn't been sure he would be welcome?

"I also didn't know if you would be comfortable having sex when your sister is down the hall," he said dryly.

"I'm not usually that noisy."

A smile joined the glint in his eyes. "I am."

"You don't howl, do you?"

"If I'm pleased, I do."

"I have no idea if you're joking or not."

His smiled widened. "I've also been known to make women howl."

Morgen *still* didn't know if he was joking. She couldn't imagine herself howling, but she admitted that their kisses had been a lot more passionate than anything she'd shared with her ex-husband in the past ten years. Or ever. Maybe she *would* end up making more noise than typical. The thought made her cheeks flush, and she rubbed her face to cover it as she imagined prim comments from Sian the morning after.

"Maybe your apartment *would* be better," she murmured, though if he truly howled, that would still be audible in the house.

"Or a distant hilltop in the woods." Amar's gaze dropped to her lips, and the heat flushing her cheeks intensified. Other parts of her flushed as well.

"When my sister is down there in the hot tub?"

"The jets are noisy. They would drown out howls from the woods." Amar returned her amulet, clasping the chain around her neck for her, then letting his fingers trace her throat and jaw.

A shiver of pleasure ran through Morgen, and she stepped closer. Amar's eyelids drooped halfway as he wrapped his arms around her, then bent his head to kiss her.

Excitement surged up inside of her. She'd wanted this—wanted *him*—for weeks.

Shivering with anticipation, she molded her body to his and ran her hands up his muscular arms to grip his shoulders. A growl rumbled in his chest as his lips moved against hers, wakening desire within her. He wanted her. Maybe he'd been thinking about her the night before, not willing to go up to her room unbidden, but hoping she would come down to visit him.

She should have. She should have been braver, more assertive. By now, she knew how he felt. There was no reason to hesitate.

His hands slipped under her shirt, warm and callused as they teased her sensitive skin. A moan escaped her lips, almost embarrassing her. She'd told him she didn't make much noise, but out here in the forest, she lost any inhibitions she might have had in the house with others around. She pushed her hands up into his thick hair, raking her fingernails across his scalp.

Amar pressed her against the tree, the rough bark hard against her back, him hard against her front. She pulled him even tighter to her, all that delicious hardness making her moan again. As their kisses deepened, her heart pounded against their chests.

"Morgen," Amar said against her lips before dropping his mouth to lick her throat, then tease her with a nip. "My witch."

"My wolf," she gasped at the sharp zing of pleasure. "I want you."

"You should have come to me," he whispered, pushing her T-shirt and hoodie over her head, the cool air caressing her skin. He warmed it with strokes from his warm hands as he slipped her bra off.

"I'm not that bold," she admitted, though she didn't feel her usual shyness as he stroked her and perused her naked chest. "And you were healing from broken ribs."

"I heal quickly." His thumb brushed her nipple, sending an electrical jolt far more pleasurable than that of the dots through her. "I've wanted you for a long time." His eyes bored into hers with intensity, and his hands left her only long enough for him to unfasten his vest. "Since you made me the talisman. No, even before then. Since I felt your power, and I saw you naked and beautiful in the grass."

"Amar," she whispered, excited by his admission. She pressed her bare chest against his warm skin as she wrapped her arms tighter around him. She could feel him through his jeans and knew he was correct, that he had no need for that pine bark. Maybe because he made a habit of licking trees.

His hand trailed down to the button in her jeans, and anticipation ran through her nerves like wildfire. But then he straightened, jerking up and turning his head toward some sound.

"No," she said, refusing to be interrupted by anything. Not again. This wasn't the first time he'd pressed her up against a tree and left her breathless. "Amar, it's *fine*," she added, though she had no idea if it was.

"I caught a scent," he said.

He hadn't pulled back and still held her against the tree, his powerful biceps by her cheek as he gripped the trunk behind her.

"Yeah, *mine*. I don't want to stop. I need—" She cut herself off, not wanting to beg, not wanting him to know his cocky statements had been true, even if they had been, even if she wanted him and she didn't care if the whole forest heard her.

"I don't want to stop either." He met her gaze, his blue eyes intense with hunger. "Trust me." He kissed her again, and she thought he might give in and ignore whatever he'd smelled, but he growled with frustration and pulled back. Then *stepped* back. "But I caught *his* scent."

"Your enemy? Didn't you look all over the forest for him last night?" Cool air brushed her chest, and she wanted to wrap her arms around him again to keep him close, but she made herself let him go. If this was the guy who'd half eviscerated poor Arturo...

"He wasn't here then." Amar bent and picked up her clothes. "He is now. I'm sorry." He handed them to her.

"It's not your fault," she said. It was his vengeful enemy's fault, the bastard.

"It is," Amar said. "I've long feared my past would catch up with me. I didn't know I'd care about and worry about someone else when it did."

As Morgen refastened her bra, he stepped farther away from her.

"Wait." She lunged and grabbed his arm. "You're not taking off and leaving me alone again."

"I have to find him."

"I'll come with you and help."

"You should go back to the house," Amar said, "and make sure your defenses are up."

"What if someone drops a rockfall on me along the way, and you're not there to help?"

Amar hesitated, glancing toward the woods before frowning back at her. She expected him to say it was too dangerous for her to come, but he surprised her by nodding.

"You're right. You need to stay with me so I can protect you."

"And because I could help you." Morgen lifted her chin and grabbed the staff, though she didn't truly know if any of her incantations would be useful.

"Yes." Amar gripped her hand. "You could."

As she followed him away from the tree, the staff buzzed faintly in her hand again. Maybe it was her imagination, but it seemed disappointed to be leaving the dots.

14

MORGEN GLOWERED INTO THE WOODS AS SHE FOLLOWED AMAR across a ridge and up another slope. The nature hike had been more appealing before her clothes had become disheveled and she'd been interrupted in the middle of slinging her arms—and legs—around Amar.

Fortunately, they didn't go far before he stopped. He pointed at the mud between a boulder and a tree.

Another large wolf footprint wouldn't have surprised her, but something more like a giant bear print—or a *sasquatch* print—was indented in the mud. Two of them. The prints faced back across the ridge.

Her glower deepened as she turned in that direction. "Is that the tree where we were... having romance?"

Amar glanced at her but didn't correct her word choice to something more accurate, like humping, groping, or moaning. The earlier humor and passion were gone from his eyes, replaced by hard determination.

"Yes," he said.

"Your old enemy was *watching*?"

"Apparently."

"What a pervert. Can't he get his voyeurism fix on the internet like everyone else?" She wasn't speaking quietly, but she didn't care. A part of her wanted the guy—the strange man-animal—to hear and feel like the deviant he was. Though if the *rougarou* eviscerated people for a hobby, he doubtless didn't care.

"This way." Amar strode off, following more prints in the mud.

Morgen paused long enough to place her shoe next to one for a comparison. She shuddered at how much larger it was and how deeply the *rougarou*'s claws had sunk into the ground.

"What *is* he?" she whispered. Amar had explained, but she didn't think the *rougarou* was anything like she'd imagined. "Isn't he a normal human during the day? Doesn't he *have* to be?"

"No. He can be a man, a wolf, or a hybrid, kind of a furry man. And he's not bound by the moon—he can shift in the day or night."

"If you have to face him as a normal man, won't you be outmatched?" Morgen didn't mean to insult Amar, but maybe tracking this guy down without more help was a bad idea.

"I will handle him," he said coolly as he looked over his shoulder. "Especially if you help. Your werewolf-control incantation may have some effect on him."

"May? As in it also may not?"

"We'll find out."

Morgen refrained from voicing more concerns. If she did, he might send her back to the house. The house where Sian and Wendy were by themselves.

She halted and looked back, afraid she'd made the wrong choice. Maybe they should *all* be at the house, kneeling behind the railing on the deck with guns.

But the wards were up. They ought to protect Sian and Wendy as long as they stayed behind the boundary. She hoped.

The sound of a car startled Morgen. Tires squealed as

someone drove off in a hurry, having a hard time gaining traction on the wet pavement.

She hadn't realized they'd come to the east side of Wolf Wood and were near the road that ran along that side of the property.

"I smell blood," Amar said.

"Maybe he ran out in traffic and got hit by a car."

Amar shook his head grimly.

The two-lane road came into view through the trees, the roar of the highway farther to the east now audible. Amar stopped before reaching the shoulder and looked down at something. A body.

Morgen's gut twisted. She didn't want to take a closer look, but she had to know if it was the *rougarou* or some innocent. After taking a deep breath, she stepped around Amar.

The dead man's throat had been torn out by claws, and his head was dented in, as if he'd been thrown against a tree. Maybe he had. Morgen spotted a tuft of hair stuck to gouged bark in a cedar near the body. Parallel black tire streaks marked the road where the driver had stopped in a hurry. Because a giant wolf monster had sprung out of the trees in front of him? The car that had made the marks was gone.

"I think he forced this man to stop, killed him, and took his car. We won't catch him on foot." Anger and disgust infused Amar's voice.

Morgen didn't say she was glad they wouldn't catch the *rougarou*, but she thought it. This poor guy had been driving along, minding his own business, and now he was dead.

Amar walked a few steps up the road and pointed to something in the ferns. A car door.

Had the *rougarou* torn it *off* to get the man out of the car? Morgen started to doubt whether her werewolf incantation could control something that powerful. Amar and the Lobos were strong, but ripping off car doors and hurling men twenty feet into the trees... That was on another level.

"I'm surprised he ran from us," Morgen admitted, then realized Amar might again be insulted by the implication. "I mean, you're formidable, but..."

Amar didn't appear insulted, only grim. "I believe he wants more than to kill me. I think he wants revenge."

"Isn't he the one who killed *your* parents?"

"Yes, but I took his eye."

"*So*? That's not the same. You should be the one wanting revenge."

"The *rougarou* weren't made to be logical. Just killers." Until that moment, Amar had been relatively calm, but he startled her by snarling and punching a tree.

She jumped. He grabbed the trunk with both hands, threw back his head, and yelled. Or maybe that was a howl. A primal howl full of anger and frustration. Blood ran from his knuckles, his skin lacerated from the punch.

Morgen, wanting to soothe him, took a step toward him, but she paused. The fury in his eyes made her afraid he would lash out at anyone who came close.

Amar pushed away from the tree and stalked down the side of the road, blood dripping from his knuckles to the pavement.

"Better give him a minute," she whispered and pulled out her phone.

Since Deputy Franklin already had reasons to consider her a troublemaker, Morgen hated to call him, but someone had to report the man's death. And that there was a crazy monster roaming the woods around Bellrock. A crazy monster in a stolen car. Maybe they could get the license plate number, find the vehicle, and descend upon the *rougarou* with every sheriff, deputy, and able-bodied volunteer in the county.

"Ms. Keller," Deputy Franklin answered. He must have finally programmed her number into his phone book. "I assume you're in some kind of trouble?"

"You assume correctly." Morgen told him about the body and gave their rough location. After she hung up, she called to Amar, "Franklin said he can be here in ten minutes."

He'd stopped a couple dozen yards up the road, his back to her. A car drove past, but the driver didn't slow down. If anything, he sped up.

Though she didn't know if Amar wanted company, Morgen walked toward him. Aware of the tension in his shoulders and clenched fists, she stopped a few steps away.

"I'm sorry this is happening. I hope you don't blame yourself for..." She glanced back at the body. "Things that you can't control."

"I should have killed him more than thirty years ago," he said hoarsely. "It's stupid to leave an enemy alive behind you."

"You said you were ten at the time, right? Could you really have killed him?"

He glared over his shoulder at her.

"Sorry." Morgen lifted her hands. "I didn't mean to bring pesky logic into the conversation." She didn't know whether to hug him or try to lighten his mood with humor. The macabre scene behind them didn't suggest humor was appropriate, but with all that tension in his body, she was hesitant to risk touching him. "Is there anything I can do? Do you want water? A hug?" She eyed his bloody hand. "For me to call Dr. Valderas and make an appointment for a skin graft?"

His shoulders slumped, some of the tension ebbing out of him. Or maybe that was a slump of defeat.

"It'll heal on its own," he muttered. "I beat up trees for a living, remember."

"You usually use a chainsaw."

Amar turned to face her, the rage replaced by weariness. He

was so fit and virile that she usually thought of him as a young member of the pack, but the gray peppering his dark hair reminded her that he was her age. Maybe older.

He walked to her, wrapped an arm around her shoulders, and pressed his forehead to the side of her head. "I'm concerned for you," he said quietly.

"I'm concerned for *you*."

For more reasons than one. She wished she had a first-aid kit for his hand.

"I have long expected him to catch up with me," Amar said.

"That doesn't make this all right. If you die, who's going to build that cat condo?"

He snorted softly, his breath warm against her ear.

They stood like that until two SUVs from the sheriff's department arrived. Even then, Amar was slow to release her. Morgen had a feeling her fearless werewolf was afraid. Maybe not for himself but for her and for those he cared about. She wished she knew how to get rid of this enemy for him.

Deputy Franklin and two other uniformed men stepped out of the vehicles, and Amar released her. Franklin looked at the body, conferred with his men, then walked over to her.

"Did you see who did it?" Franklin glanced warily at Amar.

Belatedly, it occurred to Morgen that the deputy might believe that he or another of the werewolves was responsible, but he focused back on her without making any accusations.

"I saw his footprints," Morgen said. "Amar can probably find one nearby to show you."

Amar grunted and pointed to one in the mud on the side of the road. Franklin looked at it, swore, took photos, and waved one of his men over.

"What the hell has invaded my town now?" Franklin looked at Morgen again, as if she might know. Or as if *she* were responsible.

"I just live here." She spread her hands.

He glanced toward the trees, but he must have known they were part of Wolf Wood because he didn't make any snarky comments.

"We didn't see him do this," Amar said, "but I can describe him if it helps. We've... met before."

"Wonderful." Franklin pulled a tablet out of his SUV. "A state trooper was found dead earlier this morning, his throat and abdomen torn out, a lot like that."

"He likes to kill," Amar said. "If you want an eyewitness, speak with the boy Arturo."

"Is that the delinquent kid who likes to knock mailboxes off their posts?"

"He's recuperating in Dr. Valderas's office," Amar said coolly. "He was almost killed yesterday."

Franklin scowled but didn't say anything else about mailboxes. While he tapped in Amar's information, Morgen stepped aside to call her sister. It was possible that the *rougarou* had driven off in the car, only to turn up the driveway into Wolf Wood—and to the house.

When the call dropped to voice mail, Morgen frowned at the phone. How long had it been since she'd seen Sian? Not that long. If she'd decided to use the hot tub, she might still be in there.

Morgen called Wendy and was relieved when she picked up right away.

"Are you guys all right?" she asked over Wendy's *hello*.

"Us guys? Me and Napoleon?"

"You and Sian, though I hope your ferret, Lucky, and Zorro are all well too."

"Oh, your sister is in the hot tub. With a book. She's kind of weird."

"Because she likes to read in a tub? That's not weird." At least not in Morgen's opinion.

"Because, when I said I needed to air out the van because it smells ferrety, she lectured me on how the strongly scented secretions of mustelids are used for sexual signaling as well as marking territory, and how Napoleon may desire a female. Then she told me how ferrets reproduce. Morgen, I didn't ask."

"She likes to share her knowledge. You two stay inside the wards, all right? There's been a murder at the edge of the property. It's not safe."

"A *murder*? Who?"

"I don't know who he was. Someone who was driving through in a car that now belongs to a *rougarou*. Stay at the house, and give Sian some more tips on magic, please."

"She needs an amulet," Wendy said.

"I know. I'll come see if I can make one."

Another SUV arrived, a black civilian model. Mayor Ungar stepped out.

He looked at Morgen, and she grimaced, though she was positive he hadn't come to talk about her taxes.

"I've got to go." She hung up and walked over, though her introvert tendencies—or simple common sense—made her want to hang back as the mayor spoke to Amar and Franklin.

"We'll take a hunting party out tonight," Franklin was saying as Morgen joined them. "Fully armed and armored. Will the Lobos join us?"

"Yes," Amar said.

"The Loups?" Franklin looked at the mayor.

Ungar glared at Amar, and Morgen thought he would reject the idea, but he said, "I'll see to it that they do, but I came to talk to you because some of them are missing."

"The *rougarou* could have ensorcelled them," Amar said.

"*Ensorcelled*? Like a *witch* would do?" The mayor scoffed.

"Not like a witch," Amar said. "He has other powers, ancient powers from the Old World. He could turn you into one of his minions if he wished."

Another buzz reverberated in Morgen's hand, and she frowned down at the staff. Was this still about the dots? It couldn't understand the conversation and have opinions on it... could it?

Ungar scoffed in response to Amar's comment. "He could try."

"He would succeed," Amar said.

The mayor's glare turned even harder.

"I could ask the coven if they can help," Morgen offered, though she wasn't sure she had the sway, after hosting one meeting at the house, to elicit their services.

"We'll handle this." Franklin stuck a thumb in his belt, the belt that his potbelly slumped over. He didn't appear threatening in the least, but Amar and the mayor were big strong men and nodded their agreement. "You ladies stay at home and stir your cauldrons."

Morgen frowned at the dismissal and refrained from pointing out that the Lobos had *already* taken out a hunting party and hadn't found anything. The *rougarou* was apparently good at disappearing. Maybe she could figure out a way to mark him or otherwise locate him for them.

One way or another, she vowed to help.

15

DEPUTY FRANKLIN DROPPED MORGEN OFF AT THE HOUSE BEFORE driving away with Amar and the other men for their hunt. As she headed for the front porch, Wendy hopped out of her van. The side door was open, perhaps for the aforementioned *airing out*. Wendy jogged up carrying a soldering gun and a silver chain.

Morgen pointed at the jewelry. "Is that for Sian's amulet?"

"Freshly made, yup. At first, I wasn't sure what to put on the chain, but then your sister got all pedantic on me, and I figured it out." Wendy held up the chain to show off a thick silver book dangling from it.

"That seems appropriate."

It didn't have a concave receptacle like the talismans, but neither did the amulet Morgen wore. Hopefully, that meant the ritual didn't require her pouring a concoction of kooky ingredients and her own blood into something to harden. Franklin's joke about cauldrons hadn't been far off.

"Thanks, Wendy. I really appreciate it. Sian will too."

Wendy arched her eyebrows. "Are you sure? She doesn't seem the appreciative type."

"She hides her appreciation under dry lectures."

"About embryonic diapause, I know."

This time, Morgen raised *her* eyebrows.

"It was in the ferret-reproduction talk."

"Ah."

Morgen found her sister in the kitchen. Surprisingly, Sian was on the phone and didn't have damp hair to suggest she'd just gotten out of the hot tub. Maybe that was why Morgen's call had gone to voice mail. If so, this was a long conversation for Sian, who avoided the phone even more assiduously than Morgen, claiming that email was sufficient if one absolutely needed to communicate with another person.

Morgen was about to head down to the root cellar to look for the amulet book she'd seen in her vision, but Sian held up a finger as she finished and said goodbye.

"That was my department head at the university," she said. "She's verified that I'm an acceptable candidate for the chimpanzee work. It doesn't involve teaching, so that's a relief."

"Oh." Morgen had known her sister was gainfully employed and couldn't stay here forever, but how was she supposed to teach Sian magic if she went back to Seattle? "Do you leave soon?"

"I'll have to get a ride down on Monday for an afternoon meeting."

"That's the day after tomorrow."

"Your command of the calendar is admirable."

"I'm surprised because— Well, I'm about to make you an amulet so you can become a witch." She held up the silver chain. "And you're *leaving.*"

Morgen hadn't meant the words to come out sounding accusatory—and needy—but they did. She'd known Sian still had her career and wouldn't stay that long, but after they'd worked together to battle the demon, she'd thought... Hell, she didn't know what she'd thought. That her sister would also give up her old life and move to Bellrock to become a witch? That the one sibling who mostly understood her—and whom she mostly understood—would stick around?

"Do day jobs preclude learning witchcraft?" Sian asked.

"Well, no, but day jobs two hours away might make it hard to come up for lessons."

"It's only an hour and a half, and I can visit on the weekends. Is that a book?" Sian leaned in to examine the pendant.

"Yeah, Wendy said you were lecturing her, so it seemed like a good symbol for you. You're lucky you didn't get a pulpit."

"Since I deliver fact-based discourses, not sermons, a religious symbol would not have been appropriate. I like the book."

"I'm glad you approve. I still have to magic it up for you, which will likely involve a nude ritual in the root cellar." Morgen decided not to mention her vision of Grandma performing such a ritual.

Sian leaned back. "You've gotten odder since you moved up here."

"Amar called me eccentric and said I've grown on him."

"Perhaps he's not an inappropriate match for you, after all."

"Did you think he was?"

"I questioned your choice to seek a new lover so soon after the dissolution of your marriage."

"It's *not* that soon. And Jun and I barely saw each other the last year of our marriage. Besides, Amar and I aren't lovers yet." Not that Morgen hadn't *tried* to become Amar's lover. If the world would stop hurling enemies at them, they could fornicate like bonobos in a Congo rainforest. She sighed wistfully.

"Do nude rituals not inspire randiness?"

"Not enough," she muttered. "I'll be downstairs if you need me. I want to get this done before you go so you can try a couple of incantations and experience the delight of casting magical spells."

Reluctantly, Morgen admitted that it would be better for Sian to leave the area. As long as Amar had an enemy hell-bent on destroying anyone close to him, the fewer people staying at the house, the better. Morgen wondered if she should sign Wendy up for an art school in Seattle as an excuse to send her away too. In the past, Wendy had spoken wistfully about taking classes down there.

Lucky bounded outside with Morgen but paused at the porch steps and sniffed the air while she grabbed her staff. As long as enemies were skulking in the woods, she didn't intend to go anywhere without it.

Clouds still filled the sky, heavy and gray with the promise of more rain. Lucky turned around and trotted back into the house. As Morgen closed the door, she debated if that was a sign of something. Lucky didn't love the rain, but clouds alone didn't bother him. Was it possible he'd caught a whiff of something out there that had deterred him from wanting to hunt? Could Amar's enemy have returned to the area?

Morgen listened but didn't hear any cars driving up the road to the house. Not that the *rougarou* couldn't have returned on foot.

She leaned over the railing and peered toward Zorro's nesting box but couldn't tell if he was inside. *Zorro*, she thought, focusing on it. *When you're done napping for the day, will you fly around and try to find a... guy that looks like a cross between a sasquatch and a werewolf?*

Since Morgen hadn't yet seen the *rougarou*, she couldn't share an image with Zorro. Maybe it didn't matter. She didn't even know if Zorro was in his box.

As she walked around the corner of the house toward the root cellar, she caught herself looking off to the west in the direction of the first dot tree. The staff had stopped buzzing, but the temptation to search for a fourth one that might or might not exist crossed her mind. There was, however, no way she would go for walks in the woods by herself right now. Wendy was in her van, and Morgen might have talked her into going along, but she wouldn't feel much safer with her. Even having Amar along didn't feel like enough against this new threat.

"Amulet first, magical dot hunt later," she muttered, but she pulled out her phone before opening the cellar doors and called her cousin. The cell reception under the house was spotty, so she lingered outside.

"Hey, Morgen," Zoe answered. "Did you decide to sell Grandma's house yet?"

"I'm not selling it."

"No? I heard you had a bunch of hunky contractors up there remodeling it and thought you might have taken my advice to spruce it up so you could list it for more money."

"Who told you about the werewol— the contractors?"

"Word gets around."

"Really?" Morgen wondered who in town had gossiped to Zoe.

"Sian called me," Zoe said. "She's got me looking for apartments in affordable neighborhoods near the university, preferably in extremely quiet and child-free complexes. As if *affordable neighborhood near the university* wasn't already an oxymoron without that addendum."

"*Sian* described the contractors as hunky?"

"She said there were sweaty men in tank tops wandering around your property day and night. My imagination filled in the rest. You should have invited me up. You know, to inspect the work."

"You're welcome to come up to visit." Morgen remembered the *rougarou*. "Though maybe give me a week or two to resolve a lingering... issue."

"Will do. What did you call about? Are any of those contractors single?"

"I think most of them are, and—"

"*Most* of them? Really? Maybe I'll come up next weekend."

"Is the Seattle dating scene not living up to your standards?"

"It's full of tech nerds."

"Who aren't sweaty enough for your tastes?"

"Among other things."

A raindrop splattered on Morgen's head, reminding her to get to the point. "Can you get me a satellite map of the property, Zoe? I thought about looking on Google Earth, but it would be nice to have the property boundaries on the map."

"Sure, that's easy. The county GIS system will have it. I'll save a copy and text it over."

"Thanks. I appreciate it."

"Enough to introduce me to a single hunk?"

"Sure. The guy who cooks elk balls is pretty affable."

"I prefer dark and dangerous to affable."

"Oh, they've all got plenty of that going for them. Especially when the moon comes out. I need to go. Thanks, Zoe." Morgen hung up before her cousin could pepper her with questions on the entire Lobo pack.

Once she had the map, she would figure out the precise location of the dot trees, draw some lines, and see if she could use them to find a fourth. If the house ended up being centered within a square, it might mean something. Something helpful, she hoped.

There wasn't a gargoyle statue or anything obvious to turn on the bookcase in the back of the cellar, but when Morgen tugged on it, it moved, scraping along the packed-earth floor. A mountain tapestry, the same as in the vision, hung on the wall behind it. It looked a bit like nearby Mt Baker, but for all she knew, it was one of the Alps, and a European witch had brought the decoration to America generations ago. Morgen slid the tapestry aside, found the plastic bin, and tugged it out.

"Thank you, Grandma," she said, peeling open the lid.

The contents weren't arranged exactly as they had been in the vision, but she found the book Grandma had been using on the bottom.

Crafting Power, the title read, by the Sisters of the Idyllwyld Coterie.

"Sounds promising."

Morgen took the book to the workbench to peruse the contents. Rain pattered on the wooden cellar doors. She hoped Amar and the others weren't outside being poured on. She hoped the *rougarou* was.

"Here we go. Focus artifacts."

Morgen was halfway through reading about a ritual that required dancing, chanting, and treating water with a Tusk of Taledor when scratches sounded at the door. She jumped, envisioning the *rougarou* clawing at the wood. But that guy ripped doors right off their hinges.

Something that sounded like wings battered at the wood.

"Zorro?"

Before climbing up to check, Morgen grabbed the staff. It might *not* be Zorro.

As soon as she opened one of the doors, the spotted owl flew in, beating his wings hard enough to spray water droplets onto her. He landed atop a bookcase and hooted insistently at her.

"Did you see something?" she asked. "Or are you grumpy because Amar has been too busy to hunt down mice to deliver to your nesting box?"

A vision washed over her, and Morgen gasped and bent over, dropping the staff to grip her knees for support. Usually, Zorro would share what he was seeing in the moment, but he showed her an SUV coming up the driveway, so maybe he was sharing something that he'd seen a few minutes ago. Something that had alarmed him?

The SUV rounded a bend, giving her a glimpse of the spot where the driver-side door *should* have been. A big man sat inside. He didn't look like the cross between a werewolf and a sasquatch she'd been envisioning, but Amar had said the *rougarou* could pass as a human. A human with yellow eyes. No, it would be *one* yellow eye.

Morgen swore and grabbed her phone, but she paused, not sure if she was seeing the present moment.

"When was this, Zorro?" What if the *rougarou* had visited while she'd been gone?

Outside, gravel crunched—a vehicle driving up to the house. Zorro's vision faded.

Morgen dialed Franklin and hoped Amar was with him. The call dropped to voice mail. She cursed and left a short message: *He's here. At the house. The murderer.*

After she hung up, Morgen was tempted to close the cellar doors and hide inside, but if the wards weren't sufficient and the *rougarou* went to the house, Sian would be in danger. And Wendy too. Her van wouldn't be any protection at all.

"You better stay in here, buddy," Morgen told Zorro, though he didn't look like he planned to leave his perch on the bookcase. If anything, he'd scooted farther back into the shadows.

Morgen gripped her staff and her amulet and made herself climb the steps. It was time to see this guy face to face.

16

WENDY'S VAN WAS GONE, SO AT LEAST THAT WAS ONE PERSON WHO wouldn't be in danger, but barking came from inside the house, reminding Morgen that Sian and Lucky were inside. She hoped her sister realized that trouble had arrived and didn't let the dog out.

In the driveway, the *rougarou* had parked and stepped out of his stolen SUV. He must have been aware of Morgen exiting the root cellar, but his focus was on the barn.

Did he have a name? For the first time, she wondered. Amar hadn't mentioned it.

Morgen eyed the invisible boundary line where she and Wendy had placed the wards. Would they be strong enough to deter this guy? Morgen hoped so.

The *rougarou* was even bigger than she'd first thought, seven feet tall and broad shouldered, with a damp black T-shirt stretched over his muscular torso. Even from two dozen yards away, Morgen could sense magic about him.

In the past couple of months, she'd started being able to tell when an artifact had some power, but this was the first time she'd felt anything like that from a person. If he *was* a person. There was a reptilian coldness in his single yellow eye, the other one an ugly snarl of scar tissue. His hair was white, but there was no hint of age-related frailty about him. When he turned to look at Morgen, something about him reminded her of the demon, of ancient power from another realm. Dangerous ancient power.

He smiled at her, and it chilled her far more than the rain ever could. In the house, the barking stopped. A faint whine followed, then nothing.

"This is where he lives," the *rougarou* said, his voice deep and grating. It was a statement, not a question.

"A number of people live here, but there aren't any vacancies. If you're looking for boarding, I'm afraid I'll have to turn you away." Morgen pointed her staff toward the driveway, though it occurred to her that if she could delay this guy here until Franklin's men and the Lobos arrived, she should.

"You can try." The *rougarou* chuckled and stalked closer to her. "You are his female. I saw you in the woods about to rut against a tree."

"Yeah, the trees here are good for that. Real soft against your back." Morgen gripped the staff with both hands, pointed it at him, and ran through the incantations she could try against him, starting with the werewolf-control spell.

"I thought you would be younger." He looked her up and down. "Sexier. He's powerful for a wolf. He could have any mate he wishes."

"Well, his rent is included when he picks me, so that's a plus." Morgen refused to feel insulted by this guy, though she had to resist the urge to run into the house and shut the door on him.

"I thought about killing him then, while he was distracted, but I want him to suffer first. I want to kill those he cares about." The *rougarou* smiled again as he stopped ten feet from her. His toes were almost bumping against the boundary line created by the wards. Could he sense it? That the magic would hurt him if he crossed it without an invitation?

"He's suffered enough." Morgen lifted her chin. "Under the moon's magic, turn the snarling hound from angry foe to witch bound."

His thick white eyebrows rose, then he lifted his gaze and inhaled deeply, his huge chest expanding. "I feel your power, witch. I see now why he chose you." He squinted and focused on her, then took a step forward, through the ward.

Power snapped and crackled as her defenses were triggered, but he only inhaled deeply again, as if he were breathing in the magic. As if he relished it battering at his skin.

"It's like a good massage," he said with a chuckle.

Morgen repeated the chant, louder this time, and willed it to work on him. "Go back to your car," she added, hoping a command would work now.

"Yes, I feel your power," he said, not moving. "It's delicious. Perhaps I will mate with you myself before killing you."

That threat made her want to sprint for the root cellar and slam shut the doors, but she made herself stand her ground and keep her chin up. The werewolf chant wasn't working. Time to try something else. On the chance he fell into the same category as an imp, she tried the incantation to banish one.

Nothing happened.

"My power is older than anything you modern witches wield. You have no way to defeat me." The *rougarou* took another step toward her, menace wafting off him.

Morgen lifted the staff, prepared to stab him, though she feared she couldn't best him in a physical confrontation. She needed magic on her side. What had that incantation been that Grandma had whispered in the vision? The one that had given her staff the power to blast six werewolves?

It had been short and sweet. She tried to dredge it from her mind as her heart pounded and she took a step back, not wanting him to get close enough to grab her.

A creak sounded. The front door opening.

"Stay inside!" Morgen yelled.

The *rougarou* stepped closer to her.

"Under the moon's magic, poor behavior correct and this witch protect!" Morgen blurted, the words coming to her.

The staff buzzed in her hands, but it didn't launch any power at the big man. He crouched like a panther prepared to spring. No, it had been *bad*, not *poor*.

This time, she shouted the incantation. Green light flared among the antlers, and raw power blasted the *rougarou*. It caught him in the air as he sprang for her, and it knocked him backward. He landed on the gravel, but he rolled to his feet immediately.

Terrified he would recover and attack again, Morgen yelled and ran toward him, leveling the staff to use it like a battering ram. She pronged him in the side as he stood, even as she wished she'd gotten him in the ass. Though she jammed the weapon into him with all her strength, he didn't budge. He merely snarled and spun back toward her.

He knocked the staff aside, almost knocking *her* aside since she'd tightened her grip and wouldn't let go. He stepped closer and kicked her. Morgen tried to avoid the blow, but his leg was too fast and too long. He clipped her in the side and knocked her to the ground.

Again, she kept her grip on the staff, knowing she would be dead if she lost it. Though she landed hard on her butt, she got it pointed at him once more.

A good thing, because he crouched to attack again. But he paused instead of springing, and fabric ripped. His clothes. His body twisted and morphed, sprouting fur. He didn't change completely, not like one of the werewolves taking a lupine form. He remained on his two feet, but his muscles grew even larger as his clothing ripped away. Fur covered his arms and legs, and his face twisted and cracked as a snout formed where his mouth had been. Human teeth altered into pointed fangs.

From the ground, Morgen once more chanted, "Under the moon's magic, bad behavior correct and this witch protect!"

She feared her magic would be less effective on whatever he'd turned into, but another green blast struck him in the chest. It worked, sending him flying—but not as far this time. He landed on his hands and feet, crouching like a gorilla. He faced her, snarling and somehow smiling even with that lupine snout. His yellow eye burned into her soul, promising her death—or something worse.

Again, she unleashed the power of the staff. It was the only weapon she had. Once more, her magic blasted him in the chest. He lifted his face and howled, but it sounded more like a cry of pleasure than of pain, as if he were sucking in her power and enjoyed having it tear through him.

The rumble of a vehicle came up the driveway—of multiple vehicles. The *rougarou* squinted in that direction, hesitated, then looked at Morgen again, as if he wanted to finish her off so badly that he would risk being caught here. At the last second, he spun and ran on two furry legs across the driveway and the lawn.

Several sheriff's department SUVs drove into view. The officers must have spotted the *rougarou* as he ran into the trees for several drove out onto the lawn. Doors flew open, and men in uniforms and carrying rifles sprang out and fired into the woods as they ran after him. Amar, Mayor Ungar, and several other Lobos and Loups, still in human form since it was afternoon, sprang out too. Some had axes or sledgehammers, and others had only their bare hands, but that didn't keep them all from charging after their foe.

Morgen rolled to her feet and rubbed her bruised butt. She hoped Amar and the others caught the bastard. Caught him and killed him. The fact that her power had only made him pause, not doing anything to truly hurt him, made her aware of how dangerous he was.

Sian leaned over the porch railing and held up her phone. "If it helps, I got a picture of him."

"Great. We'll have it put on a milk carton to alert the county that he's missing."

"Ha ha." Sian showed her the broom she held in her other hand. "You may want to rethink keeping a gun in the house. Even if it imperils the lamps."

"I'll keep your suggestion in mind," Morgen said, though she was positive that mundane firearms wouldn't have any more power over that guy than her magic. She wished she knew what would.

17

WHILE MORGEN PACED IN THE LIVING ROOM, SIAN MADE COFFEE IN the kitchen, enough to give to wet werewolves and law enforcers, should they return from the chase. Morgen strained her ears for sounds of howling, gunfire, or battle of any sort, but the hunt must have moved too far away from the house for her to hear.

Her sister's phone rang, and Morgen ran into the kitchen. It didn't make sense that Deputy Franklin or any of the Lobos would have called Sian, but someone might be reporting in.

"There's been an incident here," Sian was saying as Morgen entered. "This might not be the best time for you to come." She paused as whoever was on the other end spoke. "No, I don't think we're in danger now. We were in danger twenty minutes ago." Another pause. "It wasn't my intent to make you feel better."

Morgen arched her eyebrows and tried to see the caller's identity on the phone, but it wasn't a number Sian had programmed into her address book.

"Very well," Sian said. "I am certain she will appreciate it."

She hung up.

"Dr. Valderas is bringing you a book and coming to loom protectively next to us while the others hunt," Sian said.

"That was Valderas? You hang out together, and you don't have him programmed into your phone?"

"Yes, it was, yes, we do, and no, I do not. My memory is not addled, so I can recognize his number when he calls."

"Still, you guys have coffee together and argue about animal science."

"What's your point?"

"Just that you might have added him to your contacts." Morgen thought about asking if she'd friended him on the various social-media sites, as one did these days, but she doubted Sian even had accounts on them.

"Should we remain acquaintances for a suitable length of time, and should I feel compelled to purchase him gifts for his birthday, I will enter all of his contact information into my phone. What's important is that he's bringing you the book you discussed yesterday."

"I appreciate that. I haven't figured out those dots yet. It's not a priority right now, but I have this... feeling that it would be helpful to learn about them as soon as possible." Maybe intuition was a better word, though her sister might mock her for believing in such things.

"They don't look like a natural phenomenon," was all Sian said, "not like bioluminescent moss or mushrooms. Can't you appeal to the collective wisdom of the witch community?"

"Ute, one of the witches who came to the meeting, didn't recognize them."

"Collective usually refers to more than one," Sian said.

"Yes, next time they're here, I'll hand out pictures of my magical dots with the beverage glasses."

"There are presumably more witches in the world than those who exist in Bellrock. I was referring to them."

"I don't have their numbers."

"Can't you use your app? I thought you mentioned that witches all over the world had downloaded it. How many people is that?"

"A few hundred." Morgen admitted that wasn't an insignificant number of people. She tapped her chin thoughtfully. "I could make a pop-up that displays when they open the app, one that shares a picture of the dots and asks if anyone recognizes them. Maybe I could gamify it, turn it into a trivia quiz with points and a prize to entice people to answer."

Sian slanted her a sidelong look. "Or you could just ask for their help. Aren't they using your app for free? If they find it an adequate resource, they ought to be willing to help the creator."

"Uh, maybe." Morgen liked the gamification idea more. Who didn't love earning points? "I'm not sure they know my name or feel that beholden to me for the app. They can leave tips, but only a few have."

"Enough to help with your property-tax problem?"

"I've made seven dollars so far. That might protect the mailbox from being seized by the government."

Sian sipped her coffee and murmured, "The *flag* on the mail-box, perhaps."

"Regardless, your idea isn't bad."

"Naturally not."

"Your modesty could use some work." Morgen trotted to her room and grabbed her laptop. Updating the app would give her something to do besides worry.

While she worked, Wendy returned to the house, easing around the sheriff's department vehicles to find a parking spot for her van. Lucky greeted her at the door, but his usual tail wagging was subdued. He'd been quiet ever since the *rougarou* had shown up. Maybe he knew Amar's enemy was still nearby. Not comforting.

Napoleon was also subdued, drooping limply over Wendy's shoulder. The ferret's eyes shifted left and right, as if he were searching for a reason to play dead.

"Are you being arrested?" Wendy asked Morgen. "Or is Amar?"

"No, but there's a deadly enemy about."

Wendy smiled faintly. "What's new?"

"I blasted him with Grandma's staff and all the power I could summon, and I think he *liked* it."

"He also wanted to rape Morgen," Sian said.

Wendy's smile dropped.

"I was perturbed by the lack of suitable weapons in the house," Sian added.

"There are knives in the butcher block," Morgen said. "Your go-to defensive weapon doesn't need to be a broom."

"I wanted something long so I could keep him as far away as possible."

Morgen sighed and didn't point out that the *rougarou* could have snapped a broomstick with a flick of his finger. She was lucky he hadn't snapped her staff in half.

"You two are serious." Wendy looked back and forth between them.

Napoleon sat up and chittered in her ear. Morgen suspected it was only in her imagination that the ferret noises sounded like *I-told-you-so-I-told-you-so.* After a thorough tongue-lashing, Napoleon ran down Wendy's side, across the living room, and sprang onto the hearth. He sniffed at a couple of brochures that Morgen had left there to burn, and she thought he might demand another fire, but he hopped into the wood basket and hid behind a log.

"I don't think our familiars want anything to do with the *rougarou* either." After the fight, Morgen had checked on Zorro and found him still hiding in the cellar, perched in the shadows atop the bookcase. She'd left one of the doors ajar so he could leave when he wished.

"Napoleon never wants anything to do with anyone or anything ferocious," Wendy said.

"I've noticed," Morgen said.

Lucky padded over to sniff at the woodbox. Napoleon scolded him, probably telling him to find his own hiding place.

"This might be a good weekend for you to go to Seattle and check out art schools," Morgen said.

Wendy arched her eyebrows. "You want me to leave you here? With a monster that wants to... *do* things to you?"

"I've got Amar." Morgen almost added *and Sian,* but since Sian didn't know how to do anything witchy yet, maybe it would be best to send her away too. Zoe probably needed help apartment hunting for her.

Sian did not, Morgen noticed, object to not being included in her army of defenders.

"Where is he?" Wendy asked.

"Out in the woods with the deputies."

"What if he circles back?" Wendy asked.

Morgen shook her head and wanted to say that wouldn't happen, but it already had.

"And what happened to the wards?" Wendy added. "It looked like they'd been triggered."

"He walked through them without trouble."

Wendy's jaw sagged. "Seriously? You're strong, and we both put our power into them. That shouldn't have been possible. This guy must be really..."

"Yeah. He is."

"Why don't *you* come to Seattle too?" Wendy waved at Sian. "Both of you. We could have a girls' weekend out. It would be fun."

Morgen didn't want to have *fun* while Amar was up here in

danger. Judging by the distasteful expression on Sian's face, she didn't *ever* want to have fun.

Another car arrived, and Morgen peered out. "Your date is here, Sian."

"Ha ha. He's coming to bring *you* a book."

"Yeah, but he'll flirt with you."

"Date?" Wendy asked.

"Dr. Valderas," Morgen said, opening the door for him.

Lucky forgot his fears long enough to bound out, get a pat on the head, and lead the way back inside.

"Hey, Doc," Morgen said. "How's Arturo?"

Valderas climbed the porch steps and handed her a thick tome. Morgen nodded her thanks. She had updated the app with a picture of the dots in the hope that Sian's suggestion would have merit, but she still planned to peruse his book.

"He's stable," Valderas said. "A couple of the female Lobos came to take him home to watch him."

"Female Lobos?" Morgen blinked. "I didn't realize there were any, besides Maria."

"Maria is the only one who runs with the pack most of the time and works in the construction business. The others didn't come up from Mexico with the core Lobos. They were—are—citizens here who, ah, had dalliances with some of the men and fell sufficiently under their spell to want to be turned into werewolves. Unlike with the Loups—and with *me*—I understand all of the turnings were voluntary." Valderas glanced warily at Sian. Concerned she would judge him for having allowed himself to be involuntarily turned? As if one would have a choice about that.

"I had wondered," Sian said, "if there were more females about or if the werewolves simply mated with human women. A situation with so many more males than females would otherwise result in aggressive behavior."

"Territorial pissing?" Morgen asked.

"More like territorial throat-tearing-out."

Valderas snorted but didn't disagree.

"Would you like a cup of coffee, Osvaldo?" Sian asked.

"I shouldn't stay long, since I've been told to expect more patients, but..." Valderas checked his phone, didn't have any notifications, and nodded to her. "A cup would be nice."

"Excellent. I wish to show you two scholarly articles I found on the equestrian intestinal microbiome. Interestingly, they lend credence to the method of probiotic administration that you were talking about earlier."

"I look forward to reading them."

"I thought they were going to flirt," Wendy whispered to Morgen.

"They *are* flirting. That's how they do it."

"She hasn't touched him or fluffed up her hair or even made eye contact."

"It's their way."

Sian frowned at them and waved for Valderas to follow her to the kitchen, but they paused when Morgen's phone rang.

"Hey, Pedro," Morgen answered. "How's the hunt going?"

"It's me," Amar said. "I borrowed his phone to update you."

"How come he can turn into a wolf without breaking his phone, and you can't?"

"He's a more conscientious shapeshifter. I give in fully to my animal urges."

"You are a beast." Morgen smiled, relieved he was all right, at least for the moment.

"Yes."

"If I get you a phone for Christmas, will you use it?"

Sian raised her eyebrows. "You haven't even figured out how to pay the property taxes on your mailbox."

"But the flag is covered." Morgen winked. "And I have credit cards."

She was joking, but Sian scowled at her in sisterly condemnation for the mere suggestion of financial recklessness.

"Have you located the baddie?" Morgen asked Amar while making shooing motions toward Sian.

She and Valderas disappeared into the kitchen.

"Unfortunately, no." Amar's voice turned into a growl. "He is being a *coward*."

"Is there anything I can do to help?" Morgen asked, though her encounter with the *rougarou* had chilled her. She would be happy to never see him again, but as long as he was out there and a threat to Amar, she wouldn't sleep well.

"It's too dangerous. I called because... I want you to leave."

"Leave... the house?"

"Leave Bellrock. Take your sister, and go stay somewhere safe until I handle this. If you leave in the car, he shouldn't be able to track you down."

Even though Morgen had been thinking about sending Wendy and Sian away for their safety, she frowned at this suggestion that *she* leave. "What about *you*?"

"I'll let you know when I've taken care of him."

"What if you're not able to?"

"Then at least you'll be safe."

"I don't want to be safe without you."

"Morgen..."

"Damn it, Amar. I... I care about you." She'd almost said she loved him. Maybe she did, but she was aware of Wendy watching, and who knew how many werewolves and deputies were standing around Amar and listening to his phone conversation. She didn't want to say the words for the first time over the phone with witnesses around. She wanted to look into Amar's eyes, say something funny to soothe his grumpiness, then kiss him and confess her feelings to him. Then make love to him. What she definitely *didn't* want was to leave the county.

"I care about you too," Amar said. "That's why I want you to leave."

"I have to stay and help you. Come back to the house. I'll make you dinner—something fancy, with *meat*—and we'll brainstorm and figure this out. We'll come up with a brilliant plan that we'll execute together. Against all odds, we'll bravely defeat your heinous enemy."

"I do like meat." Amar didn't comment on the rest.

"I've heard werewolves are into it."

"Yes. But Morgen..."

"Look, we'll talk over dinner, all right? If you don't like my plan, I'll leave in the morning and help my sister find an apartment in Seattle."

After a long pause, he sighed and said, "Very well. We're going to take another lap around Wolf Wood, so I won't be back until dark."

"Be careful."

"You as well. Call if you see him."

"Oh, I will. Trust me." She did *not* want to face that bastard alone again.

"What's your brilliant plan?" Wendy asked after Morgen hung up.

"I'll come up with it while the meat is thawing."

A chittering came from the hearth. Lucky sat on the rug and watched as Napoleon, who'd climbed out of the woodbox, pushed one of the brochures toward the edge with his nose. It had a picture of the Space Needle on the front.

"I think your ferret is trying to tell you something," Morgen said.

"That I'm not invited to dinner?"

"That it would be a delightful time for you to visit Seattle." Morgen patted her on the back. "I hope you'll take this opportunity to visit the city and check out those art schools."

"I guess, but I *am* a witch, you know. I could help too."

Napoleon chittered and shoved the brochure to the floor.

"Even when your familiar is on strike?" Morgen asked.

"He's *usually* on strike." Wendy strode over to pluck him up. "Or being a big pain in the ass."

Lucky trotted over to Morgen, reared up on his hind legs, and planted his paws on her shoulders.

"I wouldn't know what that's like," she said.

18

WHILE THE MEAT DEFROSTED FOR THE MEAL SHE'D PROMISED AMAR, Morgen sat on the couch to watch out the window as twilight approached. She kept her phone nearby, hoping Franklin or one of the Lobos would call to give her an update, preferably one that said they'd taken down their prey and were on their way here for a celebratory feast. Though tempted, she kept herself from calling any of them. If they were facing off against the *rougarou*, she didn't want to distract them.

She *was* tempted to call Phoebe and ask her if the coven would come up to help. After watching the *rougarou* walk through her wards, Morgen feared she would need all the magic users in town to defeat him if he showed up again—especially if he showed up while the werewolves were busy hunting.

But would the witches come? It would be dangerous, and just because Morgen had sent them a free app and helped with the demon didn't mean they owed her anything. Calista had only summoned that demon because she'd been trying to get rid of Morgen. And a lot of witches had been at the graveyard that night, willing to help Calista.

Morgen sank back on the couch, afraid she had more detractors than allies among the coven. Maybe she'd made a mistake in emptying the house of everyone except her and Lucky. Earlier, she'd shooed Valderas and Sian away, suggesting Sian would be a great veterinary assistant if injured animals or werewolves came to the office, and she'd succeeded in getting Wendy to leave as well. Morgen wanted them all to be safe, but what of her?

She'd reset the wards, for what good they had done, and she'd perused Grandma's *Incantations of Power*, but she hadn't found anything that seemed stronger than the spell Morgen had already used. An incantation that was supposed to cause a foe to develop a rash and lice had been a tempting one to memorize, but it hadn't sounded instantaneous. Morgen wouldn't feel that much satisfaction if the *rougarou* developed an itchy scalp and groin three days after she died.

Though she didn't think she was tired, she found her eyelids growing heavy. Lucky hopped up on the couch with her, and she pulled the afghan down to drape over him and her legs. He burrowed between them and curled into a ball.

"Don't you think it's a little weird for a seventy-pound dog to act like a cat?"

He shivered, as if snowdrifts surrounded the house and the power had gone out. It wasn't that cold, so maybe this had more to do with the devil creature in the woods.

Morgen listened for howls, figuring it was dark enough now that the packs could have shifted into wolves to hunt, but all she heard was the sound of her own yawns. Though she didn't want to sleep, not when Amar and the others were in danger, her body disobeyed her wishes, and her head drooped against the cushions.

Warmth emanated from the amulet lying on her chest. Maybe it was responsible for her drowsiness because it wanted to impart another vision. At the thought, she stopped fighting her drowsiness and let sleep overtake her.

When she opened her eyes again, full darkness had come. A glow started up within the firebox, then expanded outward, soon morphing into a vision of a sunny morning outside, sun glinting off snow melting on the lawn. A woman in a helmet and leather jacket was riding up the driveway on a green motorcycle with a sidecar, a cat riding inside.

At first, Morgen thought it was Grandma, but she'd seen her wrecked Harley in the barn, and it hadn't been green or had a sidecar. Nor had Morgen seen litter boxes, cat toys, or other evidence that a pet—or familiar—had lived in the house with Grandma.

The woman stopped before she reached the house and climbed off the motorcycle to frown at a dark brown spot on the gravel driveway. Dried blood. This must have been shortly after the Amar incident.

Grandma walked out of the house wearing clothes that included a parka and scarf—far more appropriate winter attire than she'd had in the previous vision. She waved as she approached, something silver glinting between her fingers. The amulet she'd made? Something else was tucked under her arm. It looked like a plastic bag of food, but it was hard to tell.

The visitor removed her helmet and hung it from one of the handlebars. It was Belinda, and Morgen remembered the speakers in an earlier vision suggesting that she and Grandma had been motorcycle-riding buddies.

Grandma extended the amulet toward Belinda, who forgot about the stain as she brought both hands to her mouth, then hugged her. Grandma lifted her eyes toward the sky, patted her once, and smiled tightly as she extricated herself from the embrace.

Hah, that was where Sian had gotten her distaste for hugging. Not that Morgen was that much of a touchy-feely person herself. Their mother hadn't been either. Apparently, it was genetic.

Grandma waved for Belinda to take the amulet. She did so, closing her fingers tightly around it, and spun a pirouette like a six-year-old in a dance class rather than a woman in her sixties or seventies. She lifted her arms for another hug, but Grandma lifted the plastic bag and held it up like a shield.

Teriyaki beef jerky, the package read.

"I need to see if my furry houseguest is still here and wants breakfast," Grandma said.

"Your what?"

"There was a wolf incident on my driveway last night." Grandma pointed to the stain.

"I wondered if that was blood."

"A lot of it, yeah." Grandma took a step toward the barn, but Belinda lifted her hand.

"Is it a wolf or a *were*wolf?"

"A werewolf."

"Are you sure?"

"Pretty sure. After getting his fur and blood all over the driveway, he turned into a naked man."

"That does imply werewolf-ness."

"I thought so." Grandma started toward the barn again.

"Wait," Belinda blurted, lunging to grab her arm. "Werewolves are dangerous. Even wounded."

"No kidding."

"They're *especially* dangerous to witches. They *hate* our kind after all the fights we've been through to protect Bellrock from that nasty Canadian pack."

"I'm aware."

"Does he know you're a witch?"

"I chanted and waved my staff at the wolves harassing him, so he got a few clues." Grandma gently tugged her arm out of Belinda's grip. "It'll be fine. I'm not without means to protect myself from deadly predators."

Belinda glanced toward the house. "You left your staff inside."

"I meant this." Grandma held up the bag.

Belinda curled a lip. "I didn't know you ate things like that."

"My late husband did."

"He's been gone for years, hasn't he? Won't it be spoiled?"

"Enh, with all the salt in it, I'm sure it's preserved for all eternity." This time, Grandma succeeded in slipping away from her visitor and heading to the barn.

The dubious expression on Belinda's face said she thought checking on a wounded werewolf was a bad idea. The cat in the sidecar meowed dubiously. Belinda leaned against the motorcycle and pulled a wand out from under her familiar. She wiped cat fur off it. Maybe this event had been before she'd been elected president of the coven and received that fancy staff with the glowing orb on top.

Despite her apparent fearlessness—and her predator-defense gift—Grandma eased the barn door open slowly. She peered around before stepping inside, then turned toward a dark corner but didn't walk closer. If not for the colorful afghan, Morgen might have missed the naked man curled up in the gloom.

Grandma leaned back to slide the door further open and let in more light. Amar growled at her. His hair hung in his eyes, and he looked even wilder than usual.

"I see you're a morning person. Here's breakfast." Grandma tossed the bag to him.

His hand came out from under the blanket with impressive speed, and he caught it before it would have smacked him in the face.

"Teriyaki beef jerky?" Amar rasped, his voice rough with pain. The afghan hid his wounds, but Morgen had no doubt he hadn't healed fully during the night.

"I told you this wasn't the Four Seasons. Eat up so you can get your stamina back. As soon as you're fit, I want you off my property. I don't know why those ugly fur balls were chasing you, but I don't want them to come back looking for you. I like my peace and quiet, and that caterwauling you call howling was so abysmal, it wilted my houseplants."

Amar squinted at her. "Why did you help me, witch?"

"I don't like bullies. Where's the rest of your pack?"

Amar hesitated. This must have been right after he left because Maria chose Pedro. "I'm a lone wolf."

"Seems dangerous."

"It can be. Especially if you refuse to kiss ass."

"Given the amount of fur on wolf *asses*, that would be unpleasant."

"Extremely so." Amar eyed the jerky bag distastefully but must have been hungry for he opened it. As soon as he sniffed the contents, he sneered and read the fine print. "This expired years ago."

"Wolves eat flattened possums by the side of the road. You can handle some stale beef jerky."

"You're thinking of coyotes. They're scavengers. And the possums are freshly flattened, not *expired*."

"Technically, they're very expired. Get a dictionary, wolf."

Without waiting for a response, Grandma walked out.

Belinda raised her eyebrows.

"He appreciated my help and denigrated my breakfast offering," Grandma said.

"He said he *appreciated* you? A witch?"

"He said it with his eyes. While he was sneering at the jerky."

"Do you want me to stay with you until he leaves? To make sure you're safe?"

"No."

"Do you want me to gather the coven to help you get him off your property?"

Grandma considered the barn. "No. He can stay until he's

better. Maybe he'll catch some of the rats that are always scuttling around in there. God knows they never expire."

"You're a quirky woman, Gwen."

"So are you. It's the reason I talk to you more than the others."

"I thought you just didn't like paying Judith's dues."

"That too."

"Well, I'll be off. Holler if you need any assistance." Belinda tilted her head toward the barn, then touched her new amulet. "I owe you one."

"Damn right, you do. I nearly froze my nipples off last night because I'd been making that thing."

"That must be a ritual I'm not familiar with." Belinda waved and rode off.

The words *holler if you need any assistance* and *I owe you one* echoed in Morgen's mind as the vision faded, leaving her in the dark living room, staring at the fireplace.

She grabbed her phone to check the time. It wasn't that late. She pulled up the contact information for the coven members and found Belinda's number.

Hoping the woman would feel that the *one* that she'd said she *owed* Grandma might extend to her granddaughter, Morgen called her.

19

Two pans of spaghetti sauce simmered on the stove, one filled with mushrooms, eggplant, zucchini, and other vegetables that Morgen approved heartily of, and one laden with meatballs. She'd pulled out ground beef *and* ground pork to make them, the *fancy meat* she'd promised Amar.

Since Belinda had agreed to ask for volunteers to come up to spend the night at the house—and reinforce the wards with more power—Morgen was making more than even his voracious lupine appetite required. It was possible there wouldn't *be* any volunteers, but at least Belinda would come. She'd agreed even before Morgen mentioned amulets and how she'd learned that her grandmother used to make them.

She eyed the box of noodles and the water she'd set aside to boil for them, but she wanted to wait until Amar arrived to start them. Werewolves probably didn't like overcooked noodles any more than normal diners.

Morgen's phone dinged with a text. Zoe had sent photographs of the map she'd requested, satellite images with the boundary lines delineated. She'd sent an overview of the whole property, as well as images focusing on the various quadrants. Grandma hadn't had a printer, so Morgen emailed the pictures to herself, grabbed her laptop, and sat at the kitchen table to look at them on the larger screen.

She drew circles around the spots where she believed the dot trees to be. With the oak, she didn't have to guess. Thanks to all the evergreens around it, its spreading branches full of deciduous leaves stood out on the satellite imagery.

"There's my triangle," Morgen murmured, drawing lines on the photos. "And if there were a square, the fourth point would be about here." She drew a circle around a clump of trees. "That would put the house... not exactly in the middle but definitely *inside* the square. Coincidence?"

Lucky, who'd been under the table while she'd been cooking, slipped out. Instead of responding to her question, he sat on the floor in front of the stove and pointed his nose at the saucepan with the meatballs. He didn't even glance at the one with only vegetables in it. His tail swished back and forth on the vinyl floor with hopeful wags.

She'd already fed him, so he shouldn't have been genuinely hungry. "You can have one when Amar gets back and we have dinner."

More tail swishing followed the comment.

Morgen leaned back in her chair. "It could be a coincidence," she said, answering her own question. "There could be a lot more than three or four dot trees out there. Though, with as much as Amar roams around Wolf Wood, if there were a lot of them, you'd think he would have noticed more, right?"

Lucky wagged his tail again.

"Of course, I don't know how much time a wolf spends looking ten feet up tree trunks. *You* mostly sniff around the base where dogs, wolves, and coyotes have left their marks, right? Unless there's a squirrel chittering at you from the branches. Still, maybe

I'll ask Amar to join me for a walk in the morning to check out this area." Morgen tapped the new circle, then thought of what had happened the *last* time they'd gone for a walk to check out a tree. The kiss that had almost turned into much more than a kiss had been stimulating. Being stalked and watched by a murdering monster had been less so.

Flashlight beams outside the window caught her eye, and she jumped to her feet. The pack and Franklin's officers came out of the woods on foot, their clothing damp from the intermittent rain.

Morgen debated if propriety demanded that she invite them *all* in for dinner—they'd come to hunt the *rougarou* at her request, after all—but if all the werewolves came in to dine, her meatballs would disappear in seconds. If Amar wasn't fast, he might end up with nothing but sauce-covered mushrooms from her pot. Despite numerous conversations on the subject, and her assuring him that mushrooms had lovely amounts of protein, he refused to acknowledge them as a meat substitute.

The hunters climbed into their SUVs and trucks without coming up to the house, so Morgen didn't have to make a decision regarding dinner invitations. Only Amar headed to the porch.

Lucky abandoned his stovetop vigil and ran to the front door to greet him. Morgen turned on the burner for the water so she could start the noodles. She was digging a metal colander that had seen its prime in the 1970s out of a cabinet when Amar walked into the kitchen, Lucky galloping at his side.

"We caught sign of him several times but weren't able to catch up with him," Amar said wearily. "More than once, he took to the trees like a gorilla. The men are breaking for dinner, but they'll be back in a couple of hours, and we'll hunt again tonight."

Morgen would have preferred that Amar stay at the house—or at least in the barn where he was close—that night, but she couldn't blame him for continuing to try to find his old enemy. "I'm glad they're willing to help."

"The Loups and sheriff's department have all lost people. They want to get rid of the *rougarou* too."

"Understandable."

"The *rougarou* who's probably only here in Bellrock because he's after me." Amar sighed. "He's crossed paths with the rest of the pack in the past... but I'm the one he hates."

Morgen groped for something to say that would make him feel better. More than weariness seemed to be causing his shoulders to slump. Was that defeat? If so, it would be the first time she'd seen it on him.

"If you're able to take him down, he won't hurt anyone else ever again. Maybe it's good that you're getting the opportunity to do that." Morgen *hoped* he would get the opportunity to do that.

"If we succeed."

Lucky nuzzled his hand, trying to force head patting.

Amar obliged somewhat absently, though he did say, "Your dog is excited to see me."

"I told him he wouldn't get a meatball until you got back and we ate."

"I figured his exuberance was due to more than my personality."

"Oh, I don't know. He doesn't mind grumps." Morgen smiled, kissed Amar on the cheek, and set the colander on the counter.

"As long as those grumps drop meatballs in his gullet?"

"Exactly."

He snorted softly and sat at the table. "Have you come to your senses and realized that you'd be safer in another county and rethought leaving Bellrock?"

Morgen wondered if he knew his enemy had walked through the wards. She didn't want to worry him, so she didn't mention it.

"No," she said, "but I called Belinda, and she said she would come stay at the house tonight while you're off hunting."

Amar raised his eyebrows. "Did you have to bribe her?"

"No, Grandma handled that."

His eyebrows climbed higher.

Morgen thought about explaining the vision and the amulet, but she was more interested in him and how he'd met Grandma. If she truly had saved him from Loups ganging up on him, that would explain why he'd been willing to befriend her and had felt loyal to her. Thus far, Morgen had been trusting that the visions the amulet shared with her were accurate—they'd led her to both the hidden safe in the library and the secret nook in the root cellar. But were they exactly what had happened?

"Did you ever eat the teriyaki beef jerky she gave you?" Morgen asked.

Amar's jaw drooped. She couldn't tell if it was because he had no idea what she was talking about or he was surprised she knew about the event.

"She didn't tell you about that," he reasoned. "Because you weren't in touch with her then."

"That's right. I had a dream. I guess more of a vision, kind of like my familiars share with me. Except it came from the amulet." Morgen waved at the chain around her neck. "Did she really help you against a bunch of Loups chasing you that night? Is that why you came to be friends? You never said why you two got along, other than that you were both loners."

The water started boiling, so she dumped the noodles in.

"I was hungry, so I did eat the jerky. It was like eating a salt lick." Amar tilted his nose toward the stovetop. "Your meatballs, which I caught the scent of a mile away, smell much more appealing."

He fell silent as she used a wooden spoon to prod the noodles down into the water.

"You don't want to talk about the rest?" she guessed.

"A man doesn't like to admit that he was getting his ass kicked and was rescued by an old naked lady in flip-flops."

Morgen smiled over her shoulder. "You shouldn't mind naked people. You're in that state often enough to apply for membership at a nudist colony."

"Ha ha." He gave her a dark look.

Morgen left the stove to lean over his chair and hug him from behind. "I'm glad you and Grandma found each other and weren't completely alone these last few years."

"Hm," was all he said, not willing to go into further detail on the *ass kicking*. He did pat her arm, holding it to his chest and encouraging her to stay close. "I've not heard of many witches who receive visions of the past from their jewelry. I think your power is growing."

"I think *Grandma* is the one who had power." Morgen wondered if Grandma had made the amulet she was wearing, not only the one she'd given Belinda.

"You do as well. I can sense it, especially when you're close like this."

"I hope it's friendly and comforting, not dark and threatening."

Amar turned his face toward hers. "It's sexy and alluring."

"Even better." She smiled, though she only met his eyes for a second. Since they had an enemy stalking the woods outside and his pack would return as soon as they ate, this wasn't a good time to be titillated by him finding her—or her supposed power—sexy and alluring. Even if she was glad he did.

Aware of his speculative gaze upon her, Morgen leaned over his shoulder to tap the laptop keyboard and bring the map to life. "If, while you're out hunting tonight, you go in this direction—" she pointed at the circle, "—will you check the trees there for magical dots?"

He looked away from her and toward the screen, but his hand remained on her arm to keep her close. Morgen was happy to be close, though she would have to stir the noodles eventually.

"While I'm hunting a tremendously powerful predator," he said, "you want me to peruse trees?"

"You can't tell me you don't peruse trees left and right when you're on the hunt." Morgen tugged her arm free so she could stir the noodles, though she brushed her fingers through his hair in a promise to return. "Lucky does."

Lucky, who was now lying on his stomach in front of the stove, whined.

"*Lucky* is probably looking for someplace to lift his leg," Amar said.

"You and the Lobos don't do that?"

"Not while we're hunting. And not on magical trees. One doesn't want to risk brushing sensitive parts up against anything capable of zapping one."

"I can see how that would be alarming, but the dots have all been several feet off the ground. Unless you're doing ballet-style leg lifts, I don't think your *sensitive parts* will be in danger."

"After I've defeated my enemy, I'll look at trees for you."

Morgen removed the noodles, put the colander in the sink, and poured them into it. Steam wafted up and fogged the window. She glanced out to see if any vehicles were still there, but the men had all driven off and were likely feasting on steaks at the Timber Wolf. Fortunately, she didn't see any enemies lurking on the lawn. If nothing else, the wards she'd reapplied would warn her if a stranger crossed them.

"I suppose I could see if Belinda will go with me." Morgen set the empty pot aside.

Amar growled and rose from his seat to stand behind her, his muscles tense. "You will stay in the house while I hunt, not risk yourself wandering around in the woods with nothing but an old lady for protection."

"Old ladies can be formidable. Especially if they're naked." Morgen smiled, though she didn't intend to suggest nude hikes to

Belinda. "But I meant that I'd wait until morning." Not that the woods would necessarily be safe then. As she'd seen, the *rougarou* wasn't a vampire, and he had no trouble threatening her in daylight. "I have a hunch that the dots are important and it could be beneficial to figure out what they do." She remembered the way the staff had reacted to the last bunch of them. "It's fine if you don't have time to look for another tree. I can handle it."

"I'll do it." Amar glared at her.

"Good." She turned and kissed him, hoping he wouldn't feel that she'd manipulated him. That hadn't been her intent. "Thank you."

He caught her wrists and pulled her close, his eyes narrowing.

"Are you irked with me?" Morgen asked. "Grumpy? Do you need me to drop a meatball in your gullet?"

"I need... you."

Morgen opened her mouth to say it wasn't the best time for that, but he stepped closer, bent, and kissed her, and her admonishment died on her lips. She gripped his shoulders and kissed him back, thoughts of dinner falling out of her mind. If they didn't eat, they ought to have time for... each other.

His hands slid around her back, pulling her tight against him, and his mouth promised he was hungry for more than food. As his touch sent shivers through her, she ran her hands over his arms and up under his vest, exploring the hard muscles of his torso.

"I'm tired of being interrupted," he said against her mouth.

"Me too," she whispered, already breathless.

He grasped her hips and lifted her, startling her. She gripped his shoulders, holding on tight. He growled and set her on the counter, easing between her legs, and she realized he wanted her right here. Excitement flushed her as she tugged his vest open, then lowered her mouth to taste his warm skin. He groaned and nipped at her ear as he unfastened her jeans.

She was vaguely aware of Lucky sighing and slinking out of

the kitchen and acknowledged that she would have to give him *two* meatballs later to overcome her guilt. But that didn't keep her from wrapping her legs around Amar and—

A howl wafted in from the woods, alien and demanding. It filled Morgen with fear and stole her ardor faster than if someone had dumped a bucket of cold water over her head.

Amar thumped his palms to the counter to either side of her and snarled, "No, damn it."

"Is that him?" she whispered, still gripping his shoulders but as much from fear now as desire.

"Yes."

The howl came again, deeper and eerier than a wolf howl. She didn't know how she knew that it was demanding something, but she did. It seemed slightly taunting as well. Maybe the pervert was watching them from afar again and knew what they were up to.

"He sounds... kind of close," she said.

"He is." The tendons in Amar's neck stood out, and so much tension emanated from him that she worried they would snap— that *he* would snap. "He's commanding me to come out there, to serve him as one of his minions."

"Can you howl back and tell him to suck it?" Morgen patted his chest and tried to smile, but she was afraid. The wards wouldn't stop the *rougarou*, and even though she had her staff, and Amar could turn into a wolf, she didn't think it would be enough.

"I..." As the howl sounded again, Amar jerked away from her, half-turning toward the door. Then he halted, his fingers balling into fists.

Morgen slid off the counter and rested a hand on his shoulder. "His commands won't work on you, right? The talisman..." She brushed the chain with her finger, hoping it was giving him the power to resist, that it would be enough.

But Amar shook his head. "It's what I feared. His is a different type of magic. Old World magic from a forgotten time."

Another eerie howl sounded—was the *rougarou* getting closer?
—and Amar took three rapid steps across the kitchen.

"No." Morgen lunged after him, grabbing him with both
hands. "If you go out there, he'll kill you."

"I *know*." Amar planted his hands to either side of the door
frame, his muscles heaving as he struggled to stay in the kitchen.
The wood of the wall creaked under the pressure he exerted. "If I
give in to his power, I'll fall to my knees in front of him. He'll kill
me, and I won't be able to stop him. Or he'll kill *others* while I
watch, powerless to do anything. *Again*."

Morgen assumed he was thinking of—remembering—his
parents' deaths, but he looked back at her, meeting her eyes.
Maybe he feared having to watch the *rougarou* torment and kill *her*
in front of him.

"You can resist him." Hoping it was true, Morgen tried to think
of incantations she'd come across that might break another's
enchantment. The only thing that came to mind was when she'd
used the werewolf-control spell to override the one another witch
had cast on him. But now that he wore that talisman—

Another demanding howl echoed across the lawn. A pitiful
whine came from the living room—Lucky—even as Amar threw
his head back and roared.

Morgen wrapped her arms around him, as if she could hold
him in place, but she was afraid of all the power coiled in his body.
If he jerked an elbow back, he could break her ribs.

"Control me, Morgen," he rasped, lowering his head. The walls
creaked again. "Control me, so he can't."

"How?" She knew what he meant but didn't think it would
work. Her power wasn't greater than that of a centuries-old
magical creature who could walk through witch wards.

"Say the werewolf-control spell." Amar grabbed his chain and
pulled her talisman over his head.

"You know you hate it when I do that. And I don't want—"

"*Say it*," he ordered.

Another howl came from the woods—from the edge of the lawn. The *rougarou* was so close now.

Amar whirled and strode into the hall.

"No," Morgen blurted, running out of the kitchen after him. Her jeans sagged, reminding her how close they'd been to having sex with an enemy right outside. Cursing, she gripped them while wrapping her other hand around her amulet. "*Under the moon's magic, turn the snarling hound from angry foe to witch bound.*"

Amar jerked to a stop, but he didn't turn back toward her. His face was toward the living-room window, and he was still on the verge of giving in to the howl's demands.

Morgen whispered the words again and locked her arms around his tense body.

"Stay, Amar." She willed all the power she had into the words, making it a command and not a plea.

Some of the tension left his body, and he rotated to face her. Fear rose up within her that he would resent her for commanding him, even though he'd asked for it.

The howl came again, cranky and insistent, and Morgen imagined she could see that single hateful yellow eye through the window. She kept her arms around Amar.

"Stay," she repeated.

"Yes." Amar leaned his forehead against hers. "I am... your wolf."

Though she wanted to argue that he was his *own* wolf, she didn't. She sensed that this was his alternative to being the *rougarou's* wolf and that those were the only two options right now.

"Yeah, but don't forget that I'm yours too." She smiled at him.

"My witch."

"Completely."

"Good." He kissed her, and when the cranky howl sounded again, he didn't pull away.

Morgen slid her arms up to his shoulders and returned the kiss, half hoping the pervert out there was watching and was fuming because his power hadn't been enough to take Amar away from her. But she didn't want to be smug, and they dared not lower their guard and return to what they'd been doing before, not when the *rougarou* could crash through the front door at any second.

20

MORGEN GRABBED A NAPKIN AND LEANED OVER AND WIPED spaghetti sauce off Amar's chin. After the *rougarou's* howling, they hadn't shared the romantic—or even calm and pleasant—dinner she'd imagined. They'd eaten while standing side by side at the sink, watching out the window in case Amar's enemy appeared.

She'd barely managed to talk him into joining her for a bite; he'd wanted to charge back out and challenge his foe, but he seemed to accept that he wasn't a match for the *rougarou* and needed to wait for the rest of the pack to return. Given how little luck they'd had finding him so far, Morgen wondered if even all the Lobos and Loups together could take this guy down.

Beside Amar, Lucky sat alertly, looking up at his plate and wagging his tail. Amar selected a meatball from the heap mounded on his pasta and dropped it into the dog's mouth. That was the third one, and Lucky was enjoying himself immensely. Earlier, Morgen had put the two meatballs she'd promised him into his bowl, so he was making out better than a Roman emperor being hand-fed grapes. Normally, she didn't give him food from her plate, since she didn't like being stared at while she ate, but if Amar wanted to spoil him, so be it. Maybe they'd bonded when they'd slept together in front of the fireplace.

She smirked.

Amar noticed and lifted his eyebrows. "If you were another witch, I would assume you were contemplating servile tasks you could give me while you have me under your sway." He glanced toward his talisman, which lay on the counter next to him. It had been twenty minutes since the last howl, but that didn't mean the *rougarou* wouldn't try again to turn him into a minion.

"I'm smirking at the realization that you slept with my *dog* before me," Morgen said.

"That's because you keep forgetting to wander out to the barn and into my bed."

"I thought it was because of the proliferation of enemies that are constantly interrupting us."

"That too. I want to kill him." Amar glowered out the window.

"So we can be together?"

"For that reason and others." Though Amar didn't relinquish his glower, he set his plate on the counter and wrapped an arm around her shoulders. "I've actually expected him to find me my whole life. I won't say that it's a relief that he has... but it'll end things. One way or another." He stared grimly through the glass panes.

"I hope it ends in a particular way that leaves us both alive."

"Me too. The pack and I have moved so many times in our lives, avoiding him or even the possibility that he might find us. I've always been afraid to grow too attached to any one area. Or any one person." Amar eyed her. "But I've occasionally wondered what I've missed out on by being..."

"Wild and feral?"

"Unattached."

Morgen thought about asking if he'd ever thought of a serious *attachment* with Maria, but she didn't want to bring up his ex-lovers, especially not one who was still in the area.

"Did you ever contemplate having children?" Amar asked.

"Yes, but I'm not very maternal, and I had my work that I liked, and Jun wasn't all that paternal either. I don't know. We were always kind of... a logical match since we had a lot of common interests, but I'm not sure I was ever aching to birth his children."

"You didn't love him?"

"I did. It was just... kind of a sedate love." And she admitted it had faded over time. She'd felt betrayed when he'd filed for divorce, since he hadn't warned her or said ahead of time that he was unhappy, but it wasn't as if her heart and soul had crumbled and she'd pined for months afterward. "We never gave in—or almost gave in—to fiery passions on the kitchen counter."

Amar blinked. "Never?"

"No, do werewolves do that a lot?"

His eyelids drooped. "More the woods than the kitchen, but we do have fiery passions that we give in to."

"I look forward to experiencing them."

"Good." He kissed her, though not as heatedly as before, and when the beams of a car appeared through the trees, she knew why. His pack was returning.

"Are you sure you should go out and hunt again?" Morgen asked, though when they broke the kiss and she glanced out the window, she realized the vehicle belonged to Belinda rather than a Lobo.

"We'll find him sooner or later." Amar picked up his talisman and donned it. "He has to sleep at some point."

"Don't *you* need to sleep?"

"When this is over."

As Belinda parked her sedan, more vehicles arrived. Trucks. Those were the Lobos.

Amar hugged her, told her to make sure the wards were up, and walked out to greet the pack.

Lucky looked at Amar's plate, whined, and wagged his tail hopefully.

"You've had enough," Morgen said. "Vizslas are supposed to stay lean and trim so they can successfully hunt down their prey."

He tilted his head in confusion. Or perhaps in protest.

She put Amar's plate in the fridge with the leftovers, then walked out onto the porch.

To her surprise, Zorro perched on the railing. He hooted at her as Belinda and Phoebe climbed out of the car, Belinda opening the back door to pull out her staff.

"I don't suppose you've seen the *rougarou*?" Morgen asked the owl. She was surprised he hadn't shared any visions of the intruder wandering through the woods, but she'd admittedly given Zorro a poor description. Now that she'd actually met the *rougarou*, she might have better luck.

The owl issued an uncertain hoot. Or maybe that was an *uneasy* one.

"Are you afraid to look for him?" Morgen asked.

Zorro shifted from foot to foot, and he rotated his head to look away from her.

"He can't reach you, right? You can fly."

Maybe that was an incorrect assumption. If the *rougarou* could howl and turn people into minions, maybe he had magic he could use on a witch's familiar from a distance.

"Do you want another task?" Morgen thought of the fourth dot tree that might be out there. Zorro might be the perfect candidate to search for it. "One that involves investigating trees? Trees that might have rats burrowed in the fallen leaves at the bases of their trunks?"

Zorro rotated his head back toward her and hooted again. Maybe it was her imagination, but he sounded much more interested. She thought of the map and the spot she'd circled, trying to impart to him where she believed the tree to be and that she wanted confirmation of dots.

He flexed his wings as Belinda and Phoebe approached, then sprang from the railing and flew into the night. He took off in the direction Morgen had suggested. Even though he'd proved a few times that he could somewhat grasp her thoughts, she was still impressed when he did.

"Sending your familiar on errands?" Phoebe climbed the steps to join her.

Belinda trailed behind, the orb on top of her staff glowing as she sent wary looks toward the Lobos. Half of them, including Amar, had turned into wolves. One glanced at her—or maybe the orb—a couple of times, but most were focused on the woods and making plans for their hunt.

"Yes," Morgen said. "I'm looking for dots on trees if your Zeke is bored."

"He's at home sleeping. Ravens forage during the day and roost at night."

Belinda climbed up to join them. "I saw your request on the app."

"Nobody's sent a reply yet." That disappointed Morgen, but she was encouraged to learn that Belinda was using her app.

"I hope someone in the community will be able to help you," Belinda said, "though I assume that's not your primary concern right now."

"It's not."

Howls came from the Lobos. The sounds were startling when they were so close, but they were better than the creepy calls of the *rougarou.*

"The howling wolves in the yard would be *my* primary concern," Phoebe said.

"Are you sure?" Morgen asked. "I heard a rumor that you're not as anti-wolf as you've suggested."

"What are you talking about?" Phoebe frowned at her as Belinda looked curiously at her.

"The mayor." Morgen realized she only had Valderas's word on that. She didn't *think* the town vet had a reason to lead her astray, but for a silver-haired man and stalwart member of the community, he was a bit of a gossip.

When Phoebe leaned back, her jaw dropping open, Morgen suspected Valderas had given her the truth.

"The mayor?" Belinda sounded more amused than surprised. "I thought you stopped seeing him after he was seduced into the werewolf way—and bitten by that scruffy Loup leader."

"I *did*," Phoebe said. "No witch should have anything to do with one of *them*."

Despite her vehement tone, her cheeks grew pink, and she avoided both of their eyes.

Belinda looked at Morgen, as if she was curious and wanted more details. Morgen didn't want to out her source and could only spread her arms.

"I'm not seeing him," Phoebe repeated, staring straight at the deck boards. "He comes over now and then, but we're not *dating* or having a relationship. I don't even want him there."

"Then why don't you tell him to beat it?" Belinda frowned. "He doesn't force you, does he?"

"No, I'm not some weak-willed neophyte witch. I could handle him if he tried that. But he's..." Phoebe shifted her gaze to the roof of the porch and huffed, still avoiding their eyes. "Hot."

"Hot?" Belinda arched her brows again.

"I don't go out with him or anything. He's *such* a pompous ass. He was even before the wolf thing, but he's..."

"Hot?" Belinda repeated.

"He gets my motor running," Phoebe mumbled. "Animal magnetism, I guess. He's like no other lover I've taken, and now that he's... one of them, he's even more... I don't know." She looked at Morgen. "You know how it is, right?"

"The werewolves do seem to have fiery passion," Morgen murmured, glancing toward the Lobos.

The rest of the pack had changed into wolf form, and they were loping across the lawn toward the woods, but the gray-and-black wolf in the lead—Amar—glanced back at her, his blue eyes knowing as they met hers.

"Interesting," Belinda said. "All this time, I've assumed they're simply savages."

"They *are* savages," Phoebe said, then lowered her voice. "But sometimes, a girl likes that."

"I see." Belinda cleared her throat and changed the subject, an act that elicited a grateful expression from the stricken Phoebe. "I can sense where someone powerful broke through the ward barrier. Morgen, we'll show you how to make them stronger, and we'll do our best to add our power to reinforce them. I brought an overnight bag. You shouldn't be here alone, especially when your protector is off hunting." Belinda smirked and glanced at Phoebe. "Savagely."

Phoebe groaned.

"Sorry," Morgen whispered, wishing she hadn't embarrassed her mentor. But maybe it would keep Phoebe from informing her that werewolves were inappropriate boyfriends.

A vision came over Morgen, and she missed Phoebe's response.

"That was fast," she muttered, gripping the railing for support.

Zorro flew over the dark forest, winging between trees and thankfully not pausing to hunt any of the rats she'd mentioned to him. It was hard for her to get her bearings but easier than it would have been on foot—looking down from an owl's point of view was similar to viewing the satellite imagery. When Zorro soared over an outcropping she'd seen on the map, she knew he was in the right spot.

Phoebe touched her shoulder as the owl circled the trees, flying low and looking for dots. "Are you all right?"

"Vision," Morgen said, seeing the world through Zorro's eyes more than she did her own.

Disappointment welled up as he flew past every tree in the area twice, and there were no glints of magical dots. Maybe they didn't glint in the night the way they did during the day.

Zorro flew back up above the treetops and headed farther south. Not wanting to send him out of Wolf Wood, Morgen was tempted to call him back, but she had a feeling he knew where he was going.

He flew over a stream she knew was near the edge of the property, then dove down and landed on the branch of an old apple tree someone must have planted out there long ago. Blue and purple confetti-like dots glinted on the dark trunk.

"Interesting," Morgen murmured.

After a long moment of staring at them, Zorro took off toward the northeast. At first, she thought he was taking a circuitous route back to the house, wanting to hunt along the way, but he flew in a straight line, his wingbeats determined. He passed a rocky outcropping and landed on a branch in an old pine. He peered down at more dots on the trunk.

"Wait," Morgen whispered, "there are *five* dot trees?"

Or were there more?

Zorro's gaze shifted to needle litter at the base of the tree. With vision far sharper than her own, he picked out a mouse. So did she. He dove, talons outstretched.

"No," she blurted, raising a hand, as if she could stop the vision.

But Zorro swooped in and caught the mouse. After carrying it back up to a branch, he feasted.

Morgen's stomach roiled, and she was on the verge of spewing mushrooms and eggplants all over the bushes beside the porch when the vision faded.

"Thank you," she whispered, dropping to her knees.

"Her exchanges with her familiar seem a lot more interactive than mine," Belinda remarked.

"I can only imagine what the ones with the *dog* are like," Phoebe said.

Morgen rested her forehead against the railing and her hand over her stomach, willing the nausea to fade. Zorro didn't send any more visions, either because he was busy eating or he'd shown her all the dot trees he knew about.

After sucking in several breaths of cool night air, Morgen pulled herself to her feet.

"Will you start on the wards?" she asked her guests. "I'll join you in a minute. I need to check something."

Phoebe and Belinda waved in agreement, and Morgen hurried inside to her laptop. After pulling up the satellite image, she picked out the stream and looked for a large deciduous tree that could be an apple tree. But even at maximum zoom, the resolution wasn't good enough for her to determine species, and numerous deciduous trees grew along the waterway. It took her several minutes to pick out what she believed was the spot, just inside the property line. She drew a circle around it.

"And where's the fifth?" Morgen closed her eyes, trying to remember landmarks Zorro had flown past. That rocky outcropping. Was that it? "No, there."

She circled it with moderate confidence, then drew lines between each of the points and leaned back, tilting her head as she considered the shape.

"Hello, pentagon." Not only wasn't it the square she'd anticipated but the house wasn't in the center. She drew lines to connect all the circles—the points. "Or should I say *pentagram*?"

Was it a coincidence that she'd made the same shape painted on the floor of her grandmother's root cellar? She shook her head. Even if she was guessing about the exact locations of those trees, the pentagram was too accurate to be accidental. She was sure of it.

Morgen drew a circle in the center of the pentagram. It marked a rocky area on the map, the grays and browns almost clear of trees. The satellite image didn't mark contour lines for elevation, but it looked like there might be a cliff there.

Maybe the magic of the dots had nothing to do with the trees they were in. Maybe they'd been placed to create this pentagram and mark a location. The location *of* something.

"But what? A chest of hidden riches?" Morgen snorted, hardly believing her grandmother had set up *Treasure Island* on her own property. She didn't even know if Grandma had been responsible for the dots.

Even though the treasure idea seemed silly, Morgen couldn't help but think that a cliff would be the perfect place to hide something. There would be nooks and crannies all over it.

When Amar returned, she would ask him about the area. None of the trails she'd followed across Wolf Wood led through it, but she doubted wolves stuck to trails when they hunted. Neither did owls.

Zorro? Morgen willed her thoughts to go out to him. *Can you hear me? I have something else I'd like you to investigate.*

But if he could hear her mental calls, he didn't respond in any way. After gorging himself, he might be napping. She would have to wait until he returned to his nesting box to communicate with him again.

Morgen eyed the circle. "It's probably only a mile away."

The temptation to talk Phoebe and Belinda into a moonlit trek through the woods came over her, but she resisted it. If there wasn't a trail, it would be a difficult walk, and if they crossed paths with the *rougarou*, she didn't know if three witches would be enough to defeat him.

Reluctantly, she said, "Solving this mystery will have to wait until tomorrow."

21

"I'VE HEARD OF THE *ROUGAROU*," BELINDA SAID, KNEELING BACK FROM the ground where they'd been placing new wards. She shared a concerned look with Phoebe.

While they'd worked, Morgen had been telling them what Amar had told her.

"And that would explain the grisly deaths," Belinda added. "From what I've heard from colleagues in the South, they came over from the Old World, but supposedly, they've all been hunted down and are extinct now."

"This one isn't extinct," Morgen said. "He is *old*. Amar was a boy when he first ran into him."

"Amar isn't that old." Belinda smiled faintly, pushing a strand of white hair behind her ear. "But if the *rougarou* is one of the same creatures who roamed the European countryside centuries ago, he'll have grown very powerful. As with witches, those who are shaped by magic tend to develop more power as they age."

"Wonderful," Morgen said.

"And learn more tricks too. The *rougarou* are reputed to be impossible to find if they don't *wish* to be found."

"That's what Amar and the others are experiencing. The pack has been looking for two nights. *More* than the pack. The sheriff's department and the Loups too."

"He could be camouflaging himself with his magic and watching them from the branches of a tree, and they might never know it. They're also known to be able to control wolves," Belinda said grimly. "Their howls have magic, and they can turn wolves and even werewolves into slaves. Some of the powerful ones in Europe were seen leading dozens of wolves through the countryside, forcing them to ravage entire towns. They supposedly enjoyed killing for sport, not to eat. Those who created them wanted that."

Morgen remembered the *rougarou's* howls and shivered. "He tried to get Amar earlier tonight, tried to get him to leave the house and join him in the woods."

"I'm surprised Amar was able to resist one with such power."

"He almost didn't. He was fighting it and losing, then took off his talisman and had me chant the werewolf-control incantation."

Belinda considered her. "And that worked?"

"Yeah, but I think it pissed off the *rougarou*."

"Likely. I'm a little surprised you had the power to override *his* control spell. I suppose you truly are of Gwen's blood."

"I told you she's worth teaching," Phoebe said. "She'll help keep Bellrock safe."

"That she might," Belinda said. "She might be key in defeating this threat."

Morgen shrugged, uncomfortable under their scrutiny and not wanting to take credit for more than she'd done. "The incantation might only have worked on Amar because he so badly *wanted* me to have control. I mean, not permanently, but he would temporarily pick me instead of that freak of nature."

"Even so, I'm surprised he made the request," Belinda said. "He must trust you very much."

"We've been through a lot together in the last few months."

Phoebe yawned. "I think the wards are as strong as they're going to get. Can we call it a night?"

Morgen led the way into the house and showed them to guest rooms. But did she want to go to bed? Even though she was also tired, she hated the idea of going to sleep when Amar was out there in danger.

Belinda paused before closing the door. "Wake us if you hear anything or need anything, Morgen."

Phoebe had already disappeared into her room.

"I will. Do you think it would be all right if I try to make an amulet for my sister?" Morgen fished in her pocket and pulled out the pendant Wendy had made. "Do you know if it's a big deal if a ritual gets interrupted? I heard it was a long one."

"There wouldn't be any harm to you or backlash of any kind, if that's what you're asking. You'd just have to start over if there was a pause of more than a few seconds." Belinda considered the pendant. "You're going to attempt to make a magical focus?"

"Yeah, unless you've got an extra lying around. My sister needs one so she can start learning." Morgen realized Belinda might not approve of her and Wendy teaching a new witch their ways. It wasn't as if either of them was that experienced. Wendy had been raised from childhood to know she was a witch, but she was still so young herself.

"Is she going to join the coven and pay dues?" Belinda quirked an eyebrow. "You know Judith gets huffy about people practicing witchcraft in the county without dropping coins in the coven's coffers."

"What do you guys do with all those dues?" Morgen asked, relieved Belinda didn't sound annoyed.

"Keep the communal liquor cabinet full and help out members who grow too old to take care of themselves. A lot of us are a tad quirky and end up divorced or estranged from our families in our old age. And sometimes, our younger age too." Belinda smiled ruefully.

"I understand quirky."

"I thought you might. Good luck with the ritual. It takes a powerful witch to make amulets, but since you made those talismans and can override the howls of an ancient evil... you might be able to handle it."

"I hope so. I do love getting nude and dancing."

"Dancing?" Both of Belinda's eyebrows went up this time. "Do you refer to the stately and refined ritualistic movements that accompany a chant of power?"

"Uh, if you'd seen me around the campfire calling my familiars, you'd know there was nothing stately and refined about it. I tripped over a rock twice."

"Your sister must be honored that you're willing to go to such lengths for her."

"I doubt it. She's about to take a job back in Seattle."

"Ah. Well, one needn't be local to Bellrock to use one's craft."

Morgen doubted Sian would use incantations to clean out the chimpanzee cages but nodded, said goodnight, and headed downstairs. She paused in the living room, wondering if it was safe to leave Belinda and Phoebe unchaperoned in the house. As far as she knew, they had both been outside on the deck during the library break-in, so they couldn't have been the ones snooping. Further, Morgen hated to doubt either of them, but she couldn't know for *sure* that they hadn't colluded with the snoop. As the president, Belinda could have ordered a younger and spryer witch to infiltrate the house.

Lucky was snoozing on the couch, but he lifted his head.

"Let me know if either of our houseguests does anything interesting," Morgen whispered to him, trying to make it a magical command to a familiar, not a random comment to a dog.

Lucky cocked his head and looked toward the kitchen.

"Wandering down and opening the fridge door doesn't count."

Whether he understood her was questionable, but he plopped his head back down on his paws.

Morgen slipped outside, the air damp and cool and promising rain. It was early September, but it already felt like deep autumn.

She paused on her way to the root cellar to look into the dark woods and listen for signs of the hunt. Distant howls drifted to her ears, but they were far away, and she couldn't guess what they signified.

Her phone rang, startling her. "Hi, Sian. How's the date going?"

"It wasn't a date when we left the house, and it most certainly isn't a date now. Dr. Valderas has received a new patient, and I am assisting him."

Morgen grimaced. "Someone else who's been mauled by claws?"

"Yes. One of the Lobos who was scouting ahead of the hunting party. One of Deputy Franklin's men was also injured and is being taken to the hospital in Bellingham."

"I guess that means he's not hiding from the hunters tonight," Morgen muttered.

"What?"

"Nothing, just that this may be resolved soon."

But would it resolve with Amar still alive?

"Why don't you spend the night there?" Morgen asked. "I think it'll be safer than at the house."

"I did not bring my pajamas or bathroom accoutrements."

"Maybe the doc has a long T-shirt and an extra toothbrush."

"I do not sleep in other people's clothing—you know how sensitive I am to the harsh laundry detergents that so many use—and unless that extra toothbrush is still in the plastic container, my mouth is puckering at the mere suggestion."

"I'm sure you can make do for one night."

"Perhaps, if you wish me to avoid the house that you invited me to stay in, you could bring my pajamas and toothbrush to me."

"Perhaps I'm busy making you an amulet that will allow you to harness your witchly powers."

"I'd rather have my own toothbrush."

"You're a pain in the ass, Sian."

"I have to go. Dr. Valderas needs me." Sian hung up.

"He'll only need you until he figures out how high-maintenance you are," Morgen grumbled at the phone.

Against her sister's wishes, she continued to the root cellar to see if she could make that amulet. If trouble found Sian, she would be a lot more likely to fend it off with magic than a toothbrush.

22

EXHAUSTED, MORGEN EYED THE SILVER CHAIN AND BOOK PENDANT on the worktable as she tugged her clothes back on. It was chilly in the cellar, but the vigorous chanting and dancing—maybe Belinda was right and *dancing* was an optimistic term for the awkward steps laid out in the book that Morgen had been emulating—had kept her warm.

The bottoms of her feet ached from standing so long, and her sweat turned clammy as her body cooled. Morgen thought of the vision that had shown Grandma finishing up a ritual to make an amulet, one perhaps similar to this one, and felt close to her, or at least her memory. She didn't, however, know if she'd succeeded.

Steam wafted up from the amulet—per the instructions, Morgen had mixed a concoction of ingredients with Grandma's stirring tusk and poured the liquid on it—but it wasn't glowing or oozing great magical energy, at least insofar as she could tell. It did seem to have *some* kind of signature. At the least, she sensed that it was there.

In the morning, she would ask Belinda if the ritual had worked. Morgen didn't want to hand the amulet to her sister, promising it would allow her to channel her powers, only for Sian to find out at a deadly moment that it was a dud.

Morgen checked her phone, hoping for an update from Amar, but nobody had called during the hours she'd been performing the ritual. She grabbed the amulet and headed for the doors. It was well past midnight, and she'd yawned numerous times while chanting.

As she climbed the steps, another vision crept up on her. One from Lucky? Letting her know that one of her houseguests was doing something suspicious?

No, the dark forest came to her eyes, a view from above. Zorro was flying over Wolf Wood.

Morgen hoped he wasn't about to show her a *sixth* tree with dots. That would ruin her pentagram and leave her wondering if all her line-drawing had been for naught.

Zorro landed high in a pine and peered through the branches toward a moonlit clearing. He'd landed in a spot that made it hard to see much, but Morgen caught movement below him. She almost urged him to get closer or out from behind all the branches, but as soon as she spotted the *rougarou*, she realized Zorro was trying not to be seen. And she couldn't blame him.

The *rougarou* wasn't alone.

Six large wolves lay in a circle around him. At first, Morgen couldn't guess why they'd be lounging around in the woods, but they weren't relaxed; they were on their bellies with their tails tucked between their legs as they faced him. Was the *rougarou* taking minions? Creating a pack of his own to sic at Amar and the Lobos?

The *rougarou* was on two legs in a bipedal form, but he didn't appear human, not like he had when he first came to the house. He was more like the sasquatch with a wolf's head that he'd turned into when he attacked her. He lifted his furry snout and howled.

She couldn't hear sound through Zorro's vision, but it didn't matter. She heard that howl from the root cellar. It was off in the distance and in the opposite direction from where the Lobos had been howling earlier. That had been hours ago, so they might have moved, but she had a feeling they were hunting in the wrong part of the woods. Though it was possible that *some* of the Lobos were right there at his feet. She didn't recognize any of the wolves—there wasn't a black wolf or a gray-and-black wolf among the bunch—but that didn't mean much. Other than Amar, Maria, the black-furred Loup leader, and the silver-furred Dr. Valderas, most of them looked similar to her.

The *rougarou* lifted furry arms, and the pack rose to their feet. He pointed into the trees, and they all trotted off together, the wolves meek and docile, their tails still clenched.

Before they disappeared into the woods, the *rougarou* looked back, his yellow eye glinting as it focused on Zorro. His jaws opened, and his tongue lolled out. He looked like he was smiling.

Morgen shivered in fear for her familiar. The *rougarou* might have known he was there all along.

Zorro sprang from his perch and flew in the opposite direction, winging across the woods at top speed. The vision dissolved, and Morgen found herself kneeling on the cellar steps.

Her heart was pounding, and all hint of fatigue vanished. She didn't know if the *rougarou* was heading to the house, but she felt vastly unprepared to battle him, especially now that he had powerful werewolf minions. Her staff and incantations hadn't been enough to drive him away even before he'd gathered troops.

She pocketed the amulet and headed up to the library. Maybe it was time to consult *Incantations of Power* to see if something from its secret pages could help.

Morgen woke to sunlight streaming through the library window and across the table where she'd fallen asleep with her cheek plastered to a book page. Information about summoning imps lay before her bleary eyes, though she barely remembered reading about it. As she sat up, her neck, back, and butt all let her know how foolish it had been to sleep in a chair. Her body had stiffened so much that she almost pitched over when she stood.

If not for the appealing scent of something baking wafting up from downstairs, she might have staggered off to her bedroom to sleep for another four hours. She didn't know where the *rougarou* had gone after taking off with his minions, but he hadn't come to the house. If someone had forced their way through the wards, she would have felt it and woken up. Lucky also would have barked like a stuttering foghorn from the living room.

Morgen tucked the book under her arm so she could continue perusing it over breakfast and walked downstairs. She found Belinda and Phoebe in the kitchen, sharing coffee and smearing butter and jam on freshly baked croissants. A few more peeked out from under a cloth in a basket on the table.

"Morning, Morgen." Phoebe raised her mug. "I hope you don't mind that we found the tube of croissant dough in the fridge and helped ourselves. We made enough for you."

"That's fine." Morgen's stomach whined. After the amulet ritual and being up most of the night, she could have consumed the whole basket by herself. "Thanks."

"What is that?" Belinda's gaze locked onto the book.

"A scintillating bestseller from ages past." Morgen held it up so they could see the cover.

"That's a dangerous tome."

"I was hoping to find something to use against the *rougarou*."

Belinda shook her head. "You can't summon a demon to battle your enemies. Calista's experience must have shown you the folly of that kind of thinking."

"No problem. This only has imp-summoning rituals listed."

"You can't summon *anything*. Those creatures want nothing more than to escape into this world to wreak havoc. They can't be called forth under any circumstances. Any deals you make with them will go badly. I promise." Belinda shuddered visibly.

Morgen didn't think it was an act. That reassured her, making her suspect Belinda had strong morals and hadn't had anything to do with the snoop in the house. Phoebe was also frowning in disapproval.

"Someone in the coven doesn't feel that way." Morgen wondered if they would share ideas about who *had* snooped. "During the meeting, someone sneaked into the house and tried to find this book."

"How would they have known you had it?" Belinda asked. "I assume Gwen left it to you, but I knew her for years, and I didn't suspect she had it."

"She had it with her at the graveyard," Phoebe said.

"We found the incantation that helped us banish the demon in here." Morgen lifted the book.

"Ah," Belinda murmured. "Of course. Well, keep it someplace safe where nobody can find it. I'd like to say nobody in our coven would be tempted by such knowledge, but clearly, I can't—"

Her phone rang, and she stepped into the hallway to answer it.

Morgen grabbed a croissant and looked out the window, hoping to see Amar. The trucks and SUVs were all gone, so the men and werewolves had returned at some point. Why hadn't Amar stopped by the house?

She shook her head. He might have been too tired to check in with her and gone straight to the barn.

When Belinda stepped back into the kitchen, her face was grave. "A creature—Harriet didn't know what it's called, but I'm sure it's the *rougarou*—raced through town last night with a number of werewolves. They attacked livestock and pets, damaged property, and killed a man who stepped out of his home and shot at them. They specifically destroyed a number of wood carvings in people's yards."

"Wood carvings that Amar made?" Morgen slumped against the counter, certain the *rougarou* had been sending a message.

"I don't know. The coven will call an emergency meeting today. We're going to have to figure out a way to deal with this ourselves."

"Will the meeting be here?" Morgen pointed to the floor.

"I don't know," Belinda said with a sigh. "I'll let you know."

She and Phoebe left the house with half-eaten croissants in their hands. As Morgen smeared butter and strawberry jam on the one she'd taken, she tried not to feel alone and vulnerable. She called Sian, but her sister didn't answer. If she'd spent the night helping with veterinary procedures, sleeping late was understandable, but if the *rougarou* and his minions had been in town... something could have happened to her. Dr. Valderas's office was only a block off Main Street.

"You better just be sleeping in, Sian," Morgen told the voice mail box. "Call me when you wake up. And wake up soon."

An alert popped up as she lowered her phone. Someone had sent her a message via the rudimentary communications system within her app.

She thumbed it open. Someone with the username *Dances Under the Moon Petals* had responded to her request for information on the tree dots.

"Seems like a legit source to me," Morgen murmured.

You're likely having difficulty finding information on the tree twinklers because they are not witch magic but druid magic, the note read. *I live near an old mini henge in England that was once a popular meeting place for druids and have seen the twinklers in some of the nearby ancient trees. They are at five points around the meeting area and have the power to keep out hostile intruders and provide protection for those within its boundaries. According to legend, they can be acti-*

vated by one with power who speaks the words, "Earth Mother, protect thy sacred grove."

Morgen skimmed through the message again, not sure whether to be hopeful or not. As far as she knew, she had witch blood flowing through her veins, not druid blood. Would these tree twinklers respond to her? Or laugh at her for trying to activate them?

According to Amar, Grandma's staff was a druid tool—the name he'd given had made it sound like something to assist with evicting slugs from the garden, not to mow down powerful enemies—but she still didn't know if he'd made that up as a joke or had been telling the truth.

Still, the staff had seemed to respond to the tree twinklers on the ridge. Maybe it had been crafted by a similar type of magic.

"How would Grandma have gotten druid things? We're a long way from England, and the local henge scene is limited."

Morgen scratched her jaw. Even though she didn't know if she could activate the dots—the tree *twinklers*—the suggestion that they protected against hostile intruders was promising. Was it possible this druid magic—would it be considered *Old World* magic, like that of the *rougarou*?—could be more effective than her "modern witch" magic, as he'd called it? At least against an Old World enemy?

The thoughts made her want to check out the center point of that pentagram more than ever. She would take the staff along, in case it *was* a druid tool and holding it prompted the twinklers to want to help her.

"Hopefully, the druid magic won't be offended that I let the antler tips be sheared off." Morgen sent a response to *Dances Under the Moon Petals*, thanking her for the information.

After that, she glanced out the window for the twentieth time that morning. Relief swamped her when she spotted Amar walking out of the woods. *Limping* out of the woods. Dried blood smeared the side of his face, and a bite mark on his arm wept more blood.

Morgen grabbed the staff and rushed outside. Lucky slipped out with her to do his business.

"Amar?" She leaned the staff against the porch railing and ran up to wrap her arms around him, careful not to touch his obvious injuries. "What happened?"

"We never caught up with him, but he used his power on the pack—the very wolves I was out there hunting with. He temporarily turned several of them against us. They attacked us and also Franklin's men. Those men won't want to hunt with us again." Amar sighed and returned her hug. He leaned his face against the top of her head, and she could sense his weariness.

"Last night, Zorro showed me a vision of the *rougarou* in the forest with wolves gathered around him. Belinda got a call before she left this morning. His minions attacked and killed livestock and a man in town. And, uh, molested some of your wood carvings."

Amar's only response was a growl that reverberated through his chest.

"I'm sorry," Morgen said. "If it helps, the coven is having an emergency meeting today, and I think—I hope—they're going to throw everything they have into trying to stop him."

"This is *my* problem to stop."

Morgen kept herself from pointing out that he'd failed to do so thus far and seemed too tired to stop a mosquito feasting on his arm at that moment.

"I need to get some rest," he admitted.

"I guess this isn't the best time to ask you to go on a nature hike with me." Morgen was hardly refreshed after napping in a chair, but she felt compelled to investigate the druid magic. If they could find a secret weapon to use on the *rougarou,* a powerful ancient magic that could equal or surpass his, they would be in a much better position. "I need to call some words out to those tree dots," she added.

"While nature hiking?"

Morgen explained the trees Zorro had shown her, the lines she'd drawn, and the message she'd received.

Amar closed his eyes and rubbed his face. She could tell he didn't want to go, didn't believe that she would find anything useful, and she wished she could tell him to get some rest. But she worried about tramping through the forest alone with a powerful enemy about.

"If you come, I'll bandage your wounds and give you a massage." She smiled at him. "It won't take long. And you can nap on the boulders while I try to activate the dot magic." *Tree twinklers* was a goofy name, and she was reluctant to use it with him.

"Napping on boulders. How appealing."

"I thought the massage might be appealing."

"I don't know. Will I be sprawled across a boulder at the time?"

"Maybe two or three of them. I'll make sure they've been warmed by the sun. Hot stone massages are a popular thing, you know."

"*Boulders* aren't mentioned in the catalogs."

"How do you know? You've looked?"

"Werewolves who hunt all night and wield chainsaws and lift logs all day get stiff and sore." Amar looked wistfully toward his barn apartment, making Morgen feel guilty about her request.

"I'm sorry. I'd go by myself, but—"

"No," he said harshly. Amar wrapped an arm around her and pulled her close to more softly repeat, "No. Go nowhere alone, unless it's to leave the area completely and escape his reach."

"His reach seems long."

"I know." Amar took a deep breath and dropped his arms. "All right. Let's go."

"Wait." Morgen held up a finger. "I'll bring you something to rejuvenate you."

She ran into the kitchen, poured all the coffee left in the pot into a thermos, then spread butter on two croissants for him. Suspecting a werewolf would require something more substantial than carbohydrates, she also grabbed a tub of vegan protein powder. With her arms full, she ran outside and thrust the thermos and croissants at him.

Amar accepted them, but he didn't reach for the tub. He eyed it as if it were a snake dripping venom from its fangs.

Morgen held it up with another smile. "This has a high amino-acid profile. It's great for healing wounds."

As Amar took a long drink from the thermos, he eyed the label. "Pumpkin-seed protein powder?"

"Yeah, it's good. Vanilla-cinnamon flavor. It'll go perfectly with your breakfast." Morgen opened the jug and dug out the scooper. She thought about dumping the powder in his coffee, since she usually consumed it in a smoothie, but she didn't know how well it would dissolve in something so thin. Instead, she leaned in and sprinkled it over the buttered croissants. "There you go. Three thousand milligrams of arginine in there. That'll heal that bite wound right up."

Amar didn't jerk the croissant away, but he also didn't lift it to his mouth to devour it. "Some women bring their men ibuprofen and bandages when they're injured."

"A palliative at best. I'm looking out for your health." Morgen sprinkled a scoop on the other croissant and patted him on his stomach.

"Huh." He ate the first croissant, though not without making a face. "I think pork loins also have a lot of arginine."

"Yeah, but I don't keep a tub of those in the pantry."

"Alas."

He finished the croissants without further comment and waved the thermos toward the woods. "Lead the way."

Morgen pulled up a copy of the map on her phone and showed him the spot. She headed off in the right direction, but as they maneuvered through the woods, soon leaving the trails behind, he touched her a few times to redirect her. The trees grew densely on this side of the property, and the terrain was lumpier than the trails behind the house, so she was glad she hadn't tried to find the place alone in the middle of the night.

"Do you have any idea where the *rougarou* holes up in the day?" Morgen asked.

"No. I'm not even sure he sleeps. He's not your typical mortal."

"Not needing sleep is an unfair advantage."

"Tell me about it."

23

ABOUT TWENTY MINUTES INTO THEIR TREK, THE TREES THINNED UP ahead, more light making it through to the forest floor. Morgen picked up her pace, hoping to find the cliff and bare rocky area shown on the map.

"I see some boulders up there." She pointed with her staff—she'd been using it as a walking stick.

"Should I be getting excited for my massage?" Amar asked.

"*Obviously.*"

Morgen tried to tamp down her own excitement. It was possible there was nothing up there, that it had been chance that the dot trees marked the points of a pentagram, but she didn't truly believe that. Not after receiving the note from the British witch.

Birds chirped as they drew closer, and a falcon screeched high overhead. A chipmunk chittered from atop one of many sunlit boulders. It saw them coming and darted out of view. More chipmunks chittered, and was that the call of a pika?

Lucky would have loved this place, but since the arrival of the *rougarou*, Morgen had been scared to take him far from the house.

She also hadn't forgotten the rockfall that someone had arranged for her.

She was about to step out of the trees into the sunlight when Amar caught her shoulder.

"Hold on." He pointed upward.

The falcon they'd heard was flapping its wings and flying away from them, but she couldn't imagine that had disturbed Amar.

"Listen," he added.

At first, the chirping birds and chittering chipmunks were all she heard. Then a faint buzz reached her ears. She remembered the gyrocopter Wendy's sister had flown to attack the house, but this was a quieter buzz made by something smaller.

"A swarm of bees?" she asked.

"A drone." Amar pulled her back a few steps so they remained fully under the trees.

He was right. A few seconds later, a white four-armed drone flew into view. It buzzed as it sailed over the boulder-strewn clearing, a camera recording its flight.

But why? Who could have known about the tree twinklers and the clearing? Or was its owner simply spying on her in the hope of discovering something interesting—such as where she kept Grandma's old book?

Morgen lurched in alarm as she realized she hadn't returned that book to the secret vault. It was lying out on the kitchen table. She smacked her hand to her face and groaned as the drone buzzed over the trees above them and continued on.

"It's going in the direction of the house," Amar said, as its noise faded.

Because its owner had been waiting for nobody to be home...

"It can't get *in* the house, can it?" Morgen asked.

"Not unless you left a door or large window open."

"I didn't."

Morgen bit her lip, imagining the drone taking pictures of

Grandma's book through the windows. But she'd closed it, so at the most, it would get pictures of the cover. And the wards were up, so unless the witch who wanted it was as powerful as the *rougarou*, she wouldn't be able to break into the house to get it.

"It shouldn't be a problem," Morgen said, trying to reassure herself, "unless it can open the front door, flip out graspers, and carry away heavy books, but there's no way it could do that." She hesitated. "Right?"

"I don't know. A witch could have enchanted it. Could you tell?"

"If it was an enchanted drone? Uh, no."

"Will your wards halt it if it flies over the house?"

Morgen started to nod *yes* but caught herself. Wendy had said the wards didn't work on anything mechanical. She groaned. "No."

That had to be why the witch, if the drone did indeed belong to her, had chosen such a tool.

"Do you want to continue on or go back?" Amar looked over his shoulder.

Morgen hesitated again before saying, "Continue on. This shouldn't take long. I think this is the spot."

She waved toward what was admittedly nothing but a low cliff and a few jumbles of mossy boulders. Here and there, logs suggested there had been a rockfall at some point. Morgen hoped the area wasn't primed for another one.

A couple more chipmunks appeared as they walked out into the open. Morgen eyed the boulders, found them unspectacular, and picked her way toward the cliff. It was only about fifteen feet high, so nothing impressive.

She wondered where she was supposed to say the words the other witch had shared. Did it have to be precisely in the middle of the pentagram? If so, how was she supposed to find that spot? The dot trees were too far away to see.

"Maybe I can stand on a boulder and call out the words."

Morgen pulled out her phone to read the message again. "Maybe if I call loudly enough, being close will be good enough."

She glanced at Amar, wondering if he had an opinion, but he lay across a boulder on his back, his long legs hanging down. It didn't look like a comfortable position.

Not wanting to delay his rest longer, Morgen climbed to the top of a jumble of rocks. "Earth Mother, protect thy sacred grove."

A chipmunk on a boulder chattered at her, probably complaining that she hadn't brought nuts. Nothing else happened. She called the words again, making her voice firm and loud, though she was reluctant to shout when there were spies about.

Again, nothing happened. She turned slowly around on the elevated perch, looking for something that stood out. Something like—

"That cave." She'd missed it before, but there was a dark crevice in the cliff, partially hidden by boulders.

She scrambled down and jogged toward it. It might only be a crack in the rocks that went back a foot or two, but if it *was* a cave, it could be the spot where she was supposed to give the command.

When she reached the crevice, she almost squeezed right inside, but a giant spider perched at face level made her jerk back.

"Good thing the Pacific Northwest isn't known for venomous arachnids," she whispered, though she still didn't want to run into one.

Morgen tapped on her flashlight app and shined the beam into the dark. It went farther back than she expected, and anticipation flooded her nerves. Maybe she *had* found something.

As soon as she leaned in, a spiderweb plastered her face. Groaning, she wiped it off, then tugged down her sleeve and used her arm to clear the area ahead of her.

"If nothing else, the web means nothing has been in here for a while, right?" In case there were booby traps or a trapdoor opened over a pit, she leaned back out to call to Amar. "I'm going into a cave. You stand guard, okay?"

Amar grunted and stuck a thumb up without looking at her. Her poor exhausted werewolf.

"I should have given him another scoop of protein powder."

Morgen crept farther inside and shined her light around a stone chamber about ten feet wide and fifteen feet deep. The floor was packed earth under bits of twigs and dried grass that animals had brought inside, making nests in the corners. Despite that, the cave appeared too even and perfectly sized to be a natural formation. A couple of faded blankets were folded in a corner.

Her light played across a stone pillar near the back wall of the cave. It had a flat face with two runes carved into it. Witch runes? Druid runes? Something altogether different?

The pillar was about two feet high and embedded in the dirt. Next to it, a flat piece of wood held three stout candles, the wax melted from use.

Morgen knelt in front of the pillar but paused before reaching out to touch it. Something magical buzzed the air around her, and her skin tingled. A warning? It reminded her of the tree twinklers. What if touching the pillar sent her flying across the cave? She imagined Amar coming to look for her and finding her unconscious with blood streaming from her head.

She dragged the staff over and tapped the pillar with it. A warm energy flowed from the stone and washed over it. It didn't feel threatening, but she didn't know if that meant much. The staff buzzed in her hand, but she couldn't tell if that was its own magic or something spread by the pillar.

Morgen opened her mouth to try the command, but a shadow fell across the entrance. She jumped to her feet and spun, but it was only Amar.

He stuck his head inside. "I didn't know this place was here."

"Does that mean you weren't the one to bring the blankets and candles in the hope of luring me out here for romance?"

"I was not. There aren't any fresh scents around, besides those of small animals. I suspect any romance that happened here took place long ago."

"Maybe Grandma and Grandpa used to get randy out here." It was hard to imagine older people enjoying cave sex, especially when the house was so close, but she hoped Grandma had known about the place and that strangers hadn't been skulking about on the property instead.

The drone came to mind.

"I never met your grandfather," Amar said, "but I would think people of that age would prefer orthopedic mattresses to cave floors."

"Probably. I'm going to try that command again. I doubt anything will happen, but in case I get zapped across the cave, maybe you could catch me before I hit the rock wall."

Amar stepped fully inside. "I'm ready. Go ahead."

Morgen knelt again and spoke. "Earth Mother, protect thy sacred grove."

A faint hum came from the pillar. She arched her eyebrows as she waited for more. She'd expected something more dramatic.

She'd no sooner had the thought than the hum grew louder. Green light flashed outside, then flowed into the cave.

A gasp came from behind her. Morgen turned in time to see Amar crumple to the ground, gripping the sides of his head.

"Amar!" She dropped the staff and jumped to her feet.

The green light grew stronger as it focused around him, the glow so bright she could barely see him through it. But he groaned and rolled around in obvious pain. She ran to his side and touched him, though she feared doing so would unleash the strange attack on her as well.

It didn't. Whatever it was only targeted him.

"Make it stop!" he gasped.

"Let's get you out of the cave." Morgen tried to lift him, but it wasn't until he pushed up and staggered to his feet that she was able to maneuver him toward the exit. But he halted before he'd taken two steps, as if he'd struck a wall. "What is it, Amar?"

She swept her hand through the air ahead of him and didn't connect with anything. She tried to push him forward, but she *felt* him hitting something.

The light intensified, and he threw back his head and screamed.

"What can I do?" she cried in terror. She'd never heard him in such pain.

That pillar.

She grabbed the staff and ran back and whacked it. "Stop it!"

Nothing happened, but Amar's back went rigid as the pain intensified.

"Please, stop!" she yelled.

Desperate, Morgen repeated the druid command, hoping that would somehow turn off the power, but it didn't. She dropped down and grabbed the pillar with both hands, willing it to stop. She tried to tear it from the ground, but it didn't budge.

An image flashed into her mind, a gray-and-black wolf—Amar —leaping for her throat. But when she glanced back, he was still human, bent over and gripping his head as he gasped and groaned.

Did the pillar think it was *protecting* her? Hell, that was what it was supposed to do, wasn't it? Create an area of protection and attack hostile intruders.

"He's a friend," she told the pillar. "A friend to witches. *And* druids. A friend to me. Please, stop."

Behind her, Amar collapsed back to the ground.

24

Tears streaked down Morgen's cheeks as she gripped the pillar, pleading with it to stop hurting Amar as he writhed behind her, gasping and screaming as he'd never done before. Feeling pain he'd never felt before.

"He's a friend," she repeated, then grabbed her staff.

She'd already whacked the pillar, but maybe if she touched it while casting that incantation Grandma had used on Amar's enemies...

Werewolves are enemies to our kind, a deep baritone spoke into her mind.

"Not this one. Amar is a friend." Morgen abandoned the staff and ran to his side, doing her best to hug him as he gasped and twisted. "He's a friend to witches. And *druids*," she added, reminded that this wasn't witch magic that she dealt with.

What could she say to make the pillar understand? She didn't even know what she was dealing with. It couldn't be a *person*.

"He makes custom furniture for their familiars!" she blurted. As if *that* would help. But just in case, she thought of Amar carrying out the owl nesting box for Zorro. And making the ferret tree for Napoleon.

He is your servant?

Morgen wanted to reject that notion, but the intense green light around Amar lessened. His face was still stricken, but he stopped writhing and managed to focus on her.

"He's my friend," Morgen repeated. "A really good friend."

A servant of a druid may be protected alongside a druid.

"Then yes, he's a servant." She winced, knowing Amar wouldn't appreciate that comment, but the pillar didn't seem to understand *friendship*. "My servant."

The light faded further.

Then none here are a threat to you, and you do not need protection. Why did you call for it?

"Uh, there was a nasty drone flying overhead. And there's a *rougarou* somewhere nearby. He's *definitely* a threat."

The protection is here when a druid needs it.

The last of the light disappeared, inside and outside of the cave. Morgen wondered if it had originated at the five trees, some kind of beams shooting out from the dots and meeting in this central place.

Amar drew in a long shaky breath as the tension ebbed from his body. He didn't rise, but the rictus of pain that had stamped his face smoothed.

"I'm sorry." Morgen returned to his side and hugged him with one arm while sniffling and wiping tears from her cheeks. "*Really* sorry. I had no idea what would happen."

"That was not the massage you promised me," he rasped.

"No. It was an awful reward for your assistance."

"And I'm apparently your servant now."

"You know I don't believe that." She certainly *hoped* he did.

"I know." He lifted a hand to the back of her head and held her close. "But I want a *long* massage after this. With the hot stones, the bamboo sticks, the body scrub, the scalp rub, *everything.*"

Morgen leaned back. "I can't believe you know about all those things."

"What, werewolves can't get massages?"

"I guess you need to be pampered after rolling around on a cave floor."

"While being *tortured*, yes." Amar cast a scathing look at the pillar. "I'd apply my chainsaw to that thing if I had it along."

"You can't."

"Why? It'll zap me?"

"We need it to zap the *rougarou.*"

Amar squinted at her. "I *would* like him to suffer what I just suffered. For a few centuries."

"If that power attacked him and dropped him to the ground, you could go in and, uhm, finish him off." It wasn't in Morgen's nature to suggest people—even *enemy* people—be *finished off*, but after all the innocents that the *rougarou* had killed, it was probably for the best. Especially since Amar couldn't live in peace as long as his foe was alive and hunting him.

"I felt like that pillar was going to finish *me* off." Amar gripped the back of his neck.

"That is possible." The thought terrified Morgen. If she'd accidentally woken a power that had killed Amar, she never would have been able to forgive herself. "If what the witch in England told me is correct, we'd have to lure him here to get it to work."

"He's not going to be dumb enough to walk into a cave with our scents all over the area," Amar said. "He's as smart as a regular person and much older and more experienced. He would know it was a trap."

"I don't think he'd have to come into the cave, just this area. The magical light was outside too. I didn't see how far it extended

—" she'd been too busy being terrified Amar would die, "—but it had some range."

"Still, what would lure him to the area? Me? Maybe if he thought I was injured."

"You were just screaming loudly enough for the San Juan ferry passengers to hear you." Morgen waved in the direction of Puget Sound.

Amar opened his mouth, some sarcastic retort on his lips, but he paused. He rolled to his feet and held up a finger. "You're right. I'll check to see if he's out there."

"Don't leave me for long, please."

"Are you afraid to be alone with that pillar?"

Afraid to be alone in the same forest with his enemy was more like it. But she only smiled and said, "No, but you know how I pine in your absence."

"I won't go far. I want to see if I catch his scent. Hearing me in pain may very well have drawn him."

"If he's not busy killing other people."

Amar grimaced and nodded in acknowledgment as he slipped out of the cave. He moved speedily for someone who'd been in agony moments before. Maybe he wanted to escape the pillar.

Morgen thought about trying to communicate further with it, to see if she could learn more about it and why someone had brought druid magic to Wolf Wood, but her phone rang.

"Sian!" she blurted in relief.

"Morgen," her sister said, deadpan.

"I worried when you didn't answer."

"I slept late after being up late, assisting Osvaldo with his surgery. I only recently woke up."

"Thank you for calling back. I hope that means you slept well and that your missing PJs weren't a problem."

"They *were* a problem. All Osvaldo could lend me was a large button-down shirt. He doesn't *wear* T-shirts. He doesn't like *gym* wear, as he called it."

"What's wrong with buttons? Some pajamas are basically button-down shirts."

"They're *awful*. There's a seam down the middle of your chest. Who wants a *seam* rubbing against their bare stomach and breasts? And don't get me started on the toothbrush situation."

"Did he not have an extra?"

"He did, but it had *firm* bristles. He said werewolves like firmness. It felt like I was massaging my gums with a scouring pad."

"You lead a tortured life, don't you?"

"I insist that you allow me to return to the house today. If I can't stay, I must at least collect my belongings."

Morgen thought about the drone and was tempted to tell her to stay away, but the *rougarou* and his minions had been rampaging through town the night before, not Wolf Wood. Besides, between the wards and her magic, Grandma's house might be safer than Dr. Valderas's office.

"Why don't you come up this evening?" Morgen asked. "The coven is going to meet again and figure out how to solve the *rougarou* problem."

"You wish me to come when there are strange women milling all over the property again?" Sian asked.

"Yes. The reward for your willingness to endure such torture will be the delightfully soft bristles of your very own toothbrush."

Sian sighed dramatically and hung up.

"Everything okay?" Amar stuck his head back into the cave without setting foot inside.

"My sister is weird."

"It seems to run in the family." His smile kept it from coming across as an insult, but Morgen still glowered at him.

"I don't know where the *rougarou* is, but I don't sense him out here. It's possible he's resting somewhere and didn't hear me. Your idea to lure him here isn't a bad one. After feeling the intensity of that magic—" Amar winced as he touched his chest, "—I believe it might be enough to do him in. Even if it didn't kill him completely, it would distract him enough for me to take advantage."

Morgen nodded in agreement.

"I'll see if I can lure him here tonight," Amar added.

"Don't you mean *we* will?"

He shook his head. "I want you to stay at the house where you'll be safe."

"You can't activate the magic." At least Morgen assumed he wouldn't be able to. "I'll have to be with you."

Amar swore, no doubt realizing she was right.

"Judging by his pattern so far, he's more likely to be lured by someone you care about than by you." Morgen pointed to herself, though the idea of being bait for the scary guy who'd already proven he could kick her ass did not hold any appeal. "It might be best if you wait back at the house or somewhere else. If he sees me out here alone, he'll probably be doubly tempted. So far, he's been avoiding you."

Amar's face grew even graver. "I want to object."

"But you won't because you know I'm right."

"I won't object to you being here," he said, "but you won't be alone. I'll be at your side."

Morgen didn't know if that would work, but she didn't truly want to be out here alone, not with that creeper stalking her. "All right. We'll figure something out."

Maybe they could camouflage Amar and his scent somehow.

"Tonight," he said. "It's time to finish this."

Nerves fluttered in her stomach, but she made herself nod. "Tonight."

25

THE COUCH WASN'T THE MOST PRACTICAL PLACE FOR A MASSAGE, BUT Morgen hadn't been certain about inviting Amar up to her bedroom. That might have led to *more* than massages, something that needed to wait until after they defeated his nemesis. Besides, shortly after they'd returned to the house, Sian had texted to say that Dr. Valderas would be driving her over soon. Maybe she'd complained too frequently about the firm toothbrush bristles and overstayed her welcome.

Given how quickly Amar fell asleep after Morgen started rubbing his back and shoulders, sex might not have happened regardless. It was the middle of the day, and they had a bait-and-trap to plan, so she supposed she shouldn't be disappointed. Stroking his powerful back muscles as he lay on his stomach *was* intriguing, however. Too bad she didn't have any massage oil.

Lucky padded into the living room to check on them. When they'd returned and let him out, he'd run a few laps around the garden beds and the barn, but he hadn't ventured far from the house. These last few days, he'd been subdued, as if he knew that a terrible enemy lurked in the woods. Morgen had been relieved to find Zorro in his nesting box. After the *rougarou* looked right at him the night before, she hadn't been certain he'd gotten away.

After sniffing Amar's beard, perhaps to check for food crumbs, Lucky nosed Morgen's wrist, a mild complaint that she wasn't massaging anything of his.

"Not now," she whispered. "I need to tend my brave warrior, whom I inadvertently caused to be put through excruciating pain."

The soulful brown-eyed gaze that Lucky leveled at her promised she didn't know how difficult a dog's life was. She shook her head at him, shifted to work on a few knots in Amar's lower back, and debated on finding a cushion to kneel on. The thin living-room rug wasn't welcoming to kneecaps.

After she finished the massage, she would circle the house and look for any sign that the drone had been in the area. When they'd first returned, she'd checked the doors and windows but hadn't seen any evidence that it had forced its way into the house. Would it have if she'd left a window open? She'd hurried to return the book to the hidden wall safe, feeling that she'd been fortunate.

Lucky padded around behind her—to leave, she thought— then climbed up on the other end of the couch. Before she could stop him, he curled up in a ball between Amar's legs. Technically, he was curled up *on* Amar's legs. At seventy pounds, he wasn't the lightest vizsla in the world, or able to squeeze into tiny places, and his weight woke Amar.

"Are you sitting on me?" he mumbled, his cheek smashed into the couch cushion.

"*Someone* is sitting on you. Your new best friend."

"Not you?"

She smiled, happy to be under consideration as his *best friend*. "Someone furrier. Someone you bonded with the other night."

A familiar van rolled up the driveway, and Morgen frowned out the window. Wendy was supposed to be looking at art schools in Seattle, or at least staying out of the area until they dealt with the *rougarou*. Not only was her van arriving, however, but other vehicles followed it. There were a few trucks in the mix—some of the Lobos?—but most were sedans, minivans, and other mom cars. Or maybe *witch* cars. There was Belinda's sedan.

"We have visitors," Morgen said.

Lucky lurched to his feet, put his front paws on the back of the couch, and barked out the window.

"You don't say," Amar mumbled, shifting his legs so that Lucky wasn't standing on him.

"You can rest." Morgen patted his back. "I'll go out and talk with them."

This had to be the emergency meeting Belinda had promised to call.

"Hello, ladies," Morgen said when she reached the cars. Phoebe, Belinda, and numerous other witches had stepped out. Several bent to pull out canvas grocery totes. Bottles clinked inside. "You brought snacks for the meeting?"

"For the night, in case we need to stay," Belinda said, waving the grocery-bag carriers toward the house. "There are lamb and beef kebabs to cook on the grill, and Marlene is going to make her chimichurri sauce. It's delish. There's no need to starve while plotting the demise of one's enemies."

"Amar would approve of that meal." Morgen hoped for a few mushroom kebabs.

Belinda blinked. "I suppose he could have a skewer. If he helps with the plotting. We're going to come up with a plan and use our magic to *ensure* the werewolves catch their prey tonight."

"You think the *rougarou* and his minions will come here instead of ravaging the town again?" Morgen asked.

"We do." Phoebe pulled something out of her pocket, a leather thong with a couple of crystals and green and blue feathers tied to it.

"Is that a dreamcatcher?"

"It's a lupine lure," Phoebe said. "I selected a couple of my best crystals, and Wendy and Belinda helped me make it."

"A lupine lure?" Morgen glanced toward the living-room window, wondering if Amar felt himself being drawn outside.

"We're not sure if it'll work on the *rougarou*, but it *should* work on those werewolves without protective talismans." Phoebe squinted at Morgen.

"I think the Lobos will come on their own to help Amar." Morgen didn't point out that the meat kebabs would be more likely to lure them than the trinket. "But speaking of magically crafted charms and such, could you take a look at this and tell me if my ritual worked? It *seems* magical to me, but I don't trust my fledgling instincts."

Morgen drew the amulet and offered it with both hands. Phoebe gave her the lure to hold while she took the new piece to examine. She waved several other witches over, and the group emitted *oohs* and *ahs*. Morgen hoped that was promising.

"The only way to test it for certain," Belinda said, "will be to grasp it while chanting incantations, but I can sense that it is indeed magical. It feels similar to the one your grandmother made for me several years ago. You may have a future as a crafter."

"And to think I spent all that money on college learning to program databases."

"Well, I've found your app handy a few times, too, but it lacks magic that I can detect."

"I'll have to find a book that teaches me how to weave that into the code. An app that oozes magic might get me more than seven dollars in tips."

"Hi, Morgen." Wendy said as she trotted up with Napoleon in her arms. He sniffed the feathers dangling from the lure, then drew back. It must not have been meant to attract ferrets.

"I thought your familiar wanted you to go to Seattle," Morgen said.

"He was suggesting it, but when I met with the others, and Phoebe asked if I could help craft something, I was glad to." Wendy waved at the lure. "I also didn't want to run away and hide, especially when you might be up here getting mauled."

"Going to check out an institute of higher learning and making plans for your future isn't hiding."

"It is when a wolf is noshing on your landlady at the time," Wendy said.

"We'll start setting up." Belinda thumped her staff on the ground. "With so many here to help, we can further improve these wards."

She and Phoebe wandered to the side of the house, pointing at the grass and murmuring to each other.

With so many people with power here now, Morgen wondered if she and Amar needed to risk themselves going out to that cave. But would some trinket made in the *Crystal Parlor* truly draw the ancient *rougarou*? This guy had survived a long time. Morgen suspected he would see through a bunch of witches trying to trap him. Unfortunately, he might also see through a witch and a werewolf in a cave trying to trap him.

Gravel crunched, announcing the arrival of more vehicles. Several of the Lobos' construction trucks rolled into view and parked in front of the barn. The witches who were still outside paused, frowned at each other, and then frowned at the newcomers.

"I need your help." Morgen touched Wendy's arm and nodded toward the trucks before starting toward them.

"Uh, to do what?" Wendy asked.

Napoleon saw Pedro get out of a truck, squeaked in alarm, and buried his head in Wendy's armpit.

"Make a truce between witches and werewolves. At least *these* werewolves."

As she headed toward them, Morgen spotted Arturo sitting in the passenger seat of Pedro's truck, though he didn't get out. He was still pale and had to be in pain. Even with a werewolf's ability to heal faster than a typical human, it hadn't been that long since his surgery. Still, he rolled down the window, smiled, and waved at Morgen as she approached, Wendy trailing tentatively behind her. Maybe he'd come along for moral support.

"We came to prepare for another hunt," Pedro said. "Where is Amar? And why are all these *witches* here?" He curled a lip as he surveyed the women working on the wards.

"They're going to lure the *rougarou*, or at least his minions here, so you can hunt from right here at the house." Morgen glanced back, wondering if she should call Amar, but he'd come out and was heading their way.

"You cannot *hunt* your prey from a house," Pedro said.

"Why not? If you feel the need to skulk and pounce from the shadows, you could crouch under the deck."

Pedro gave her a baleful look, as if she were a foolish woman who had no idea about such things, and shifted toward Amar, but a witch had stepped into his path and stopped his progress. Morgen watched, worried she was accusing him of something, especially when she spread her arms and started gesticulating expansively. It was only when Amar lifted his gaze toward the sky and gave a terse price quote that she realized the woman might be requesting pet furniture.

"We also do not work with witches," Pedro said. "They would be a distraction, and they would happily enslave *us* if we gave them the opportunity."

"But you won't, right? You've all got your talismans." Morgen smiled and pointed at his chest.

"We do." Pedro's eyes were narrowed as he looked at her. "We have not forgotten this favor you did us. That's why we extend our protection to you. But *not* to them. We—" He lifted his nose in the air and sniffed. "Someone is cooking meat."

"Ah, has that started already? I believe lamb and beef kebabs with chimichurri sauce are on the menu. I'm sure the witches will share."

At the least, Belinda had said Amar could have a skewer.

Several other Lobos sniffed the air. Morgen hoped the witches had brought a lot of meat and a lot of skewers.

Amar reached her side, and she leaned against him.

"Did someone order another cat condo?" she asked.

"She wants a wooden dog-bed frame with a cushion on top and drawers underneath," he said.

"Did you agree to do it?"

"I said it would take a while because I'm busy."

"You might not be tomorrow," Morgen said. "The witches are combining forces to lure the *rougarou* and his minions here and thwart them from the comfort of the porch."

"I saw how they thwarted that demon. I might be *dead* tomorrow."

"Does that mean you want to continue on with our plan?"

"I don't want you to be hurt, but... I think I need you and your killer tree magic. These old ladies waving their wands won't do anything."

Morgen wasn't as sure about that, but she did think luring the *rougarou* to the cave was their best bet. If they had indeed uncovered ancient druid magic, it seemed the ideal tool to use against a centuries-old creature from the Old World.

"You coming to hunt, brother?" Pedro asked Amar as a few of the younger werewolves drifted toward the back deck and the grill.

"I'm going to hunt with Morgen tonight," Amar said.

Pedro arched his eyebrows. "I know she's your mate, but she's just a witch."

"A witch who banished a demon that we could barely bite with our fangs." Amar wrapped his arm around Morgen's shoulders. "She's a powerful ally."

Morgen expected a dismissive look or comment from Pedro, but he shrugged and said, "Yes. But she is not the pack. You will not hunt with your own kind?"

"The *rougarou* has been avoiding me when I hunt with you. He'll be more likely to attack a lone pair in the woods."

"But will you survive that?"

"We'll see. I'll call to you if we get in trouble. In the meantime, help the witches defend the house. They've come up with some magic to lure werewolves, and you know the *rougarou* commands a bunch of the Loups now."

"Magic? You mean the skewers of meat on the grill?" Pedro sniffed again.

Even Morgen could smell the cooking meat now. She would have preferred portabellas slathered in chimichurri, but she could see why this would draw carnivores.

"Something like that," Amar said, then walked up to Arturo. They fist-bumped through the open window.

"I hope you kill him, Amar," Arturo said.

"I'll try."

"I don't blame you for this, okay?" Arturo waved at his abdomen. "He hates all the Lobos. That's what Pedro said. You're just his special project."

"He hates everyone." Amar sighed, and they switched to Spanish for the rest of the conversation.

Another vehicle rolled up the driveway. Morgen was starting to wonder if there was anyone left in town. This one belonged to Dr. Valderas, and after parking, he stepped out. Sian opened the passenger-side door but didn't set her feet on the driveway. She frowned bleakly around at all the people and gripped her seat belt. Thinking about refastening it and leaving again?

"Your toothbrush is calling to you," Morgen said.

Sian's frown didn't leave, but the words must have reminded her of her mission, for she slid out of the car and shut the door. "My brutalized gums are receptive to that call."

Valderas spotted Arturo and walked over to check on him—or perhaps admonish him for not being home in bed.

As Morgen headed toward her sister, one of the younger witches trotted past her on the way to an open car trunk. She pulled out a couple of grocery bags, shuffling them into one arm. As she reached up to close the trunk, something white inside caught Morgen's eye, something mechanical with four arms.

Morgen sucked in a breath. Was that a *drone*?

The trunk thudded shut before she could get a better look. The witch—Mandy was her name, Morgen recalled from earlier introductions—turned toward the house.

"Was that a drone in your trunk?" Morgen asked.

Mandy halted, alarm flashing in her eyes, though she hid it right away. "Yeah. I do real-estate photography for my day job. Everyone wants views of the property from above these days, and drones are the way to do it. I need to go. I've got the tequila for tenderizing the meat. Funny how all of Vicki's recipes have alcohol in them."

Mandy hurried away without waiting for a reply. She wore jeans and sneakers instead of the dresses and pumps or sandals that many of the older witches favored, and she looked young and spry enough to have climbed out a second-story window and down from the roof. But she didn't radiate the menace of a conniving villain, not the way Calista had. Surely, someone who tried to bury innocent people in rockfalls and graffitied threats on cliffs would wear menace like cheap cologne.

Still, she did have that drone...

"Why do you keep inviting people to your house, Morgen?"

Sian stopped beside her with a dramatic—make that *melodramatic* —sigh.

"They invite themselves. I think the hot tub and outdoor kitchen call to them."

Sian's upper lip curled with distaste. "I'll be sure never to install such amenities."

"You're welcome to leave once you've gathered your belongings." Morgen slipped her hand into her pocket. "But I made something for you." She pulled out the amulet, hoping Sian appreciated it more than the friendship bracelet Morgen had braided out of colored embroidery thread in their youth.

Sian cocked her head. "It looks the same as it did yesterday."

"Yeah, but now it's magical. I did a special ritual and danced and chanted until my feet ached and my voice was hoarse."

"You danced? You who never attended a school dance or even had music at your wedding?"

"Jun doesn't like music, and I don't have any rhythm."

"I hope rhythm wasn't integral in the creation of this then." Sian accepted the amulet, but she didn't seem certain what to do with it.

"What I lack in coordination and aptitude, I make up for in vigor. You should have seen the sweat flying."

Actually, Morgen was glad there had been no witnesses to the sweating, dancing, *or* chanting. It was likely that even the nonjudgmental Lucky would have put his head under his paws.

"Sweat?" Sian mouthed, now holding the amulet chain by one finger stretched as far from her body as possible. "I'll make sure to sanitize this before putting it on. That won't nullify the magic, will it?"

"I don't think so, but you better stick to organic cleaning agents. Things that aren't harsh and won't cause rust."

Morgen was joking—she didn't think silver *could* rust—but Sian nodded sagely and said, "Good idea."

She dug into her purse and pulled out a few tissues and a spritz bottle of pale purple liquid. She squirted the chain and pendant, then rubbed them with the tissue.

"Should I ask?" Morgen raised her brows.

The bottle didn't have a label, and the contents appeared homemade.

"It's a vinegar-based, lavender all-purpose cleaning spray. I carry it for emergencies."

"Why am I not surprised?"

"Because it's a practical item, and I'm a practical woman. Here." Sian handed the bottle to her.

"Why would I need it?"

"You're constantly traipsing around in those woods. Nature is dirty."

"I'm not the one who licks trees." Morgen glanced at Amar.

Sian followed her glance, and her jaw dangled open in horror at whatever mental image formed for her. She waved the bottle. "Take it. I insist."

"It's a thoughtful gift, but I think you need it more than I do."

"I have a larger bottle in my suitcase." Sian placed it in Morgen's palm, wrapped her fingers around it, and headed for the house. "Let me know if you need a refill," she called back.

Morgen shook her head, having no idea if Sian would wear the amulet or ever try an incantation. Her sister might return to Seattle and never think of witchcraft again. The thought saddened her, and not just because she'd put all that effort into the ritual.

Amar returned to her side. "Are you ready to go?"

"To the cave?" Nerves tangled in Morgen's belly. "So soon?"

"It might be wise to set up before dark and make sure he has time to find us."

"It would be a shame if he didn't crash the party."

"Yes." There was no hint of humor in Amar's eyes, only flinty steel.

"All right, but I want to do one thing first." Morgen eyed the second-story library window and pulled up her app. If there was an incantation for preventing a thief from climbing out after absconding with a book, she wanted to find it and cast it before they left.

26

Before heading into the woods with Amar, Morgen did her best to convey messages to Lucky and Zorro to keep an eye on Mandy, the witch in sneakers, and also to let her know if werewolves approached the property. The idea of something happening to Sian or Wendy or anyone else she cared about while she and Amar were twiddling their thumbs in the woods distressed her. She couldn't help but feel their plan was woefully inadequate and that the *rougarou* might strike in town again instead of showing up in Wolf Wood.

Morgen was, however, prepared to spend the night waiting for him if necessary. She'd put two water bottles in a backpack, as well as numerous snacks, both vegetarian and meat-based. If Amar grew hungry while he was with her, she would prefer he unwrap a pepperoni stick rather than turning into a wolf and dragging a carcass back to their campsite to gnaw on. Not that he'd done that yet, but it seemed like a thing a werewolf might casually do.

As they neared the cave, Amar raised a hand and stopped to sniff.

"He's been here," he said. "Since we were here."

"He gets around, doesn't he?" Morgen frowned, worrying the *rougarou* might have followed their scents to the cave, gone inside, and destroyed the pillar or done something else that would sabotage the magic.

He shouldn't have *known* about the magic—Amar had said he hadn't been around when they'd triggered it—but if he'd found the pillar with runes on it, he might have suspected it did *something*.

Amar growled and stalked into the clearing. He peered all around, including at the top of the cliff, and when he halted near the cave, he squinted down at rocks beside the entrance.

"Did he sabotage something?" Morgen approached warily. "Or lay a trap of his own?"

"He pissed there." Amar pointed at the rocks, then walked to the other side of the cave entrance. "And there."

"Ew." Morgen could still see the damp spots. It hadn't been long since the *rougarou* had passed through. "Is that the werewolf way of telling someone to screw off?"

"Something like that."

Morgen leaned her staff against the cliff, pulled out one of her water bottles, and thoroughly doused both spots.

"Not good enough," she muttered and rummaged in a pocket of her backpack. She snorted when she found the condoms she'd thrown inside weeks earlier, the day Amar had told her to meet him by the spring for a tryst. Maria showing up and kissing him had thrown a wrench in those plans. Morgen wished she and Amar had come into the woods for a romantic dalliance tonight, not to face his decades-old enemy.

She pulled out the item she'd been looking for: Sian's lavender cleaning liquid. She crouched and spritzed it liberally over the damp rocks.

"Is that *your* way of telling someone to screw off?" Amar asked.

"Absolutely." Armed with the water bottle and the spritz,

Morgen crept into the cave. If that asshole had peed on the magical pillar or anything else in there, she would lop off his penis at the first opportunity.

When she shined her phone's flashlight around the interior, she didn't spot any suspicious dark spots, nor did anything appear to be disturbed.

"I don't think he went inside," Amar said from the entrance. He eyed the pillar and also didn't enter. "I don't smell any sign of him in here. My nose would be better if I turned into a wolf, but it's too early for that."

He glanced back at the late-afternoon sun.

"It's also harder for me to chat with you when you're a wolf." Morgen put away her cleaner and set her backpack and staff in a corner. "I wonder *why* he didn't come in here. Wouldn't you have been curious to find out about a cave your enemies had been lurking in?"

"Yes, but it's got a repelling vibe."

"A repelling *vibe*?" Morgen turned to face him.

"It's hard to explain. It's not a scent but more of a feeling, a feeling this place is not for our kind. It raises your hackles. I almost didn't come in yesterday." He snorted. "I should have heeded the warning from my instincts."

Morgen winced at the memory of him in pain and stepped forward to rest a hand on his chest. "I'm sorry about that."

"I know you are. I wasn't looking for sympathy, just letting you know why he might not have come in."

"Oh." She started to lower her hand, but he caught it and pressed it back against his chest.

"I wasn't looking for sympathy, but I do appreciate it."

"Good." She kissed him on the cheek and wished again that they were here for a romantic tryst. "Is there anything I can do to make you more comfortable? Maybe I can spray the lavender stuff around the cave to get rid of the vibe."

"I don't think *that* will be sufficient."

"Too bad. I'm sure my sister would like it if I sanitized as much nature as possible." Morgen imagined Sian back in Borneo, spritzing all around her tent or cabin or whatever she'd had in her orangutan-studying camp. She must have bemused her colleagues.

"I'll build a campfire outside," Amar said. "If it's clear we're here waiting for him, I doubt he'll come, unless he's certain he has a big advantage. He'll likely be wary of the cave."

"How are we going to get him to believe we're doing anything except waiting for him?"

"It crossed my mind to hide in the woods nearby. If he thinks you're here alone, doing some witch ritual..." Amar extended a hand toward the pillar.

"It would have to be a druid ritual."

"I doubt he could tell the difference. Like me, he's experienced a lot, but I doubt he's an expert on witchcraft. Most of what I learned came from living near your grandmother for three years." Amar tilted his head. "Would you be able to make me invisible with that spell of yours?"

Morgen closed her eyes, seeing the incantation and the page in the book that had described it. "I think it would only work on me. And it doesn't hide sound or scent, so..."

"Right. It was just a thought. I'll hide the old-fashioned way."

"By covering your scent with a spritz of lavender cleaner?"

That made him curl a lip and draw back. "Downwind after hiding my trail in the stream."

Outside, Amar built a campfire and pulled over a log for her to sit on. He placed everything close to the mouth of the cave so she could lunge inside and speak the command at the first hint that the *rougarou* was approaching.

As the sun sank toward the horizon, Morgen used a pine branch as a broom to sweep out the dead grass and other detritus brought in by small animals. With the thought of adding verisimilitude to their ruse, she swiped through her app to look for a ritual she could perform that wouldn't do much. Unfortunately, all of the witch rituals required nudity. She wondered if the *rougarou* knew that. The idea of being alone in a cave with a predator stalking her was scary enough without being naked. Even if Amar would be nearby, she didn't want to be that vulnerable. Especially not in front of someone who'd talked about *mating* with her.

"Here's one that's supposed to bless a home and garden," she murmured. Did caves fall into that category?

"Morgen?" came Amar's soft voice from outside. "The sun is setting. I'm going to pretend to leave. I'll act as if I'm heading back to the house, then change into a wolf, circle back, hide my trail in the stream, and find a nearby place to wait for him."

Morgen took a deep breath to steady her nerves and nodded. "Okay."

"I'll be watching, but shout if anything scares you."

"Trust me. I will."

Amar hesitated, giving her a long look up and down before nodding and leaving. Morgen banished the feeling that she wouldn't see him again. That was silly. He wasn't leaving the area.

After he left, she walked around outside, not going far from the cave as she gathered a few pinecones, twigs, and leaves. She picked a mushroom, as if she'd found something glorious, and took the items back inside. It was doubtful the *rougarou* had arrived yet, but if he was spying on her from afar, maybe he would believe she'd been gathering ingredients for a ritual.

Even though the campfire burned cheerily outside, she couldn't bring herself to sit beside it. Instead, she grabbed her staff and hunkered down against a wall of the cave where she wouldn't be visible to anyone outside.

The queasy sensation of the beginning of one of her familiar's visions came over her. She almost willed it away, not wanting to be distracted if the *rougarou* arrived, but Lucky or Zorro might be giving her important intelligence. Though at the moment, she didn't care much if that witch Mandy was skulking in the library.

The vision that formed before her eyes showed her the forest, not the house, and it was from an owl's point of view. With the arrival of darkness, Zorro had left his nesting box to hunt. Or to spy on her enemies for her?

He soared over the treetops toward the lingering light from the sunset and perched high up in a fir overlooking the train tracks. A dozen wolves sat on their haunches on the ties, their tails toward the strait, their snouts pointed uphill—toward the house. Since so many of the Lobos were already up at the house, Morgen suspected these were the Loups and that someone had rounded them up.

Belatedly, she realized those wolf snouts also might be pointed toward her cave. It was hard to tell from Zorro's perch. Which was their most likely target? Morgen and Amar? Or the house?

If they came to the cave, would the druid magic be able to stop multiple enemies? Or only one?

Zorro? Morgen willed him to hear her across the miles. *Is the* rougarou *there? Can you tell?*

One wolf lifted a hind leg to scratch a pointed ear. Morgen wondered if it was petty to hope the creosote from the railroad ties seeped through their fur and gave them butt rashes.

The vision shifted as Zorro rotated his head left and right, giving her a view up and down the railroad. It was empty of arch-enemies and sadly also trains bearing down on the pack.

A dreadful howl floated through the woods, and the wolves surged to their feet. They ran into the trees, up the slope, and out of Zorro's view.

Only when the howl sounded a second time did Morgen remember that sound never accompanied her familiars' visions. Hearing it meant that it—that *he*—was nearby.

27

After Zorro's vision faded, Morgen called her sister. The reception in the cave was poor, but she didn't want to step outside. She hadn't heard any more howls since the first two, but she was sure the *rougarou* was nearby, and she wanted to warn her sister.

"I lit a candle," Sian answered.

"Uh, congrats?"

"With a magical incantation from your app."

"Oh, good."

"Belinda said the amulet worked."

"Good," Morgen repeated, keeping her voice low. "I called because a bunch of Loups are heading up the slope from the train tracks. I'm not sure if they're going to the house or coming to me, but you need to be ready. And call me if they—and the *rougarou*—show up there, please. Amar and I will come back to help."

"You're breaking up. You said Loups are coming?"

"Maybe."

"I'll tell the others." Sian hung up before Morgen could repeat her request to be informed if the *rougarou* showed up.

She frowned at the phone, tempted to call back, but the single bar of reception came and went. Too bad she couldn't call Amar. She wanted to warn him, though he would have heard the howl, so maybe it wasn't necessary. He probably already knew that the *rougarou* had ordered his minions to get going.

Morgen risked creeping to the narrow cave entrance and peering into the night. The campfire burned lower now, but it provided enough light to make it hard for her eyes to penetrate the gloom beyond it.

Long moments passed with the occasional snap from a log the only noise. The certainty that the *rougarou* was heading to the house and might get past the witches to hurt Sian or Wendy nagged at Morgen, and she worried they were making a mistake by staying here. She wished there was some way to make *sure* the *rougarou* came here.

Wait. Maybe there was.

Morgen bit her lip. When he'd shown up at the house, he'd commented on her power and had even seemed enticed by it. If she performed a ritual—not a pretend ritual but a *real* ritual—might he sense her power from a distance and be enticed by it again? Maybe she could do the ritual to call a familiar from the forest. Amar had admitted that he'd felt that call from miles away and been compelled to leave his hunt to come to her. Would that work on someone as powerful as the *rougarou*? And if it did, would he show up with all those Loups?

"It would keep them from attacking the house," Morgen muttered, though for all she knew, the Lobos would also be drawn. "No, they've all got talismans to protect them from my magic." But the *rougarou* didn't. And the Loups didn't. She might be able to call them all here.

Once more, she peered into the gloom, wishing she knew where Amar had gone so she could consult him. But maybe it would be better to act on her own. The *rougarou* would be less likely to come if Amar's scent was fresh around the cave.

Since he also wore a talisman, she wouldn't have to worry about him being affected by her magic. He could still do as they planned, wait and sprint out to attack the *rougarou* when she activated the druid magic. This wouldn't do anything—except hopefully draw their enemy to them.

Though nervous, Morgen stepped back into the cave and removed her clothes. She was on the verge of stepping out to repeat the chant from the book when she realized she didn't have any of the ingredients the ritual required. She groaned. The three pinecones she'd picked up wouldn't do anything.

"All dressed down and nowhere to go," she muttered, eyeing her nudity. "Well, might as well try it. That guy is a perv, right? He might get excited by *any* girl dancing in the woods."

The fact that she *wanted* to lure a guy in with her nudity made her question her sanity, but she had a secret weapon here. Tree twinklers.

Morgen snorted, took a deep breath, and grabbed her staff. Willing her doubts to take a hike, she stepped outside.

She would faithfully perform the ritual and hope that some magic seeped out into the woods even without the ingredients. After all, the *rougarou* had said he could sense her power.

The familiar-calling ritual didn't say anything about staffs, but Morgen liked having it in hand and incorporated it into her chanting and dancing. As she pranced around the campfire, she did her best not to feel like an idiot, instead focusing on summoning the power within her and casting it out like a lure. It was hard, however, not to imagine her sister's face—and snark—if she somehow caught word of this. It was bad enough that Amar was out there and would witness her ungainly dancing.

The cool night air kissed her bare skin, but her movements kept her warm, and sweat soon dampened her body. She finished the ritual and started it again, deciding she would give it two shots before giving up. The urge to check in on Sian again came over her, and she almost missed seeing someone creeping through the shadows along the cliff.

At the last second, she spun and pointed her staff at... Amar.

"What are you *doing*?" he demanded in a low husky voice.

He stepped forward, reaching for her, but eyed the antlers and stopped before grabbing her. He looked her up and down, and embarrassment flushed her body.

"Trying to make sure he comes *here* instead of leading his minions to attack the house," Morgen whispered, lowering the staff. "By performing a ritual." No need to mention the lack of ingredients and that she was likely dancing foolishly, not performing any kind of magic.

"All you're doing is making me crazy," he growled.

She gave him a puzzled look.

"*I* am the one watching you." Amar looked down again, his gaze lingering on her breasts before he wrenched it back to her face. He must have decided she wouldn't prong him, for he took her arm and led her into the cave.

"I'm trying to call him," she whispered.

"*No*," he said harshly, his grip tightening.

He swallowed and made his touch gentler, but his voice was still husky, and he was breathing heavily. Had he sprinted across the woods to reach her? Or was she... arousing the wrong guy?

"You will not dance or be naked for that pervert," he said.

"I know it's weird and dangerous, but the rituals all require—"

"No." Amar pressed a finger to her lips to silence her. "You will not be naked for anyone but me. I do not even like that you are here endangering yourself."

His finger left her lips to trail lower, and gooseflesh rose along her arms. It had nothing to do with the cold air.

"It does please me that you are willing to risk yourself for me," Amar rumbled, stepping closer, his chest brushing hers. "You are like one of the pack. Loyal to the death."

"You're worth the risk," she whispered, her gaze snagging on his mouth. "Though I'm hoping we all live and—"

He cut her off with a kiss, a hungry kiss full of desire, and she felt bad for her dance, for inadvertently using her body to distract him. Another time, his response would have been flattering, but tonight, it might get them both killed. He had to be alert, ready to pounce on his enemy. And she... couldn't keep herself from returning the kiss, not when his hands lit fires that raced along her nerves and heated her to the core.

But being distracted was a bad idea. They had to stop this.

Or did they? If the *rougarou* thought they were in here having sex, he would *believe* them distracted. He might try to take advantage of that and come close to attack them. Then she could say the command and unleash the druid magic on him.

But if he was as fast and deadly as she believed, she might not have time to get the words out. And what then?

Amar broke the kiss with a growl and stepped back, releasing her. His muscles were taut, and he let his gaze linger longer this time when he looked her up and down. She wanted to reach for him and pull him back, but he shook his head and took another step from her.

"Put your clothes on." Amar turned his back to her and took several steadying breaths. "I will go back outside, and if he comes, I will spring. I will *kill* him. Then we will mate."

He prowled toward the entrance, but she lunged and caught him.

"Wait," she whispered. "We can *both* be bait. And then you'll be right here with me when he comes."

"He will not come when I'm here, waiting to pounce. He has been *hiding* from me, attacking those around me. He must *fear* to face me."

"I'm sure he does, but that's not the point." She gripped his arm, his muscles taut under her fingers. "He'll come if he believes you're distracted. If you're busy, uhm, mating." She patted his flat stomach and reached for the zipper of his leather vest.

Amar caught her hand to stop her. "We *would* be distracted if we did that."

"We won't really. We'll just pretend."

He eyed her skeptically.

Morgen pulled him to the side where they wouldn't be visible to someone looking in. "We'll kiss noisily and groan a lot."

Had the situation been less serious, Morgen would have laughed at the idea of her making convincing sex sounds. When she'd told him she was typically quiet in bed, she hadn't lied, and she hadn't so much as acted in a school play as a kid. Maybe she was a fool to believe they could convince a stranger of anything.

Amar shook his head, as if he could read her thoughts. "Put your clothes back on. We'll try another—"

His head spun toward the entrance, and his nostrils flared.

"Amar?" Morgen whispered.

"He's coming."

28

"How far away is he?" Morgen breathed, not sure if Amar had smelled the *rougarou* or heard him.

"Close." His voice was so soft, she barely caught the word.

Morgen reminded herself that his enemy's ears would be keener than a normal human's and resolved to keep her whispers soft too.

She gripped Amar's shoulder, about to suggest it was time for the ruse she thought might work and that he hadn't agreed to, but Zorro chose that moment to send her another vision. She barely kept from hissing in frustration and almost attempted to will her familiar's touch away, but what if something was happening at the house? Something she needed to know about?

Zorro sent her a view of the house and the lawn from above. He was perched on the barn roof, watching as the Lobos tore off their clothing and turned into wolves. They stood outside of the wards while Wendy, Belinda, and Phoebe appeared at the railing of the front porch. Belinda had her staff, the orb on top glowing, and Wendy and Phoebe pulled out wands.

Sian was with them, though she stood back, uncertainty in her eyes. Fear jolted Morgen. Why was Sian out there? She didn't know how to do anything yet. She ought to be in her room, reading a book. Or better yet, hiding under the bed.

On the back deck, the witches had abandoned what had been an outdoor dinner around the grill to crouch behind the railing and peer into the dark woods. Shadows stirred out there. Wolves. *Dozens* of wolves. Was that the entire Loup pack? Or had the *rougarou* found and summoned even more werewolves?

The intruders loped out of the woods toward the Lobos with their hackles up and their fangs visible. Fearless, the Lobos charged across the grass to meet them. Belinda chanted a spell and thumped her staff on the porch, and blue light streaked toward one of the enemy wolves in the lead. The first shot had been fired.

It struck the wolf in the chest, knocking him back. Not deterred, others surged forward. Some wolves ran in to meet the Lobos while others angled for the porch and deck.

Unless Wendy or Belinda had done something, the wards ought to be up, but if the werewolves sprinted through, willing to endure the pain to reach their prey, would the magic be enough to stop them?

"Are you *sure* he's here?" Morgen asked, barely seeing Amar's chest through the vision.

"Yes."

"His minions are attacking the house."

"What?" Amar had been frowning at the cave entrance, but he looked sharply at her.

The vision faded from her eyes. Before, Morgen hadn't wanted it, but now she cursed its loss. She needed to know what was happening at the house and if Sian was in danger.

"I have to go back," she whispered.

"You can't." Amar's nostrils flared as he shook his head. "He's in that direction."

Amar pointed the way they would have to go to get back to the house. Through the *rougarou*.

Morgen rocked back, the cold cave wall hard against her back. "He's baiting us—setting a trap of his own. He wants to get us out of the cave he won't enter."

"Does he need to get us out?" Amar's eyes narrowed. "How far from it does the magic extend?"

"I'm not sure, but we'd better get him close before activating it. We'll only get one chance."

Amar held up a finger. "He's coming closer."

He backed away and ripped off his vest. Her first ridiculous thought was that he wanted to act out the sex ruse, but she realized he was stripping down to shift into a wolf and face his foe.

As he reached for his jeans fastener, Morgen grabbed him and shook her head. "You can't go out until he's close enough to capture within the magic zone."

He bent close and growled into her ear, "I'll *drag* him into the magic zone."

Morgen shook her head again. Amar was an amazing warrior, and she wouldn't deny that, but she didn't think he could best the *rougarou*, not thirty years ago and not now. She wrapped her arms around him and kissed him. Noisily.

He stiffened and gripped her arms to push her away, but he paused, and his gaze shifted toward the cave entrance. Morgen hadn't heard—or smelled—anyone yet, but that meant little.

Though she could sense the frustration in Amar's tense body, he returned her kiss and issued a noisy groan. It didn't sound much more convincing than hers, and unlike before, there was nothing romantic about this. She felt like an idiot and was certain it wouldn't work. Then a clunk came from outside. A log shifting in the fire? Someone throwing a rock to try to trigger a trap?

Amar groaned again, but his eyes were locked to the cave entrance, his lips far from hers. He leaned in to whisper in her ear. "There are wolves with him. One is by the fire. The *rougarou* sent it ahead. A sacrifice. The coward won't come close. I have to—"

A huge gray wolf raced into the cave, and Morgen couldn't keep from shrieking. Amar reacted instantly, kicking it into the rock wall. He looked at her, their gazes meeting, and nodded curtly before tugging off his jeans to shift forms.

Morgen grabbed her staff. The enemy wolf had already recovered, and it lunged toward Amar as he was still shifting, its jaws snapping for his throat.

There wasn't time to say an incantation, but Morgen cracked it over the head with the staff. Snarling, the wolf focused on her. But by then, Amar had finished shifting. Larger and more muscular than the enemy wolf, he sprang onto it, his jaws fastening around its throat and sinking in.

It yelped, tore away from him, and ran back outside, blood spattering the cave floor behind it. Amar chased after it.

A terrible howl came from the clearing outside—the *rougarou*. Other wolves joined in. His minions.

Morgen lunged close to the pillar as the sounds of battle started up. The wolves ought to be close enough for the magic to affect them. She hoped.

Snarls, thuds, and growls sounded—a *lot* of them. A cry of pain rent the night. Amar.

"Earth Mother, protect—"

A wolf surged into the cave.

"—*thy sacred grove!*" Morgen finished and pointed her staff at the intruder.

The wolf sprang for her. There wasn't time to shout the incantation that cast a beam of magic from the antler tips, so she swung her staff like a club. She connected, but the wolf had a lot of mass and kept sailing toward her. Cursing, she sprang away, barely avoiding him.

Her shoulder smashed against the rock wall. Power flared all around her, green light filling the cave and brightening the night outside.

The wolf had been about to lunge toward her, but it threw its head back and yowled. More lupine cries of pain came from outside, so she knew the magic was extending beyond the cave, but she didn't know how far. Had it caught the *rougarou*?

Morgen pushed away from the rock wall and pointed her staff at the wolf, but the druidic power had captured it—had captured it and was hurting it. Eyes squinted shut, the wolf thrashed and clawed at the earthen floor. If it hadn't been trying to kill her, she would have felt sorry for it.

Remember, she thought to the pillar as she ran for the exit, *Amar is a friend. A friend to witches and druids.*

Staff raised, Morgen stepped outside. The green light was even brighter, forcing her to squint as she peered around, afraid she would find Amar writhing on the ground with the other wolves. Several big grays *were* rolling about, but she didn't see the *rougarou* or Amar's gray-and-black form.

One wolf rolled into the fire, sending sparks flying, and she stepped back. A snarl came from the side of the clearing. There.

At the edge of the light, Amar and a giant sasquatch-like figure were locked in battle, biting and wrestling among the rocks. The *rougarou* had taken his bipedal form and had clawed hands instead of paws, but his snout was that of a wolf, and long fangs snapped for Amar's throat.

They weren't inside the green light, and the magic was only affecting the minions, not the master. Damn it.

They were close but not close enough. Already, blood flowed from dozens of bites and gashes on Amar's flanks and head. He was fighting ferociously, but his enemy had more than a hundred pounds on him, with claws and fangs longer than his. Worse, tremendous magic emanated from the *rougarou*—Morgen could feel it. What it did, she didn't know, but he had the power of a super villain as he smashed Amar into the ground.

Morgen crept toward them, hoping she would get an opening, a way to help. Right now, they were too entwined for her to dare casting a magical attack at the *rougarou*. If she struck Amar by accident, his enemy could take advantage.

"You can't best me, boy!" the *rougarou* snarled. His wolfish snout mangled the words, but Morgen got the gist.

And she was sure that Amar, as he snapped and clawed and struggled to keep his enemy from landing a deadly blow, understood them too.

"You failed decades ago, and you'll fail again today." Slavering snarls interspersed the mangled words. "I will slay you, and then I'll take your mate for my own!"

Morgen paused as fear blasted her, fear of that threat playing out, of him forcing her—not as a man but as a horrible furry monster. If Amar didn't win the battle, the *rougarou* would have his way with her. As long as he was outside the influence of the druids' magic, she would be helpless to stop him.

Amar roared in defiance and fury, sounding more like a lion than a wolf. He snapped, fangs sinking into his foe's furry shoulder, but the *rougarou* only howled, as if he relished the pain. His leering snout seemed to grin as he punched Amar in the head.

Stunned, Amar paused for a second, his blue eyes glazed. Taking advantage, the *rougarou* gripped his torso with his hands, claws sinking into his flesh, and shoved Amar to the ground underneath him. With Amar pinned, the *rougarou* opened his great fanged maw to end his life.

Though terrified, Morgen found enough courage to yell and

run at them with her staff raised. She envisioned cracking the *rougarou* over the head, grabbing him by the tail, and yanking him into the influence of the magic. But the thought evaporated in the face of reality. He was far too large for her to move.

Further, he looked at her as she approached, saliva dripping from his fangs. If she tried to hit him, he might snap the staff in half. At least she'd distracted him from tearing out Amar's throat.

Mouth dry, Morgen circled him, staff still raised, hoping for an opening. If she could get behind him and prong him in the ass, he might be startled enough to jump into the light of the druid magic.

Her movement distracted the *rougarou* long enough to allow Amar to bite him in the chest and squirm out from underneath. His enemy must have wanted him more than Morgen, for he turned his back on her and sprang after Amar.

She ran behind them and turned, squinting at the dark shapes wrestling with the brilliant green background behind them. She pointed her staff at the *rougarou* and chanted, "Under the moon's magic, bad behavior correct and this witch protect!"

A beam shot out of the staff and struck the *rougarou* in the side. The same as when she'd used the incantation on him at the house, it didn't hurt him much, but he did fly forward several feet. It was enough. He entered the green light of the druid magic, and his snarls turned to yowls of pain.

For the first time, the *rougarou* didn't seem to enjoy the power wrapping around him. Like the other wolves, he writhed as the light intensified all about him.

Not hesitating, Amar took advantage. This had been their plan all along. He sprang upon his nemesis, jaws biting with lightning speed.

Morgen, not wanting to see anyone torn limb from limb, not even an enemy, looked away. At that moment, another vision came to her.

Zorro had flown from the top of the barn to a tree, giving an even higher view of the battle below, of wolves biting and wrestling on the grass, of witches casting spells to keep them on the other side of the defensive wards. But damn it, who'd lit the garden beds on fire? Unfortunately, they and the barn weren't within the wall of protection.

Thankfully, the witches were careful about whom they targeted, and none of their attacks seemed to strike the Lobos. Several wolves lay on the ground, though, and Morgen couldn't tell if they were alive or dead, or who had taken them down. She also couldn't tell who was winning. Not until a dozen of the wolves abruptly backed away, as if they'd been called by a whistle, or maybe a howl.

But that couldn't be it. Caught between the druid magic and Amar's fangs, the *rougarou* was too busy screeching—and dying? —to call out to his minions.

Maybe his distraction caused his link to them to break. At the house, the Loups turned and ran into the night, leaving behind their fallen comrades. The Lobos grouped together, tilted their snouts toward the sky, and howled.

The call drifted all the way to the cave as Zorro's vision faded. Morgen shook away the vestiges of it so she could check on Amar. She was glad the other battle had ended, but he—

No, he'd come out on top too. The *rougarou* lay at his feet, blood staining the rocks, his body no longer moving.

As Morgen opened her mouth to ask if Amar was all right— the green light bathed his gray-and-black fur, but he didn't seem to feel pain from it—the magic vanished. Darkness returned to the hillside, only the remains of the fire providing a hint of light.

The wolves that had been writhing in pain stirred. Amar backed toward Morgen, putting himself protectively in front of her and growling at the remaining Loups. Morgen didn't think any of them were dead, which left six enemies here with them, six enemies who didn't like her *or* Amar.

His hackles were up, and his growls would have frightened her if they'd been directed at her. But they were for the wolves rising to their feet and looking at them. The one she'd battled limped out of the cave to join its brethren.

Morgen stepped up beside Amar, resting one hand on his back. With the other, she pointed her staff at the Loups. If they wanted to keep fighting, she had plenty of incantations left. And Amar might be bleeding from his wounds, but when he growled, muscles bunched to spring, he emanated raw power.

The Loups whined, clenched their tails between their legs, and ran or limped off into the night.

Amar prowled forward to stand over the body of his foe. He tilted his snout to the night sky and howled. It sent a shiver down Morgen's spine.

Answering howls came from the direction of the house. She didn't know if Amar was telling the others what had happened, or merely announcing his victory.

Realizing she was standing outside naked with only her staff, Morgen started toward the cave entrance. Amar turned and stared at her with his piercing blue eyes. That power still emanated from him, and she paused, enthralled, wondering if some of his enemy's magic had somehow transferred to him.

His outline blurred, and he transformed from wolf to man. He stood naked before her, the orange of the fire casting light and shadow over the contours of his muscles. Blood dripped from numerous gashes, but his wounds didn't seem to bother him. His eyes gleamed with inner power and drew her toward him.

"My witch," Amar said, holding her gaze.

"My wolf," she whispered, a shiver of anticipation going through her.

He growled, stalked toward her, and pulled her into his arms.

He kissed her deep and hard, leaving her breathless, then swept her from her feet.

She almost cracked him on the head with her staff as she flung her arms around his shoulders to hang on. "Are we going somewhere?"

"Where we won't be interrupted." His mouth found hers again, and he strode into the cave.

29

FOR A FEW SECONDS, MORGEN WONDERED IF SHE SHOULD OBJECT TO being carried into a cave by a naked man who had, minutes before, killed someone in front of her eyes, but hadn't the *rougarou* deserved to die after all of those he'd murdered? And hadn't she *helped* Amar vanquish him?

Yes, she had, because she loved him and didn't want anyone to hurt him. And she knew he felt the same way about her. And if he wanted to celebrate by kicking the folded blankets into a semblance of a nest and lowering her into it...

"Hang on," she whispered, groping for her backpack.

"To you? Gladly."

She fumbled at the pockets, pulling out the damn lavender spritz instead of the condoms.

"You're *not* going to sanitize me," Amar said.

"No, no. Just want to be safe."

"From germs?"

"From baby wolves. At least for now." She pressed a condom into his hand.

He snorted and accepted it, probably relieved she hadn't tried to spray him down with disinfectant. "For your information, they don't come *out* that way. We would have normal children."

"That's a relief."

"As normal as *your* children could be." Amar's eyes glinted with humor as he put on the condom. "Quirky woman."

"Says the weird werewolf."

"I'm a *normal* werewolf, not a weird one."

"If you say so."

"I will *show* you so." His eyes narrowed, and he kissed her with passion that left her breathless and very aware of his strong naked body scant inches from hers.

She pulled him down onto the blankets with her, returning the kisses as she slid her hands over the hard muscles of his back. He growled again as he cupped her breast, teasing sensitive skin with his thumb. He sounded as much like a wolf as a man as his gaze ran down her bare body with appreciation, as if she were the sexiest woman he'd ever known. It was hard not to be flattered and aroused by his primitive interest—by *him*.

He stroked her as he gazed at her, his calloused touch an exhilarating blend of rough and gentle, and she squirmed and shifted toward him, enjoying this but wanting to pull him back down so they could return to kissing.

"I've wanted you for a long time," Amar whispered, smiling at her movement, at her growing need for him. "Since long before I believed I should. And especially since *this*." He touched his talisman as it dangled from his throat beside the tooth he always wore, both surviving his shape-changing in a way his clothing never could.

"As long as you know you should now." Morgen didn't know if that made sense but didn't care. She reached up, sliding her hands around the back of his head, his soft shaggy hair teasing her fingers as she tried to pull him down. His mouth was too far away.

"I know now that you're my witch, and I'm your wolf. Nothing can stop us when we fight together." Those words came out like a contented purr rather than a growl.

She wanted to agree, but one of his hands drifted lower, and her words turned into a gasp. She lunged up, wrapping her arms around him, and kissing him. They could chitchat later, damn it. She wanted him now.

He smiled against her mouth but didn't deny her the kiss. She knew he wanted this as much as she did—it wasn't as if there were any secrets when they were both naked. But he stroked her with languid patience that left her panting even as he refrained from sliding into her.

Waves of desire washed over her, and as his fingers made her squirm, she cried out for him, and it had nothing to do with ruses for enemies. He growled again, nipping at her throat and then her ear, the tiny bites lighting her every nerve on fire. She dug her fingers into his scalp, wanting his mouth back on hers but also relishing his teeth grazing her, the delicious pulses of pleasure that throbbed within her.

The urge to bite *him* came over her, from some animal part of her mind that had never considered such things before. She strained closer to him, finding the powerful tendons of his neck with her mouth and tasting his salty skin. Feeling daring, she nipped at his throat.

His grip on her tightened. "Again," he ordered.

She grazed him with her teeth, licking and biting as she dragged her fingernails over his muscled shoulders. His body coiled like a spring as he panted, as aroused by her touch as she was by his.

"Amar," she whispered hoarsely, pressing up toward him, her grip tightened on her wild wolf man.

"Morgen," he whispered back just as hoarsely, inhaling deeply, breathing in her scent. "My witch."

She reached down and grasped him, shaking with desire, needing more than his fingers and his kisses. He moaned his approval and pressed his hands to the ground on either side of her, powerful body gleaming with sweat as he looked down at her with his intense eyes. He eased into her, his body quivering from the effort of going slowly, making sure she was comfortable, but she pulled on his shoulders, wanting him without pause, needing what had been building between them for weeks.

As if released from a starting block, he plunged into her. With equal fervor, she rose up to him, and animalistic ecstasy rocketed through her. She gripped him, needing to hang on as they drove together, as pleasure coursed through her. She caught herself panting his name, instructions mingling with pleading groans. She needed him more than she'd ever needed anything before.

When she came, she cried out loudly enough that the wolves back at the house might have heard. If she hadn't felt so good, and so safe in Amar's arms, she might have been embarrassed, but her expression of pure pleasure made him throw back his head as he reached his climax, his own cry bordering on a howl.

"I'll take that as flattering," she whispered afterward, touching his face. "And a sign that you are definitely not normal."

He lowered himself, shifting her until she lay atop him instead of on the thin blankets. "I'm perfectly normal for a werewolf," he said, caressing her butt and grinning wickedly. "And *you* are not the quiet, subdued woman in bed that you said." He slid a hand across his pecs, fresh fingernail marks standing out on his chest and shoulders.

She would have felt bad about that, especially since he'd received more grievous injuries in his battle, but he looked utterly pleased and like he was already contemplating a second round.

"Well, this isn't a bed." She smirked at him. "Apparently, caves get me excited."

He eyed her through his lashes. "*I* get you excited."

"Yeah, you do, my sexy wolf."

He pulled a blanket over them, and she knew they wouldn't be going anywhere for some time.

30

As Morgen was snuggling with Amar in the aftermath of their second lovemaking session, her phone rang. She thought about ignoring it, but she had started noticing the hardness of the cave floor and was having fond thoughts of her bed. Maybe it was time to adjourn to the house, assuming it wasn't too much of a mess after the battle.

"Hey, Sian," Morgen answered, stroking the back of Amar's head when he stirred. It had grown cold as night deepened, and she was glad for his body heat.

"Where are you?" her sister asked.

"Uhm... not far." It occurred to Morgen that she should have called earlier and let the others know that she and Amar had survived. She'd been a touch distracted.

"The Lobos said the bad guy was dead, and that's why all the other wolves fled, but nobody's certain if *you're* dead." Barks were audible in the background on Sian's end. Was that Lucky going on about something?

Amar lifted his eyebrows, silently asking if he should leave and give her privacy for the call. Morgen shook her head and slung a leg over him under the blanket, liking having him close—and also not wanting her radiator to go anywhere.

"Sorry," Morgen said. "I thought the Lobos heard Amar howl —and vice versa—and that they communicated everything that way."

Morgen raised her own eyebrows, wondering if she'd assumed too much. Amar twitched his shoulder and wobbled one hand in the air. Maybe that was *sort of* how the howling worked.

"You thought werewolves howling at each other was a sufficient form of communication?" Rare exasperation tinged Sian's usually deadpan voice. "Morgen, we were *worried* about you." She lowered her voice. "I was worried about you."

"I'm touched that you care." And she was. Her sister so rarely admitted to her feelings, and Morgen appreciated hearing the words.

"Many care for you now," Amar whispered gently and kissed her bare shoulder. "You are one of the pack."

"I don't want you to be touched," Sian snapped, no hint of gentleness in *her* voice. "I want you to get your ass back to the house to deal with things."

Morgen frowned with concern even as she enjoyed Amar's tenderness. "Is there still trouble?"

"A witch has locked herself in the library, possibly because your dog is barking outside the door, and he won't calm down for any of us. We have no idea what's going through his head."

"Oh. Distract him with some of the leftover meatballs, please. And ask Belinda to go up there. If there's a woman named Mandy inside, she may have been trying to steal Grandma's book. *Again.*" If Mandy *was* inside, Morgen hoped she was trapped because the incantation she'd used to lock the library window earlier had prevented her from climbing out. And because Lucky had kept her from escaping through the door. "I'll be home soon."

"Good. I can't imagine what you've been doing in the woods for hours."

"Vanquishing an enemy and... tending Amar's wounds." Normally, Morgen wouldn't have lied, but Sian would give her a hard time if she knew what they'd truly been doing out here.

"The grievous injury to his penis, no doubt," Sian said and hung up.

"Hm." Morgen eyed the phone. "She's not as oblivious to the relationships of those around her as you might think."

Amar kissed her, then slipped out from under the blankets to grab their clothes. "What's going on in the library?" he asked as he handed hers to her. "Is there another enemy that needs to be *vanquished*?" His eyes crinkled with humor as he used her word.

"Probably just slapped on the wrist. Belinda can decide." Even though the rockfall had been terrifying and dangerous, neither Morgen nor Ute had been injured, so Morgen wasn't inclined to ask that Mandy be arrested. As long as she stopped trying to steal Grandma's book, Morgen would be happy.

Once they were dressed, she and Amar headed back through the dark woods toward the house. Since he had better night vision, he nudged her now and then to guide her, occasionally stealing a grope as he did so. She swatted him each time, though she was far more amused than offended. Once, she pretended to trip and fall against him—lips first. Though she felt a little silly—like teenagers in love—she enjoyed the playful side of Amar and looked forward to spending a lot more time with him. He must have felt the same way, for he pressed her against a tree for a long kiss before they stepped out of the woods. It left Morgen breathless again—and hoping she could resolve the witch problem and send everyone home soon.

But the number of vehicles in the driveway and people laughing and sharing drinks on the deck made her believe the party might not break up for a while. Some of the Lobos and witches had departed, but more than a dozen remained to celebrate.

José Antonio, always ready for a gathering, had pulled coolers of beer out of his truck. Going into battle together—not only here at the house but also at the demon fight a couple of weeks earlier —must have caused the witches and Lobos to lose some of their animosity toward each other. They were mingling openly, hardly any of the witches sneering at José Antonio's offerings.

As Morgen and Amar walked across the lawn—thankfully the fire in the garden beds was out—she didn't hear any barking. Lucky was outside, milling around near the grill, so his vigil at the library door must have ended.

Sian stood on the front porch with her arms crossed. Morgen started in that direction, but then she spotted Phoebe and Belinda near one of the cars. *Mandy's* car. And Mandy was with them, gesticulating and arguing.

Though Morgen was tempted to let the senior witches handle it, she wanted to know if Mandy had succeeded in finding the book. If so, Morgen would have to find a new hiding spot for it.

"Morgen is a member of the coven now," Belinda was saying as Morgen approached. "She's paid her dues, given everyone a useful app for free, and is learning our ways. She helped defeat a demon, and if the Lobos are to be believed, she was also integral in defeating the creature that's been attacking—and *killing*—people in our town."

"You can't believe *werewolves*." Mandy's back was to Morgen, and she didn't notice her approach. "And if she hangs out with them, she's not a proper witch. That's why I tried to get her to leave, to scare her away. She isn't one of us."

"Did you start that rockfall?" Belinda demanded. "You almost crushed *Ute* in that, as well as Morgen."

Mandy scowled at the ground. "I didn't know Ute was there. I just wanted Morgen to leave so I could look freely for that book. It shouldn't be in the hands of someone like her. It should be with someone who respects our ways."

"You?" Belinda had noticed Morgen but didn't draw attention to her. "You're too young, and the fact that you covet it means you can't be trusted with it."

"Can't be *trusted*? Belinda, I've been practicing witchcraft for more than ten years."

"Experience isn't the problem. Get in the car, and go home. Do not invade Morgen's privacy again."

"It's in that library somewhere," Mandy grumbled.

Morgen stopped a few feet away, relieved that it didn't sound like the woman had found the book.

"If you trespass in Wolf Wood again," Amar said, his voice a menacing growl, "you'll have to worry about more than Morgen's *dog*."

Mandy shrieked and spun around.

For a werewolf in his human form, Amar growled very convincingly. If he'd been looking at her, even Morgen would have shivered. Mandy backed up until she bumped against the car door.

"He's threatening me," she whispered, pointing at Amar and looking at Belinda and Phoebe. "Do something."

"It's Morgen's property." Belinda didn't appear worried by Amar's menace. "And he's loyal to her."

Morgen thought Amar might object to the statement—even if it was true, it hinted of subservience, and Amar was definitely *not* subservient to anyone. But he stepped closer and wrapped an arm around her as he kept glaring at Mandy.

"Yes, I am," he said.

Mandy scooted around the car without turning her back to him. Not until she reached the driver-side door and lunged inside did she look away. The car started up, and she roared off, tires flinging gravel.

"I don't think she put her seat belt on," Morgen observed, leaning into Amar and hoping he didn't let her go. "Very irresponsible."

"We'll talk with her," Belinda said.

"Safety is important," Phoebe said.

"Indeed."

"Morgen..." Phoebe eyed her and Amar. "Are you aware that your loyal werewolf has his hand on your boob?"

"Yeah, I like it there," Morgen said casually, though her cheeks flushed with warmth. She waited for Phoebe to chastise her for impropriety or let her know that a werewolf wasn't an appropriate lover for a witch, just as a dog wasn't an appropriate familiar.

But Phoebe smirked. "I bet you do."

She chuckled, and she and Belinda got in another car, leaving the partying to the younger witches. Maybe Phoebe would call Mayor Ungar later. Morgen grinned at the thought of her fifty-something mentor getting a booty call.

"Your problem has been resolved," Amar said, wrapping his other arm around her. "Come to my apartment."

"I should talk to my sister first."

Sian was scowling at them from the porch, her expression not exactly inviting.

"She will be in a better mood in the morning." Amar kissed Morgen, his lips promising an enjoyable rest of the night, if only she joined him upstairs...

"She *is* a more amenable soul after coffee," Morgen murmured against his mouth.

Amar bent, swept her into his arms, and headed for the barn. Morgen looked toward the porch, not wanting to leave her sister hanging if she still had something she wanted to discuss, but Sian was looking at the driveway now. Someone new had arrived. Ah, that was Dr. Valderas's truck. Some of the Lobos must have been injured in battle, and he was coming up to treat them. Or maybe he simply wanted to check on Sian.

"Valderas will talk to her," Amar said, nudging the barn door open with his foot while he held Morgen. "He doesn't care if his patients are amenable."

"That must be true. He treats werewolves, and they're all kinds of grumpy."

"Yes," he agreed, kissing her again as he carried her toward his apartment.

EPILOGUE

WHEN MORGEN AND AMAR WANDERED INTO THE HOUSE IN THE morning, someone had already made coffee and bacon and eggs. Since Morgen kept neither bacon nor eggs in the house, that meant the chef had either made an early run to the store or José Antonio had brought more than beer in his coolers.

Several of the Lobos' trucks and a few of the witches' cars were still parked outside, with guests crashed all over the house. Sian would likely have cross words for Morgen. Dr. Valderas's truck hadn't been out there, so he must have left after tending his patients.

Amar piled a plate high with the still-warm food. While Morgen fished granola out of the pantry for herself, she eyed her tub of pumpkin-seed protein powder, wondering if Amar would like more of it—he'd received numerous wounds the night before, after all—but the vanilla-cinnamon flavor might not go well with eggs and bacon.

Laughter came from the back deck, as well as the rumble of the hot-tub jets firing up. Sian stepped into the kitchen wearing her robe and looking like she'd just woken up.

"This place is like a frat house." As expected, her voice oozed disapproval. Her fast pace toward the coffee maker suggested she meant to pour a mug as quickly as possible before returning to her room and locking the door.

"I'm sure everyone will go home soon." Morgen stepped into the laundry room to peek out the window and see who was in the hot tub. Wendy, José Antonio, Pedro, Maria, and Judith. "It's worth having the property overrun with visitors if it means the witches and werewolves of Bellrock are mending fences. There's been so much bad blood between them. Isn't this nice to see?"

Sian squinted out beside her but only glanced at the tub before frowning at the rest of the deck. "There's vomit on that bench."

"I think that's spilled oatmeal."

"Disgusting nonetheless and a sign of overly rambunctious testosterone-filled men who can't be bothered to clean up after themselves."

Ute the herbalist wandered into view, juggling a bowl of oatmeal and a mug of coffee.

"Or perhaps a sixty-something witch without a paper towel."

"Frat house," Sian grumbled and turned back toward the stairs.

"Does that mean you're still planning to leave?"

"As soon as possible. Your chaos-drenched house and odd new life are making me yearn for the ordered quiet of a laboratory."

Morgen smiled sadly but didn't try to change her sister's mind. Thanks to her own introvert tendencies, Morgen understood a preference for a quieter life, and she looked forward to her guests leaving so she could spend time alone with Amar.

"I do appreciate that you made that amulet for me," Sian said. "It actually helped me do something. I was disinterested in harming anyone, but I made a few of those wolves believe they had fleas. Or maybe I actually *gave* them fleas. That entry in your database wasn't entirely clear. I'm guessing it was the former, because I can't believe witchcraft could defy the laws of physics and create matter where there was none before."

"You used my app? *And* my amulet?" Morgen grinned, touched.

"I did. I wouldn't say my contribution turned the tide in the battle, but I trust I'll have a way to torment any co-workers at my new job who steal my soda out of the fridge or otherwise irk me. I would also be interested in visiting on some weekends to continue learning about witchcraft. Mind you, I insist you keep me apprised of scheduled meetings, gatherings, festivities, and parties at the house—and that there won't be any *unscheduled* ones—so I can avoid unnecessary exposure to strangers when I come."

Morgen grinned wider. "May I hug you?"

Sian frowned. "I understand one need not have fur for the flea spell to work."

"So, you'd prefer a handshake?"

"Perhaps a fist bump," Sian murmured.

Morgen patted her on the shoulder and went back into the kitchen, hoping to fulfill her hugging urges with Amar, but he was gone. Banging noises sounded outside. Had he gone out to the barn to start one of his projects? She admired his work ethic, but surely he deserved a day off after all those long nights of hunting.

When she headed outside to check on him, Morgen found a familiar lady standing in front of the barn. It was Sakura, the woman who'd ordered a cat condo. Morgen grimaced. She hadn't expected Amar to find time to work on it while he was hunting down his archnemesis, had she?

As Morgen walked over to let Sakura know it would be a few days, a black SUV came up the driveway. She couldn't believe how many people were still on the property—it was starting to feel like a mall on Black Friday. No wonder Sian couldn't wait to return to work.

The driver's-side window rolled down, and Morgen couldn't stifle a groan. It was Mayor Ungar.

Since she hadn't been at the house for the big battle, Morgen didn't know if he'd been one of the invading minions, but she wouldn't have minded never seeing him again. A gash at his temple and a black eye suggested he'd been involved in the fighting somehow.

After Ungar parked, he got out and strode straight toward Morgen. She forced a smile as she glanced at the passenger side of his vehicle to see if the tax assessor had come along. He hadn't, but she doubted that meant this meeting would go well.

"If you're looking for Phoebe," Morgen said, "she went home late last night. She's probably at the Crystal Parlor this morning, pining for werewolf love."

Ungar blinked slowly. Maybe his booty-call preferences weren't supposed to be an open secret.

"I came to bring you this," he grumbled, holding out an envelope. "You'll get an official invoice in October, when the rest of the tax assessments in the county go out, but I thought I'd be polite and give you a heads-up with a preliminary estimate."

Polite. Funny how that wasn't the word that popped into Morgen's mind.

"Are you this polite with all of the county's citizens?" she asked.

"No, but you're special."

"We've barely met, and you already know that?"

"Word gets around."

More bangs came from within the barn. Sakura was still waiting out front with her arms folded over her chest, her cat sniffing at the tufts of grass growing up near the doorway. Sakura eyed the mayor warily and didn't come over. Morgen wished she had that option.

"I trust your Lobo lover won't be inviting any more of his old enemies to town," Ungar said.

He was scowling, but she couldn't keep from grinning. She *was* Amar's lover now. In all senses of the word. The urge to run inside and kiss him came over her. All she had to do was get rid of Ungar and Sakura first.

"I think that was his only old enemy," she said. "Now, he can settle down and start a family."

That wasn't *exactly* what Amar had said he wanted to do, but he had brought up the topic of children. Maybe he did dream of a sedate and settled future, inasmuch as a werewolf could have those things. Sedate and settled with passion-filled hunts whenever there was a full moon.

Ungar grunted and waved at the packed hot tub and the people milling on the deck. "If your place turns into some kind of party facility, the tax assessor will give it a commercial designation, and then you'll *really* owe a lot."

"We're just having a little celebration. There might be room in the hot tub if you want to join us." Since Morgen was positive he wouldn't accept that invitation, she felt safe making it.

"Not in the least."

Ungar turned to leave, but he paused when Amar walked out carrying what Morgen could only call a *super deluxe* cat condo.

Sakura gasped and clasped her hands together. "Rikido," she called to her cat as Amar set it down. "Come check this out."

The cat was already sauntering over. He sniffed at the shag carpet covering the various levels, then sprang up and climbed into one of several cubes with holes in the sides. Purrs soon emanated from the cube.

When had Amar found time to make that thing? And had he used the special carpet scraps again to ensure feline approval?

"What the hell is that?" Ungar asked.

"A gift," Morgen said, not wanting to mention that money was being exchanged, not after Ungar's threat about commercial property taxes. "Do you have pets, Mayor?" Maybe it was a dumb question, since he was a werewolf, but Lucky got along with Amar, so who knew how cats and dogs felt about lycanthropic masters? "Amar is a sublime woodworker and can make all manner of pet furnishings."

Amar must have heard their conversation over the purring of Sakura's familiar, for he glowered over at her. A reminder that he preferred carving mermaid mailboxes from logs to making ferret trees and cat condos. Still, if they could do something to win the mayor over to their side, or at least ensure that Ungar didn't make them a special project, Amar might consider crafting him something.

"My mother has cats," Ungar muttered. "*Four* cats. And those are just the ones that live inside. It's a menagerie."

"So, you'd need the super *super* deluxe model."

"Do you have a catalog?" Ungar surprised her by asking. Well, Christmas was only a few months away. Maybe he needed something for Mom.

"Not yet, but we will. We're just getting started with our business."

Sakura's cat came out of the cube, hopped to a platform near the top, and rolled on his back on the carpet.

"Huh," Ungar said before returning to his SUV and driving away.

Morgen opened the envelope, looked at her new tax assessment, and did her best not to faint.

"That's... almost what my starting salary was out of college. And it's due *every year*. I either need to go back to Seattle and get a *very* high-paying new database-programming job or figure out how to be a super successful app developer and entrepreneur." Morgen looked toward the hot tub when laughter rang out. "Maybe I can turn this place into a bed and breakfast. But then my sister would *never* visit. And I'd get that commercial tax assessment." She groaned.

"Problem?" Amar asked, coming over. "Besides that you're pimping out my woodworking skills?"

Morgen tilted the page toward him.

"That's a lot of cat condos."

"Tell me about it. Even the fancy bioluminescent moss isn't going to cover all of that. I—"

Sakura walked closer, and Morgen paused. Taxes seemed like a private matter between her and her roommate who would be out in the street—or out in the woods—if she couldn't figure out how to pay them.

Sakura handed an envelope of cash to Amar. "Will you load it into the van? I borrowed it from a friend so I wouldn't have to wait for delivery."

"Of course." Amar folded the envelope, stuck it in his pocket, and hefted the cat condo with the cat on top of it. A complaint of *merowww* came from the perch, but Rikido didn't spring free.

"Do you make familiar and pet charms?" Sakura asked Morgen.

"Pet what?"

"Charms. There used to be a witch in town who made them, but she retired to Palm Springs. Belinda said you've got a knack for crafting talismans and amulets and the like. Charms for familiars should be easy."

"What would you want such a charm to do?" And—the more pertinent question—how much could Morgen charge for such a thing?

"I'd like a flea-and-tick charm. Rikido is outdoors a lot, running errands for me and terrorizing the neighbor's bird feeder. He has a tendency to come back infested, and I do hate using chemicals on him. Betty used to make flea-and-tick charms."

"Uh, I could look in Grandma's books and see if I can find that."

"And hunters love the locator charms that go on their dogs'

collars and let them know how to find them when they get lost in the woods. Betty used to do a pretty good business. It's how she could afford to retire in the sunny south."

"Interesting. I'll look into it and let you know."

"Good. See you at the next meeting." Sakura waved, tucked a five-dollar tip in Amar's waistband, then got in her van and drove off, cat and cat condo loaded in the back.

Amar removed the bill with a bemused expression. "Witches are strange."

"Strange and not without financial means. How would you feel about going into business with me?"

His eyes narrowed. "You want me to make *more* cat condos and ferret trees?"

"I do, and I'll learn how to make pet charms. If they're as popular as Sakura seems to think they could be, maybe I'll be able to pay my taxes and continue to buy groceries. And you'll be able to continue living in the barn. Or... maybe you could even move into the house." She raised her eyebrows.

"Hm. I *would* want to contribute my fair share to the housing costs if I were to start living inside. I'd be reluctant, however, to give up my other work."

"You wouldn't need to. Maybe you could just do a doghouse here and a cat condo there. You know, on the side."

"A doghouse?"

"Yes, some owners make their dogs sleep outdoors. In little boxes with roofs."

"Would your dog sleep outdoors if I made him a box with a roof?"

"Not unless it came with a king-sized bed and a human in it. Vizslas are special."

"Like witches."

"Yes." Morgen grinned at him. "It's a good thing you like that in a woman."

"I do." Amar wrapped an arm around her shoulders and gazed at her, his eyelids lowering seductively. "Come into the barn with me. I have something I want to show you."

"Is it also special?"

"*Extremely* special."

"I'm intrigued."

"Good."

THE END

Printed in Great Britain
by Amazon

79939952R00169